Facing It

Look for these titles by
Linda Winfree

Now Available:

What Mattered Most

Facing It

Linda Winfree

A SAMHAIN PUBLISHING, LTD. publication.

Samhain Publishing, Ltd.
577 Mulberry Street, Suite 1520
Macon, GA 31201
www.samhainpublishing.com

Facing It
Copyright © 2010 by Linda Winfree
Print ISBN: 978-1-60504-545-0
Digital ISBN: 978-1-60504-488-0

Editing by Anne Scott
Cover by Anne Cain

First Samhain Publishing, Ltd. electronic publication: April 2009
First Samhain Publishing, Ltd. print publication: February 2010

Dedication

For the class of 2009, with love and best wishes.

Chapter One

"Come into the bedroom."

At her husband's cool command, Ruthie Chason's body went cold and stiff. Before he or the children noticed, she molded her posture into one of relaxed grace. Not looking around at Stephen, she closed her eyes for the briefest of moments and smoothed her youngest daughter's wispy bangs. When the instantaneous urge to give into hopeless tears was under control, she lifted her lashes to find her John Robert watching her with a resignation old beyond his seven years.

He laid his book aside and came to kneel beside his sister. "I'll keep her quiet, Mama."

She tipped his chin with fingers that shook only a little and leaned down to kiss his nose. "Thank you. I'll be back."

Hard-won experience told her not to add the word "soon" to the assurance. Time and its management belonged to Stephen alone. Unfolding her legs, she came to her feet and straightened her sleek sheath. She didn't have to touch her hair. Stephen liked her all pulled together and she didn't need a mirror to know not a single strand escaped her neat chignon.

She met her husband at the door and with a tight gesture he indicated that she should precede him. Down the hallway, he closed the bedroom door, not bothering to lock it. The children wouldn't leave the playroom without express permission to do so.

Without speaking, she managed to unzip her dress and slip out of it. She arranged it with pinpoint neatness over the back of a wingchair. Behind her, cloth rustled as Stephen removed his own clothing. Leaving her pumps by the chair, she slid off her panties and bra, laid those aside as well. Naked, she waited.

"On the bed, Ruth. I don't have all day; my flight leaves at seven."

Head high, she walked to the tall bed with its lush coverlet. She placed a knee on the mattress, prepared to kneel and grasp the headboard.

"No." His voice was even, almost indifferent. "On your back. I want to see your face."

Once more, she held in any reaction. She climbed onto the bed and lay down, a hairpin digging into her scalp. Good. She could concentrate on that pinprick of discomfort, use it to take her mind away from sordid reality.

He sat on the foot of the bed, between her feet, and ran a hand up the inside of one leg. Already semi-aroused, his penis rested above his thigh, the bulbous head red and angry.

"Beautiful," he murmured and pushed her thighs wider apart, sifting his fingers through the curls at her mons, trimmed just the way he liked. He trailed a finger along her vulva, flicked at her clit. She stared at the ceiling, tracing the plaster swirls there with her eyes, picking out fantastical patterns, the way she and Tori had done with clouds when they were little girls, lying on the dock at their grandparents' home.

He played with her, his other hand easing up her torso, skipping over her lower abdomen where she bore stretch marks from three pregnancies, stopping at her breasts. He pinched and rolled at her nipples. She kept her palms flat on the bed; if he wanted her to touch him, the command would come.

A pair of fingers wormed deep inside her, twisting and thrusting. The hairpin pressed against her scalp. She imagined the skin there, growing red and irritated, individual cells scraped away by the metal tips. His breathing changed, growing deeper and rougher, coming almost in pants, his fingers driving into her body, his thumb and forefinger clamping onto her nipple. Her body responded to the stimulation, fluid flowing over those fingers, but she let her mind wander where it would, keeping enough awareness to make sure she gave him what he wanted.

The mattress dipped and he rose between her thighs, palming and tugging at his heavy erection. Coming down on her body, he slammed inside her. She sucked in a gasp, swallowed it, and focused her eyes on his. He'd expect her to do so, wouldn't allow her to close her eyes when he wanted to see her face.

He rutted into her, hard stabs that had him grunting with exertion. She stared into his brown gaze, a shade lighter than her own, and tried to remember what it had been like at first, if there'd been tenderness or love, if she'd been a person then, instead of his doll. Tried to remember if there'd ever been an inkling of the love and passion and respect she'd witnessed in her parents' marriage.

How had she been drawn into him, so deep and so far that she'd never realized what he was until it was too late?

Finally, he tore into her with one last impossibly intense lunge, his body pulsing inside hers as he moaned. He collapsed atop her, rested a moment then pulled away. Seconds later, the bathroom door closed and the shower ran. She lay, staring at the ceiling. Semen slipped from her in a slow, syrupy trickle. A shuddery breath rasped from her lips.

The bathroom door opened, the odor of expensive French-milled soap wafting over her.

"I'll be back Friday evening." He didn't cast a look in her direction as he reached for his clothes. He pulled the backing free from the transdermal patch he used whenever he flew and smoothed the patch into place behind his ear. "You need to clean up and pull yourself back together, darling."

No. What she needed was to get the hell away from him before he destroyed what little of her remained.

"Don't worry about us, Lorna." Ruthie pinned on her

brightest smile. "We'll be fine."

The housekeeper looked doubtful. "But Mr. Chason—"

"Will be out of town until Friday." If her luck would only hold. Lord, please let him stay gone until then. No "surprise" early returns. "I assure you, I can handle the house while you see to your mother. Please, Lorna, go take care of her."

Lorna twisted her neat white apron in both hands, the wrinkles by her mouth deepening. "If you're sure..."

Ruthie smiled so widely her face hurt. "Positive."

An answering expression bloomed on Lorna's weary face. "Oh, thank you, Mrs. Chason. I did so want to be with her, but I know Mr. Chason doesn't like for you to be alone."

She bestowed a fierce hug on Ruthie, who returned the embrace despite her surprise. When was the last time anyone other than the children had touched her with affection? What she endured from Stephen didn't count.

Ruthie pulled away, blinking back a rush of silly tears. Crying wasn't her style, hadn't been for a very long time now. All crying did was give her a puffy face and burning eyes. It didn't change a darn thing.

She gave Lorna a tiny push toward the back door. "Tell your mother I asked about her."

After another round of reassurances and goodbyes, she locked the door and rested against it. She couldn't have asked for a better opportunity. With her legs shaking beneath her, she slipped from the kitchen with its to-die-for granite countertops and professional stainless appliances she was never allowed to use. Late-afternoon sunlight shone through the tall windows of the foyer and splashed on the Italian tile floor. She hurried up the stairs, holding on to the banister, questions and doubts beating in her head.

What if he came home? What if he caught her? What if he didn't? What if she managed to get away?

The latter was the only one that mattered, the one that spurred her on. This might be her only chance and she meant to take it.

She found the children in the spotless playroom where she'd left them. As always, they were too quiet, John Robert on the window seat with his nose buried in a book, Camille dancing a pair of dolls through the dollhouse, Ainsley curled into the rocker with her stuffed bunny on her lap and her thumb in her mouth. Studying them from the doorway, Ruthie longed for the noise and laughter of her childhood home, for that warmth and joy for her children.

Three more reasons to escape while she could.

She walked to the center of the room and sat cross-legged on the rug. John Robert glanced at her over his book; Camille didn't look around. Ruthie reached up and pulled Ainsley onto her lap, rubbing her chin against the soft dark hair. "How would you like to go on an adventure?"

Camille dropped the dolls and stared, lips parted, a glimmer of excitement in her eyes. John Robert closed his book. "Is Daddy coming?"

Ruthie sucked in a breath. "No. This is a mommy and kids adventure."

Ainsley hugged her rabbit. "Will there be pirates?"

"Maybe." Ruthie kissed her youngest daughter's cheek. "But we need to leave today. Are you ready?"

"Can I take Bun-bun?" Ainsley clutched the lovey harder.

"Yes, and John Robert can take his book and Camille can pick something to take along. But we must hurry."

She took Ainsley with her to the master suite, aware John Robert trailed her, his small face set in worried lines. "Don't we need to pack, Mama?"

"I have what we need here." Standing on her shoe shelf, she tugged the small tote from its hiding place. "I thought we might pick up new clothes along the way." She needed the house to look as normal as possible, for there to be as few clues as possible to her destination once Stephen returned. "John Robert, we will need Ainsley's go-bag. Can you get that for me? You can add some juice and snacks, if you like. I'll be right back."

13

He nodded, his eyes still troubled, and her breath caught. Already, he looked so much like her brothers, nothing like Stephen. Please, *please*, let it not be too late to get him away from his father's influence. She didn't want her firstborn, the joy of her heart, to grow up like her husband. She didn't think she could bear it.

She deposited Ainsley in the playroom again and slipped down the backstairs into Stephen's office. For once, his absolute arrogant faith in her obedience was going to come back to bite him. She slid open the unlocked credenza and removed the three leather-bound ledgers there. With them securely tucked into the tote, she gathered the girls and went in search of John Robert.

He sat at the island in the kitchen, the plaid monogrammed bag they'd termed Ainsley's "go-bag" since her infancy, in front of him. Ruthie smiled softly and forced a note of gaiety into her voice. "Ready?"

She secured them in their booster seats, lifted the garage door via remote and backed down the drive. The neighborhood was deserted and she sent another grateful prayer heavenward. Just to be safe, she took a circuitous route downtown and left the luxury SUV in a high-rise parking garage. Carrying the stylish tote and Ainsley's bag, she should appear as if she were merely going shopping, children in tow, if and when anyone looked for them on the garage security cameras. With the children gathered around her, she took the back exit and walked two blocks over to a second long-term storage garage.

There, she settled the children in the aging minivan. She cranked it, thankful when it started on the first try. With her fingers wrapped around the steering wheel in a painful grip, she looked over her shoulder at the children. "Okay, first stage of the adventure. We'll stop in Atlanta for something to eat."

Once Charleston faded behind her, she relaxed her death grip on the wheel. She'd done it. There was no going back now. Exhilaration mixed with a banked sense of dread.

She drove straight through, making only brief stops for food and restroom breaks, at shabby locations not likely to have the latest security camera systems, taking care to pay using small bills. Ainsley was asleep by the time they reached Jonesboro. Camille dozed around Macon. By Cordele, John Robert had finally nodded off.

Ruthie drove and didn't relax until she saw the sign for Chandler County. With the ease of familiarity, she navigated the back roads. There'd been changes since the last time she'd been here, just before John Robert's birth seven years before, but not so many that the intimacy of home didn't bring tears to her eyes. This time, she didn't blink them away. They slid silently down her face.

She made a right onto a gravel turnoff. The long drive opened up to a large yard and an old frame farmhouse glowing white under the moon and a bluish mercury light. A sweet sigh of relief escaped her. She'd be safe here. Her children would be safe. The house, too, had changed—a large sundeck now gracing the area next to the back porch, new plants joining the ancient azaleas and oak hydrangeas her grandmother had lovingly tended.

Ruthie stopped the van behind a dusty white Chevrolet Z71. A Volvo sedan sat next to it. She glanced over her shoulder. The children slept quietly, peacefully. Not wanting to disturb them, she slipped from the driver's seat, her lower back and legs protesting the hours spent behind the wheel. Leaving the interior light on so they wouldn't wake in the dark in an unfamiliar location, she hurried up the brick walkway, another change. When she'd been a child here, visiting her grandparents, a packed clay path had led to the back porch.

This late at night, the house was mostly dark, but squares of soft golden light spilled from the keeping-room windows. Nerves twisted in her stomach. It had been so long since they'd really talked. She didn't know him anymore, not really. What if he wasn't happy to see her, willing to help her? What would she do then?

She squared her shoulders. If that turned out to be the case, then she'd find a way to do this herself. Taking the first step necessitated that she not fail. The stakes were too high.

At the back door, she rang the doorbell and waited. Behind her, crickets and frogs sang in the dark night and beneath their song she could hear the distant whisper of the river. Oh, she'd missed this, missed the softness of these Georgia nights and the pure safety of this place.

Long minutes passed and she was preparing to push the bell again when a dark silhouette appeared at the door, backlit by the interior lights. The door swung inward.

"Ruthie?" Shock colored Tick's deep, drowsy drawl.

She blinked away more of the silly tears. His black hair sleep-mussed, clad in navy pajama pants, he held the door open with one hand, his other behind his back, securing his handgun there, she was sure.

Suddenly blinking didn't work anymore and the tears rushed free as she threw herself against his chest. "Oh Lord, Tick, I'm so glad to see you. I couldn't go to Mama's, didn't want to risk that, because I'm sure he'll look there first..."

She felt him falter once before he closed his arms around her, and sure enough, the weight of a gun in his left hand rested against her. "Ruthie, my God, what are you doing here? Are you all right?"

With an effort, she tried to pull herself together. He was married now, a father, although she hadn't even attended his wedding, hadn't seen the little boy named for him. He pulled back and used his free hand to brush the damp hair from her face. "Honey, talk to me. Come inside—"

"I c-can't." Her voice cracked and she caught his start of surprise. Oh, heaven above, he was going to think she was crazy. Maybe she was now. Maybe Stephen had driven her insane and she simply didn't know it. A half-hysterical giggle escaped her and she clamped her lips closed, took a deep breath. She waved over her shoulder. "The children...I can't leave them in the van."

"Of course not." He darted a quick look beyond her and spun to place the sleek semi-automatic in a kitchen drawer. "Come on, I'll help you get them inside. Have you eaten?"

She nodded. "In Atlanta, then a snack in Perry."

Thankfully, he didn't ask any further questions but followed her to the van and gathered John Robert into an easy hold while she lifted Camille. Her son, cradled by the uncle he didn't know, never stirred. Inside, Tick stopped in the kitchen with an uncertain expression.

"Do you think they'll wake up?" he whispered. She shook her head and he nodded. "Let's put them in the guest room upstairs and we can put your little one in the nursery with Lee."

"I'm sorry I woke you," she murmured, trailing him up the staircase, cataloging the changes in the house. Their grandmother's outdated decorating was gone and the home now bore the distinct stamp of Tick's strong personality, probably tempered somewhat by his wife's tastes as well. The sister-in-law who was merely a face in a photograph, a signature on a Christmas card.

"You didn't. I was up with Lee, had just put him back to bed when you rang." He nudged open the first door on the right off the landing. He grinned over his shoulder as he settled John Robert beneath the covers on the double bed. "My night to get up."

She slipped Camille beneath the sheets on the other side. Stephen had *never* gotten up with their children. That had always been her job, taking care of them, keeping them quiet.

"Tuck them in." Tick brushed his knuckles over her cheek, his dark eyes concerned. "I'll get the little one."

She did, tucking the sheet and thin coverlet around them, kissing them, sending up silent prayers for them. She left the small lamp burning on the dresser and eased into the hall, just as Tick topped the stairs with Ainsley cradled to his chest. He tilted his head toward the room opposite and Ruthie opened the door.

It was definitely a boy's room, with deep blue walls and wide white trim. A pine crib with white bedding stood against one wall, and a twin bed shared the space, outfitted in a quilt embroidered with an array of boats. As she flipped the quilt back for Tick to settle Ainsley down, she glimpsed a dark-haired baby snoozing in the crib, his arms laid out by his head, his lips pursed.

After she'd repeated her bedtime ritual over her daughter, Tick laid a hand on her back and ushered her toward the door. "Come on."

Her stomach knotted all over again.

In the hallway at the bottom of the stairs, he gestured toward the kitchen. "Want something? I can make some coffee or there's milk or juice—"

"Coffee would be great."

The few minutes it took him to secure his gun and start the coffee brewing gave her a chance to pull herself and her thoughts together. She leaned against the kitchen island, a new addition to the keeping room area, and glanced around. The green linoleum was gone, replaced by shining hardwood. A rustic pine table graced the dining area and in the living room, a red couch and comfortable leather chairs provided a conversation area. Pine tables held baskets for magazines and books. Photos covered the walls in neat arrangements. A play yard and infant swing sat near the living area and another basket held baby toys.

She cupped her elbows and rubbed at her arms. "It looks like you. The house, I mean."

A grin lit his face but didn't dispel the seriousness of his chocolate gaze. "That's what Cait says."

At the mention of his wife, she darted a look at him. "She won't mind, will she, us being here?"

"No, of course not." His eyebrows winged upward. He poured coffee into two mugs and slid one across to her. "Black, right?"

She nodded and lifted the warm cup. He indicated the living room. "Come on. Let's get comfortable and you can tell me what's going on."

Oh, she couldn't wait. Clutching her mug, she took one chair and he waited for her to sit before he sank into the other. Silence dragged between them and she sipped at her coffee, the rich liquid doing little to settle her nerves. She laughed, a short, humorless sound. "God, Tick, I don't know where to start."

"The beginning?"

At this gentle prompting, she laughed again. "Do you have all night?"

"I have however long you need."

She pressed her fingers against her brow. "I've made such a mess of things. Stephen...I thought he was a great catch, a good man, and he's not. He's..."

How to tell her brother she'd married a crook and a monster?

"Ruthie?" Tick covered her knee, his touch strong and warm. "Does he hurt you?"

"Not physically." She lifted her head. "That's not his thing. He...controls me. Where I go, who I see, what I do. And the children too. I don't want that for them, Tick, I don't. I want them to have what I had, what we had..." Her voice broke and she swallowed against the tightness in her throat. "Verbally, he's vicious when he's angry, when things don't go the way he likes. I've been planning to leave for a while, but I needed a plan and an opportunity, and I wasn't sure where to go, what to do... I'm sorry for showing up like this, dumping this all on you—"

"No, don't be sorry." His voice hardened. "Don't you dare be sorry, Ruthie. Holy hell, I should be apologizing to you, for not—"

"Don't." She knew what he was thinking. "It's not your fault. It's not anyone's fault but mine. And Stephen's, for being the absolute monster he is. But I need your help now, Tick."

"Anything."

"Don't say that yet. You don't know what I want." She looked at her brother, who'd been awarded the FBI award upon his graduation from Quantico. He was all about integrity and what she was going to ask would test that.

"Ruthie, just ask, honey. I'll do whatever I can."

She took a deep breath. "I want you to help me disappear."

"Disappear." He nodded and exhaled audibly. "It's not like on television. You can't just pick up a new identity—"

"Tick, when he finds out I'm gone, when he realizes what I've taken, he's going to kill me."

Her brother shook his head. "I won't let that happen. We'll find a way to keep you safe, to keep the kids safe. We'll get you a lawyer, find a way to keep him from taking them back."

"He's not going to want to kill me over the children." She shook her head. "He doesn't care about them except as photo props. It's the ledgers."

Tick's dark gaze sharpened. "The ledgers?"

"He's laundering money. A *lot* of money. And I took the records when I left."

"How do you know he's involved in this?"

"He's incredibly arrogant, Tick. He thinks I'm completely under his thumb and he talks about it, brags about it, about what he's doing."

Tick quirked an eyebrow, intrigue glinting in his eyes. "Show me."

Quiet voices and the scent of fresh coffee roused Ruthie. Eyes closed, she tensed before memory flooded back. She wasn't in Charleston anymore. She was safe, she was home. Her neck ached from her cramped position on Tick's couch, where obviously she'd dozed off while he pored over the financial books she'd filched from Stephen's office.

"Ruthie?" A touch on her shoulder accompanied the husky female voice. Ruthie opened her eyes to beautiful face surrounded by a thick fall of black hair. Caitlin, Tick's wife, whom she knew only from photos. "I'm sorry to wake you, but Ainsley was stirring when I went up to get Lee."

"Thank you." Ruthie straightened and cast a look toward the kitchen/dining area, where Tick sat at the pine table, his dark head still bent over the ledgers. He remained in his pajama pants but had added a white T-shirt. Lee, secured in a high chair at Tick's elbow, babbled and stuffed dry Cheerios into his mouth.

"I'm going to see about getting us some breakfast." Caitlin retreated to the kitchen.

Ruthie rose and hurried for the stairs. She didn't want Ainsley waking alone, in a strange room. Her daughter was clingy under the best of circumstances, but when she was upset, she turned into the human equivalent of beggarweed.

It was early, darkness still hovering outside the windows. Upstairs, she slipped into the nursery. Sure enough, Ainsley had rolled to her stomach and was stretching, a certain sign of her imminent waking. Ruthie perched on the bedside and touched her baby's silky brown hair. "Good morning, Ains."

Ainsley giggled. "Are the pirates here?"

Ruthie reached for the toy bunny and danced it up and down Ainsley's little back. "Um, I haven't seen any yet. Would some breakfast do instead?"

Ainsley made a moue of dissatisfaction and Ruthie found herself laughing for the first time in days. She rose and swung the little girl into her arms. "Come on. Let's wash your face and see what your Aunt Caitlin is making for breakfast."

In the small bathroom next door, which retained its cottage feel from her childhood, she helped Ainsley wash her hands and face. She caught a glimpse of her weary, pinched features and averted her gaze. She looked old, haggard, worn out.

Ainsley clung tighter to her neck as they descended the stairs and once they reached the keeping room, refused to be set on her feet, burrowing her face into Ruthie's shoulder with a tiny whimper. Tick glanced her way with a small smile.

"Sit." Caitlin gave her a slight push toward the table. "I'll get you something to eat. Ainsley, do you like waffles?"

With a slow, cautious movement, Ainsley lifted her head and studied Caitlin. Finally, she nodded.

"Would you like to come show me what you want for toppings?"

Ainsley released Ruthie's neck, an indication she was ready to be set free. With her thumb in her mouth, she placed her other hand in Caitlin's outstretched one and let her aunt lead her to the kitchen island, Caitlin talking softly the entire way.

At the table, Ruthie chose the chair to Tick's left, allowing her to be close to his steady presence and keep an eye on her daughter at the same time. He reached for her hand, rubbing his thumb across her knuckles in a quick caress. "I'm glad you came to me."

She tightened her fingers around his, the warm comfort of the touch bringing tears to the surface. "So am I."

Releasing her, he tapped the ledger with one long finger. "Do you know what you have here?"

"I have an idea." An ache pulsed at her temples. Caitlin set a mug of fresh coffee before her and Ruthie gave her a grateful look.

Tick held her gaze, his own troubled, his face set in tense lines. "Ruthie, you said he'd kill you. You understand that if Stephen's doing this, your having these books puts you in danger."

Her stomach clenched, all vestiges of hunger invoked by the smell of fresh, crisp waffles disappearing. "I was in danger when I walked out the door without permission yesterday. I'm not stupid, Tick, I'm fully aware what he's capable of and I knew what I was doing when I took those books. Maybe, just maybe, someone who knows what to do with them can keep him too busy to look for me, until the children and I are so far out of his reach that he can never hurt us again."

His expression tightening further, Tick nodded. "Right now, he doesn't have a clue where you are, even if he's discovered you're gone. Like you said, he's going to look at Mama's first. I want to get you somewhere safe while I get in touch with the South Carolina authorities, see if we can use this to help you."

Ainsley clambered onto the chair next to Ruthie's. Caitlin set a plate of waffles topped with bananas in front of her and a plate bearing a plain waffle before Ruthie. She set the syrup down nearby. On her way back to the kitchen, she squeezed Tick's shoulder and he glanced up, unspoken communication passing between them. She lifted an eyebrow at him. Frowning, he sighed.

"If that's what you want," he said, turning his attention to Ruthie. "Unless you had another plan?"

"I just want my children to be safe...and away from him and his influence."

"I have an idea." Tick tugged a hand through his disheveled hair. "I'll have to make a call."

Chris stowed the final bag in his SUV. The moist predawn air wrapped around him and he dragged in a deep breath. A few hours, and he'd be sucking in sea-salted air. He couldn't wait. God, he needed this time away, after the weeks of overtime he'd been putting in.

Inside the phone rang, the imperious shrill carrying through to the garage from the open kitchen door. For a half-second, he considered ignoring it. He was on vacation, damn it. His ingrained sense of duty wouldn't let him, though. With a harsh sigh, he strode inside and grabbed the offending object on the fourth ring. "Hello."

"Chris." Relief vibrated in Tick Calvert's deep voice. "Glad I caught you before you left. I need a huge favor."

Why wasn't Chris surprised? Visions of his vacation spiraling down the tubes danced through his mind. He rested his forehead on the doorjamb. "Yeah?"

"Do this for me and I'll make it worth your while—equal to full pay this week and I'll schedule you another week off whenever you want."

"Who am I covering?" He slumped into a chair and reached for a pad and pen to jot down the shift times. Hell, he should have ignored the damn phone. He would have been out of the driveway by now, headed for his version of paradise.

Tick cleared his throat. "I don't need you to work."

Suspicion tickled Chris's spine. "What do you want then?"

"I need you to take my sister Ruthie and her kids with you to St. Simons."

"What?" It had to be a joke. "Did Cookie put you up to this?

Or Troy Lee?"

"I'm serious, Chris." Tension tightened Tick's words and Chris could almost see the older man pulling a hand through his hair. "She took the kids, left her husband and I just need for him to not know where she is for a few days while I help her sort some things out. It's a bad situation and I want her with someone I can trust to keep her safe."

Chris dropped his brow into his palm. "And that's me?"

"That's you."

Something niggled at the back of Chris's mind. "Why do you need me to take her to the island? You don't think she'd be okay at your place?"

A rough exhale rumbled over the line. "Looks like her husband is involved in some pretty shady stuff. When she left, she took the evidence of that with her. This is more than what's sure to be a nasty divorce. I need some time and I need her safe."

Silence stretched over the line.

"I wouldn't ask if it wasn't important, Chris."

Chris pinched the bridge of his nose. "How much time do you need?"

"The week would be great. I might be able to sort it out in less."

"All right, I'll do it." He was such a sucker.

"Great. Knew I could count on you."

He didn't bother to touch that one. "Am I picking them up at your place?"

"Yeah. How soon can you be here?"

He rolled his neck in a slow circle, tension attacking his nape and shoulders. "Give me fifteen minutes."

Ruthie listened, her apprehension growing, as Tick, dressed now for the day in his investigator's uniform of green department polo and khakis, outlined his plan. A week, with a man she didn't know? The idea sent frissons of something akin to fear down her spine, the worry pooling into an icy knot. Maybe she'd jumped from the frying pan straight into the fire, as her grandmother used to say.

She pulled in a deep breath and dismissed her doubt. She'd come to Tick because she trusted him to help her, to keep her safe. She simply had to hold on to that trust. Slanting a glance at the dining table, where Caitlin sat with the children, trying to draw Camille and John Robert out of their shells over waffles and milk, Ruthie bit the inside of her cheek.

"Does he have someone?" she asked, turning her attention back to her brother. "A wife or girlfriend who might object? I don't want to cause problems for him."

Tick shook his head, discomfort twisting his face. "He hasn't had a serious relationship the whole time I've known him. Goes out on a date every so often, but that's about it."

She frowned. Something about that didn't.... "Why?"

Tick shrugged. "Don't know. We've wondered if he's not in the closet still—"

"He's gay." Relief washed through her. Somehow that made the situation easier, although she couldn't explain why.

Obviously uncomfortable discussing his colleague's personal life, Tick rubbed a hand over his neck. "He's never outright said it, but that's the scuttle, yeah."

An engine rumbled outside and purred to a stop. Tick rose and held out a hand. "Come on. That'll be Chris. I'll introduce you before we spring the kids on him."

She took his hand, hating the way she wanted to cling like Ainsley as he drew her outside. She forced her spine straight and dropped his hand. She wasn't a three-year-old in need of constant reassurance. Somehow, she would face this, find a way back to the woman she'd been before Stephen had cowed her.

A nondescript blue Jeep Cherokee sat in the driveway under the just-rising sun. As she and Tick stepped onto the porch, a tall man clad in jeans and a T-shirt unfolded himself from the driver's seat. His face set in serious lines, he moved up

25

the walkway, his stride one of proud bearing and easy authority. Close to Tick's side, Ruthie studied him—muscular arms and shoulders, trim waist above long legs, square jaw shadowed by a couple days' growth of stubble, short brown hair, a tan highlighting ice-blue eyes.

That cool gaze flicked over her as he mounted the steps and took Tick's outstretched hand in a brisk shake. "Tick."

"Hey, Chris, thanks for coming. I really appreciate it." His palm warm at her back, Tick drew her forward. "This is my sister, Ruthie Chason. Ruthie, Chris Parker."

"Hello." She forced herself to hold out her hand, aware she was trembling. "And yes, thank you. I can only imagine how we've ruined your vacation plans."

His palm, warm and dry, closed around hers briefly. "No problem."

She liked the even tone of his low, quiet voice, even if the size of him did make her nervous. Unlike Stephen, with whom she was nearly eye-to-eye, she had to look up at this man, making him nearer her brother's six-foot-three height.

He tucked his hands in his pockets and rocked back slightly on his heels as he turned to Tick. "We've got a four-hour drive ahead of us, maybe longer if we stop along the way."

Tick nodded. "I pulled some stuff together for you. Want some coffee while I go over that? Cait can help Ruthie get the kids ready."

A slight grimace crossed Chris Parker's face at the mention of her children and the tension tautened Ruthie's being. Not another man for whom she had to keep her babies "under control". Once more, she forced herself to relax, to trust Tick. This was the man he'd chosen to keep her and the children safe.

She accompanied Tick inside, aware of Chris's watchful gaze on her the entire way. She left the two men in quiet conversation at the kitchen island and ventured to the second story.

Upstairs, Caitlin, dressed for work, was getting Lee ready,

keeping up a steady stream of mostly one-sided conversation with her son while she washed his face and brushed his tiny teeth with a small red toothbrush. Ruthie pulled clean clothes from her tote, aware that somewhere along the way, she'd need to purchase several days' worth of clothing for the children and herself. She gnawed at the inside of her cheek. She was pretty sure she had enough cash for that, but she needed to be able to help Chris Parker with expenses as well. The tidy little sum of money she'd squirreled away over the last three years while she'd planned her escape suddenly seemed more little than tidy.

The doubt and insecurity, reinforced over and over by Stephen's snide voice, fell on her, a heavy, shattering weight.

Oh Lord, she was so in over her head.

Shivering, Harrell Beecham stepped from yet another cold shower and grabbed a towel. He rubbed the water and gooseflesh from his skin. He wasn't sure how much more of this he could stand. Sharing a bed, a bathroom, hell, the freaking *house* with Jennifer much longer was going to kill him.

Pretending to be her husband, getting to touch her when they were out socially, then having to revert to the reality of professional distance was slowly driving him out of his ever-lovin' mind. He should be able to draw hazardous duty pay for this assignment.

He toweled the excess moisture from his hair and dressed quickly—brown suit, blue shirt, no tie. Too bad he couldn't claim he needed to be at work early for the housekeeper's benefit and slip out before Jennifer returned from her morning run. She'd want to discuss her surveillance of the Chason house, although nothing ever changed there and hadn't for the past six months, before he left for his day pretending to be an up-and-coming businessman in Charleston.

The scent of just-perked coffee filled the luxurious home's lower floor. When he entered the state-of-the-art kitchen,

Teresa, their live-in housekeeper and the reason he was trapped sharing a platonic bed with Jennifer, bustled about fixing breakfast. She smiled at him. "Good morning, Mr. Beauchamp."

"Morning, Teresa." He poured a cup of coffee and glanced involuntarily toward the French doors that opened onto the patio. Sure enough, Jennifer was there already, clad in her running shorts and tank top, her long bare legs toned and tanned. God, what he wouldn't give to be between those thighs...

No, that wasn't true. He wouldn't give his career with the FBI, or Jennifer's. He wouldn't sacrifice her respect as his partner or the easy give-and-take friendship of that partnership. That was exactly why he was going to keep his pants zipped and his raging lust for his partner under control.

"I'll take that out, Teresa." He added his mug to the heavy tray and lifted it, smiling at the maid as she held the door open.

"Good morning, darling," he greeted Jennifer and settled the tray on the table. Leaning over, he brushed his mouth over hers, for Teresa's benefit, because the door remained open behind him, he told himself. Under his lips, Jennifer's were warm and soft, supple and mobile. Desire tingled to life in his groin; he squashed it ruthlessly. "How was your run?"

"Very nice." Her sleek blonde ponytail bobbed as she leaned forward to pick up a muffin. "But I didn't see our chickadees this morning. I hope they haven't flown away somewhere."

Unease shivered over Harrell's skin but he refused to look toward the house next door. They'd been watching the Chasons, particularly Stephen Chason for months now. The man had left town, supposedly on business, two days ago. But if his wife, whom he controlled like a puppet, was gone, did that mean Chason was on to them?

Harrell sipped at his coffee. "Maybe they're off looking for food, hon. Doesn't mean they've gone anywhere permanently."

"Hmm." Jennifer shrugged, her bright hazel eyes flickering to his. "I'll go for a walk later, see if I spot them about the neighborhood. Plus I wanted to drop in on Ruthie, see if she'd like to go shopping with me."

Bustling onto the patio with a plate of fresh fruit, Teresa clucked at Jennifer's words. "Not likely, Mrs. Beauchamp. You know Mr. Chason. That man keeps a tight rein on Mrs. Chason. The things Lorna says about that house." Teresa shook her head as she turned toward the door. "And those children, having to be quiet as little mice all the time. Poor things."

Frustration tightened Jennifer's pretty, full mouth, a familiar annoyance Harrell knew well. She didn't like the situation Ruthie Chason lived in, hated that they had to watch and couldn't do anything to help her or the children. Harrell could empathize—he'd been shocked to realize Chason's wife was the sister of an agent he'd attended Quantico with, worked alongside in the FBI's Organized Crime Division, considered a friend. Somehow, he knew Tick Calvert, now working with a small sheriff's department in his Georgia hometown, wouldn't appreciate Harrell knowing Ruthie lived in hell and not doing anything about it.

"Well, I'm going to shower." Jennifer unfolded herself from the chair and stretched. Harrell glanced away from the sleek perfection of her body. My God, the woman was in fantastic shape. She leaned over to drop a kiss at the corner of his mouth; he gripped the chair arms to keep from dragging her onto his lap and exploring every last inch of that gorgeous mouth of hers. "I know you're going in early. I'll look for our little birdie friends... If I don't find them, I'll give you a call on your cell."

He'd barely made it to the end of the street that led to their cul-de-sac when said cellular phone rang, his caller ID displaying Jennifer's encrypted line. "Beecham."

"Beech?" Stress tightened Jennifer's rich voice. "They're gone."

"You're sure?" He slowed for the stop sign.

"Definitely. Her car's gone, the housekeeper isn't there. This isn't good, partner."

"Maybe she just went for groceries or something." One could hope anyway. If she truly had given them the slip...this might not be pretty.

"Right. If she's out of milk, she calls for delivery, remember? The woman doesn't go anywhere without Chason's permission. Besides, yesterday's mail is still in the box and today's paper is on the front step. I'm telling you, she's gone."

"Okay." He rubbed a hand down his face. "Let's give it an hour. If she doesn't come back, you call me and I'll come home. In the meantime, I'll get a bulletin out on her vehicle."

Goddamn, he really hoped Ruthie hadn't finally defied the controlling son of a bitch and instead had only run out for a gallon of milk while Chason was gone. For some reason, the idea of Ruthie Calvert Chason as a wild card made him really, *really* nervous.

Chapter Two

"She's definitely gone," Beecham said and Jennifer didn't miss the stress darkening his voice. "She hasn't returned to the house, her SUV is in a parking tower downtown, and according to the attendant, it's been there since yesterday afternoon."

Curled into one end of the plush leather couch in Beecham's home office, she tucked her feet under her and eyed the phone on the big mahogany desk. As he'd promised, once Ruthie Chason failed to return, Beecham had come back to the house. Now they were embroiled in a quiet, doors-closed conference call with their supervising agent, Greg Weston.

"Well, she's not with Chason in Virginia Beach." The speakerphone made Weston sound as if he were speaking at the end of a tunnel. "The agents there have visually confirmed he's still at the hotel."

"Wonder if he knows she's gone," Jennifer mused. She didn't see how he couldn't. The man kept tighter tabs on his wife than the federal government did known terrorist groups. The level of his control over Ruthie made Jennifer's skin creep with nerves. She glanced sideways at Beecham, elbows on the polished desk, head bent, face buried in his hands. The taut line of his shoulders screamed with tension. She would almost bet she knew what was going through his head—he was berating himself for this perceived failure.

"Any idea where she is, Harrell?" Weston asked, his voice grim. Jennifer sloughed off a hint of pique that he seemed to be ignoring her. Beecham was the senior agent in their partnership, and he and Weston had a long working relationship. Besides, Weston's disdain toward female agents in the FBI wasn't exactly a state secret either.

"My guess?" Beecham lifted his head, his blue eyes narrowed. "She'll go to Calvert for help. She'll think Chason would look at her mother's first, and she's probably right. She knows Tick would help her."

"Right. Good thinking. We'll do an initial sweep with him. I'll put in a call to the Albany office—"

"No." Beecham shook his head. "Tallahassee or Thomasville. Calvert's wife is at the Albany office, remember?"

"You think he'll be uncooperative?"

"You know he plays his cards close to his chest, Greg. I don't think we'll get a lot out of him on initial contact."

"Tell you what, then. No point in you two being there if she's gone. We've got Chason covered in Virginia. Keep the cover intact, but make arrangements to fly into Albany, head down to that hole-in-the-wall county of Calvert's so you can talk to him. He might be more willing to open up to you, Harrell, if the initial dialogue doesn't go well."

"I wouldn't bet on it," Beecham muttered out of Weston's range, then lifted his voice. "Will do. Keep us posted on Chason, Greg."

He reached over, lifted the receiver and let it drop to end the call. Again, he rested his face in his hands, blowing out a long breath.

Jennifer frowned. "Why are you so worried?"

"If she's gone to Calvert, that could be a problem." His words emerged tight and muffled.

"Why?" Jennifer shrugged. "He used to be one of us. He knows how things work."

Beecham lifted his head, a wry expression twisting his face. "She's family. You don't know what that means to this guy. He'll do whatever it takes to protect her, even if that's counter to our objective." He cleared his throat. "Which it probably will be. And Tick Calvert as an unknown? Not a good thing."

Jennifer slipped to her feet with a stretch. "So I guess I need to pack?"

He nodded and reached for the phone. "Seems like we're off on a spur-of-the-moment trip."

She opened the door and pitched her voice a tad higher. "I'll pack a bag for you too, honey." He grimaced at the endearment and she grinned. She used them whenever she could, just because it seemed to get under his skin. Ruffling her partner's eternally calm exterior was one perk of this undercover gig. She winked at him. "Should I throw in my little black nightie?"

Beecham rolled his eyes. "Oh yeah, baby, you know I love when you wear that."

Teresa was dusting at the end of the hall. Jennifer rested an arm along the open door and struck a sex-kitten pose. "You love taking it off, you mean."

Beecham waved her toward the hall. "Let me book our flight. Go pack."

Blowing him a kiss, she sauntered to the stairs. An image lingered in her brain, of the nonexistent black scrap of lace, of Beecham's hands sweeping it from her body. Ruffling his composure was a perk of the gig—having to live with him while her jones for him got stronger every day was not. She'd been drawn to Beecham's quiet, steady persona from day one—he'd soothed her rookie-agent nerves and over the last two years, they'd settled into a strong working bond and even forged a relative friendship of sorts, although she knew far less about his personal life than her colleagues knew about their partners.

Living with him for nearly a year? He'd gotten under her skin, big time. She'd found herself drawn into the role-playing with a vengeance, using every opportunity she received to touch the warmth of his skin, to tousle his wavy auburn hair, to kiss his hard lips.

Upstairs, she pulled two carry-on bags from the huge walk-in closet. Her instincts whispered that the Chason case was about to break wide-open, with Ruthie's disappearance serving as the catalyst. The agent side of her tingled with anticipation. The female part of her who'd gotten used to living with Harrell

Beecham day in and day out cringed with dread. How was she supposed to go back to being simply his partner?

And what if she couldn't? She was damned if she did, damned if she didn't. Either way, it looked like she just might lose Beecham for good.

Tick leaned back in his desk chair, the ancient springs squawking, and watched as his fellow sheriff's investigator Mark Cook perused the black leather ledger. Cookie pursed his lips and blew out a long, low whistle. "This guy's smart. Doing it the old fashioned way too. No computer records to trace."

"Yeah." Tick rubbed a hand down his face, feeling the lack of sleep, reliving for a moment the shock of having his uncommunicative sister turn up on his doorstep at one in the morning. "And Ruthie's right. He'd probably kill her over those."

"If not for leaving him." Cookie tossed the ledger on Tick's desk. "Wish you hadn't told me, though."

Surprised, Tick quirked an eyebrow at him. He told the other man almost everything, did tell him everything in a professional sense. "Why?"

"Because now I have to *not* tell Tori."

Tick grimaced at the mention of his other sister—and Cookie's fiancé. Almost a year into the relationship, Tick was still getting accustomed to the fact that his partner was going to be his brother-in-law. It was good, though. The relationship seemed to be standing up to the test of time and stress, and even he had to admit the pair seemed good for one another, despite his initial misgivings.

Cookie gestured at the book. "So what are you going to do with that?"

Tick shrugged. "Still trying to decide. If Stephen is on the FBI's radar at the Organized Crime Division, and from some of the names in there, I'd say that's likely, then it's equally likely someone may show up here."

A tap sounded at the door. Tick lifted the ledger and stowed it in his desk drawer. "It's open."

Troy Lee, one of their younger deputies, stuck his head inside. "Hey, Tick, you've got visitors at the front desk. A pair of Feds."

"Show them to the conference room." A grin pulled at his mouth and Tick gave Cookie a knowing look. "What did I tell you?"

Cookie trailed him to the conference room with its makeshift, mismatched furniture. Two somber-suited men waited inside, their posture tight and stiff. Handshakes all around followed introductions as Agents Lewis and Freeman of the Tallahassee office tried to appear approachable. Tick waved them to sit. "What can I do for you gentlemen?"

Freeman folded his hands atop the scarred wooden table. "We need to know if you've had recent contact with your sister Ruth Ann Chason."

"Why would I? She doesn't stay in close communication with the family. Besides, why would the FBI be interested in my dealings with my sister?"

The two agents exchanged a glance. "It's possible she may have information relevant to an open case at the Organized Crime Division."

Tick feigned surprise. He leaned back, arms folded behind his head. "Really. An open OCD case. Care to share the details?"

"You know we can't do that."

"Then I'm afraid I really can't help you."

Another terse look between the two Feds. Freeman pulled a card from his wallet. "Please call if she does contact you."

Tick and Cookie stood as the two agents exited the room. Tick leaned against the table and folded his arms over his chest. He sighed. "They gave up too easy and they didn't try to work me. I'll have a tail by the end of the day."

Cookie nodded. "Yeah."

"And next Stephen will show up." His voice came out grim and tight. He was actually looking forward to that little interlude.

35

With a frown, Cookie shrugged. "Why not just tell them what she has? Obviously, they're interested in what he's doing."

Tick slanted a look at him. "Because. I wasn't a Fibbie for ten years for nothing. Those ledgers are Ruthie's ace in the hole and I'm not ready to trump it yet. Besides, I only want to share those with someone I trust."

Three hours into the trip, they stopped in Waycross for food, a rest stop, and the clothing and supplies Ruthie would need for the children. Chris chose the relative anonymity of a large retail discount store where they could handle all those needs in one trip. Inside, Ruthie settled Ainsley in the child seat of a buggy and lifted Camille to ride in the cart. John Robert trailed alongside, a hand on the metal as if he was afraid his mother and sisters would disappear if he let go.

As Ruthie went up and down the wide aisles, Chris walked behind, watching as she chose lesser-priced items and forewent others. Mentally tallying money. He caught up to stand beside her, on the side opposite John Robert. He placed a hand on the cart handle to slow her down but didn't touch her.

"Stop worrying about money," he whispered, low enough he hoped the children couldn't hear. A slight frown wrinkling her smooth brow, she turned inscrutable eyes up to him. "Tick figured you'd need some stuff. He gave me enough cash to take care of it. Just get what you think they'll need."

Something indefinable—discomfiture, maybe—tightened her expression, but she nodded. "Thank you."

He released his hold on the cart. Yeah, no short supply of Calvert pride there. She didn't like the idea of being beholden to anyone, even her brother. She was strong—he could see it in the regal carriage of her tall, graceful frame, the way she held her head. How had this woman ended up in the situation Tick described—cowed, controlled, conquered by the son of a bitch she'd married?

Chris shook his head. Appearances could be deceiving and love—or what masqueraded as love—made a person do strange things. Hadn't he learned that lesson well enough himself?

Ruthie lifted a thin pink sweater from a rack and held it aloft for Camille's inspection. The little girl frowned over it for a second and nodded. Chris folded his arms over his chest. John Robert stood quietly to the side, his gaze trained on his mother's face, and Ainsley clutched her battered stuffed rabbit, her thumb in her mouth. It had been a long morning, all of them crowded into his Jeep, but there'd been none of the "he's touching me" or "you're on my side" fussing he remembered from car trips he'd seen in movies. Now, in the store, they were quiet and incredibly well behaved. Nothing like the kids around them, he realized, as a mother two clothing racks over bribed her toddler with a sucker.

He thought about the handful of times he'd run into Ruthie's brother Chuck and his brood of five at the grocery store. Chuck and his wife kept their kids in line, but they were a noisy, chatty little group with more than their share of mischief. Tick's boy, at about a year old, was a handful too, and Chris had witnessed more than once the easy way Tick and Caitlin were trying to mold his already headstrong nature. In contrast, Ruthie's children were *too* well behaved. No whining, no fussing, just an eerie children-should-be-seen-and-not-heard perfection. It made him nervous.

Ruthie was that quiet too. She'd barely said two words to him once they'd left Tick's. He frowned. Actually, the only times she'd spoken had been in response to his questions, which granted were few and far between. Unlike Troy Lee and the others, he wasn't much of a talker, which got him ragged constantly around the department as the "strong, silent type". So he was quiet. He just didn't see a point in talking unless he had something to say. His old man had been the same way.

But Ruthie's silence spoke more of withdrawal, a turning inward of a strong personality. What had she been like before she'd married the bastard who was her husband? Bright and sparkling with laughter and conversation like her little sister Tori, maybe? Now there was a Calvert who never stopped chattering.

He tilted his head, watching Ruthie as she selected jeans in both little girls' sizes and placed them in the cart. She looked like Tori, that was for sure. Although, where Tori's sunny personality shone in her eyes and face, emphasizing her natural beauty, Ruthie's isolation seemed to overshadow hers, so that someone not looking for the innate loveliness of her might miss it completely.

And she was beautiful, with strong features framed by thick strands of black hair that had escaped her loose topknot and balanced by big brown eyes and a wide, full mouth.

Her figure wasn't half-bad, either. Like her siblings, she was tall, but she had definite curves, probably enhanced a little by motherhood. Her waist nipped in between full breasts and softly rounded hips. Someone who would fit perfectly against a tall guy, the kind of woman with a hint of softness, the kind of woman it felt oh-so-good to hold when dancing or kissing or—

Jiminy Cricket, what was he doing thinking about that, about her, anyway?

This was Tick's sister, the one he was supposed keep safe. She was *married*, for God's sake, even if she'd run from the mockery of a union. The last thing Chris needed was to look at Ruthie Chason with any kind of male interest.

Because the last woman he'd looked at that way had almost done him in.

By the time they reached St. Simons Island, Ruthie wanted to scream. The quiet in the truck, broken only by the radio and Chris Parker's occasional question and her short answers, smothered her, pressing against her ears, the tension inside her winding tighter and tighter with every mile.

She wanted…well, she wasn't sure what she wanted. Maybe for John Robert and Camille to get into an argument, the way she and Will had as children. Or for Ainsley to pitch a fit, like Tori had been prone to do as a toddler. She'd possessed a perfectly ordered life, had been forced into it every damn day for the past eight years or so.

Now she wanted normal so bad she thought she could literally bite down and taste it. Darn it, she wanted that for her children. They'd have it too. She hadn't risked everything to get this far and fail.

John Robert drew in a sharp, audible breath as they started up the Sydney Lanier Bridge, its apex five hundred feet above the water. She glanced at him over her shoulder. Eyes wide, he pressed his nose to the glass and stared down.

She laughed, the sound feeling a little rusty. "Pretty incredible, isn't it?"

He nodded but didn't pull his attention from the view. Chris darted a look at her son and the hard lines of his face softened. She reached back to pat John Robert's knee. "Maybe you'll get to play on the beach later. Wouldn't that be nice?"

Another sharp nod. "We've never done that before."

This time, Chris's gaze settled on her for a split second before he shifted his attention back to the road.

"I thought y'all lived in Charleston," he said, his voice pitched low.

She folded her arms, trying to smother the grinding tension. "We do. I mean, we did."

His eyebrows winged upward in silent inquiry. She sighed. "Stephen doesn't like the shore. He hates everything about it."

She regretted invoking his name as soon as it left her lips, as John Robert subsided against the seat with a troubled expression. "But I like the beach. All that sand between your toes and salt to wash off later."

"Seaweed to wrap around your ankles." Chris's gaze lifted to the rearview mirror. "We'll be within walking distance of the pier. Maybe we'll do some fishing or go crabbing while we're here."

"Crabbing?" Camille perked up then, shifting forward in the seat.

Chris nodded. "Yeah, we'll need some crab baskets and some bait. Hot dogs or chicken or something."

"Real crabs, with big claws?" Impishness lit Camille's eyes. She curved her hands into an imitation of those claws and moved them toward John Robert, who giggled.

Chris laughed, a resonant, pleasant rumble of sound that lasted mere seconds. "Really big claws."

The bridge ended, opening up into the island's main entry thoroughfare. Chris navigated the interplay of streets with the ease of someone intimately acquainted with a location, taking them farther into the island until they reached the historic village area with its narrow streets, big trees, old houses and glimpses of the bay.

Ruthie couldn't resist rolling down her window for a whiff of salt air. In the backseat, John Robert and Camille indulged in one of the quick sibling tussles she so longed for, to see who could get closest to the window to see the water, although it was much quieter than the ones she remembered from her own childhood.

At a stoplight, Chris squinted up at a street sign. "Have you been here before?"

She nodded, the sweet warmth of memories wrapping around her—playing in the waves with her brothers, holding her father's hand as they walked along the bay front, sharing a family picnic in the park at the town square. "It's been forever, though. Right after Tick graduated from high school, so it's been almost twenty years. It's changed a lot."

"I'll bet." He swung into a right turn followed by two lefts, taking them deeper into the crowded neighborhood around the village area. The knot of coiled stress in Ruthie's abdomen relaxed slightly. It would be difficult for Stephen to find them here, even if he knew she was on the island.

She trusted Tick enough to believe he didn't.

Chris slowed to pull into a long, thin driveway fronting several tiny cottages. He parked beside the last, a small whitewashed building with faded turquoise shutters and a minuscule screened porch. It was the furthest thing possible from the kind of trendy condo Stephen would have chosen.

She loved it.

Sliding from the truck, she marshaled the two older children to help unload and even found a way for Ainsley to pitch in, having her open and close the front door once Chris unlocked it. Together, they made short work of unpacking the cargo area.

Inside, the house was small but spotless, making economical use of the limited space. The first bedroom held a double bed with a smaller single pushed against the opposite wall while the second smaller room contained a pair of twin beds. A tiny bathroom stood between them.

Chris paused in the small hallway outside the bedrooms, his duffle slung over one shoulder. "If you need both rooms, I can bunk on the couch."

"No, that's not necessary." Ruthie tucked a stray lock of hair behind her ear. "The girls and I can sleep in the double and John Robert can have the single. There's no sense in your not having a real bed."

"All right."

She got the children started on stowing their things in the bedroom and wandered through to the small galley kitchen. Beyond that was another small porch and from the window over the sink, she could see the bay, the waters gray and a little choppy under the overcast sky. Chris appeared with the bags of kitchen staples they'd picked up in Waycross. Without speaking and with economical movements, he began putting them away. Ruthie moved to help, casting quick looks at him while she placed canned goods in the small pantry.

"I can do the cooking while we're here," she said, aligning the cans in tidy rows. She glanced at him. "I'm pretty good at it."

"Deal." He shrugged. "Because I'm pretty bad at it. But I'll clean anything we catch."

She laughed, with the realization that she'd done more of that, real laughing, today than she'd done in ages. "That was always my parents' arrangement."

"Mama." John Robert appeared in the doorway between the kitchen and combined living and dining area. His eyes shone with muted excitement. "Did you mean it about going to the beach? Can we?"

"Well..." She looked toward the sky again. No thunderclouds, but a good drizzle seemed likely. John Robert's eager face fell.

"They're going to get wet anyway." Chris leaned against the counter and rested his hands along the edge. "Right?"

"Right." She reached out to tousle her son's thick dark hair. "Let's go."

It didn't take long for them to gather what they needed and drive the few blocks to a public beach. In minutes, Camille and John Robert's excited shrieks filled her ears as they dipped their toes in the waves and ran along the shore. Ainsley, more reserved than her siblings, clung to Ruthie's leg, but jumped up and down in vicarious exhilaration with each of their yells. Ruthie's eyes burned as she found herself caught between warring desires to laugh and cry.

His shoes dangling from one hand, Chris chuckled beside her. "They're having a blast."

"Yes, they are." She glanced up at him suddenly. He stared across the sand at her children with his customary serious expression, but his eyes glinted with good humor. She started to reach for his hand and stopped. What was she doing? But the gratitude bubbling through her wouldn't be silenced. "Thank you."

He looked down. "For what?"

She waved toward John Robert and Camille, splashing each other, the droplets of seawater sparkling under the weak sun fighting through the clouds. "For this. I know we're intruding, probably ruined your vacation."

He stiffened, his face seeming to shut down. She tensed, a damper falling on her newfound sense of momentary joy. Oh Lord, now she'd offended him. She took a step back. "I didn't mean to—"

"Stop." If anything his features tightened further, but he smiled, although the expression was definitely forced. "It's not...you're not ruining my vacation, all right?" His gaze drifted to the children. "I'm glad I was around to help."

She nodded, still feeling as if something was off between them. Between them? She barely knew him. They weren't even fledgling friends. He was watching over her only as a favor to her brother. Turning her attention to Ainsley, she tilted her head toward the water. "Let's go see what all the fuss is about, shall we, Ains?"

"Beecham, you didn't answer the question." Jennifer scrambled from the rental car and met her partner at the hood. "What makes you think Calvert will talk to you?"

"We got history, babe." He tossed the keys in the air and caught them with a grand gesture. "Lots and lots of history."

Jennifer shook off the momentary shock of his offhand "babe". A carryover from their undercover work for sure, since he'd used the endearment she normally hated when they'd been posing at social functions. It had fit his persona then, and because it was so at odds with his staid Bureau personality, she liked hearing *him* say it.

She fell in beside him as they mounted the steps to the Chandler County Sheriff's Department, a small two-story building with a rather forlorn air behind a gleaming new courthouse. "What kind of history?"

He shrugged. "We were at Quantico together. Spent a couple of years both working OCD after I left the behavioral unit. We're friends."

Jennifer gave him a cheeky grin as he pulled open the door. "I wasn't aware you had friends, Beech."

He shot her a quelling look. Inside, the scent of over-brewed coffee hung in the air, mixing with the low murmur of a busy department. At the small front desk, a brunette in a sleek navy suit argued with the young officer manning it. "Roger, I'm not asking for the keys to the jail. I just need to get in his office for two minutes—"

"Agent Falconetti, I'm sorry, really I am, but rules are

rules." Roger held out his hands in a helpless gesture.

The brunette tilted her head back, thick black hair falling over her shoulder blades with the movement. "I don't believe this—"

"Well hello, darlin'." Beecham rolled out the greeting and Jennifer gaped at him. The word "darling" was in his vocabulary? "It's been a long time."

At his voice, the brunette spun to face them, surprised pleasure lighting her features. "Beecham."

Her argument with the deputy forgotten, she moved to embrace Beecham. Jennifer bristled. Who was this woman, anyway? Returning her hug, Beecham took it a step forward, planting a kiss on her mouth and actually *dipping* her in his arms with a flourish as he did so. Jennifer stared, a slow burn of jealousy starting in her chest. This was not the Harrell Beecham, stolid FBI agent, she knew so well. This wasn't *her* Beecham.

The door squeaked open behind Jennifer.

"Hey, buddy, unhand my wife." The deep drawl held a slight edge of menace beneath the teasing note.

With a slow chuckle, Beecham restored the brunette to her feet but didn't release her, his arms looped lightly about her waist. "Knew I should have stolen you away from him when I had the chance."

Sure she'd stepped into the twilight zone, Jennifer glanced backward. The lean dark-haired man standing just inside the door was at least four inches taller than Beecham. Clad in khakis and a dark green polo, he grinned at the tableau, but the expression didn't quite meet his brown watchful eyes.

Thumbs tucked in his pockets and his stance one of forced relaxation, he lifted his eyebrows. "What chance?"

Beecham returned his grin. "Hey, I had chances. Didn't I, Cait?"

The brunette patted his arm in a gesture of friendly comfort before she stepped away. "Sure you did, Beech."

Beecham seemed to return to himself with a start.

"Jennifer, let me introduce you. Caitlin Falconetti, one of our fellow agents, and her husband, Tick Calvert." He waved a hand behind him. "Lead investigator here now, right?"

Calvert nodded and Beecham continued, "My partner, Agent Jennifer Settles."

Once the murmured hellos subsided, Calvert eyed Beecham. "So what brings you to this neck of the woods? The wilds and badlands of south Georgia usually aren't your stomping grounds."

"You have to ask?" Beecham glanced toward the front desk, where the young deputy was taking everything in with keen interest. "Is there someplace we can talk?"

Calvert gestured at the hallway. "We can use the conference room."

Conference room was a generous term for the cramped area he ushered them into, filled with mismatched furniture and crammed with storage boxes. Jennifer took a seat, as did Falconetti, but the two men faced off on foot at opposite ends of the table once Calvert closed the door.

Beecham shook his head. "Damn it, Tick, I'm here because you've already given two agents the runaround today."

With a careless shrug, Calvert dropped into the chair next to Falconetti. "What makes you think you're getting anything different?"

"I can help. You know that—"

"What I *know* is that if you're here, you were aware she was in trouble and you didn't do a damn thing to help her."

"Tick—"

"Why don't you cut the bullshit, Beecham, and tell me what's really going on?"

"I can't do that."

"Then I can't help you."

His attitude grated its way under Jennifer's skin. She leaned forward. "We could charge you with obstruction. Sitting in a cell for a couple of days might change your mind."

He laughed aloud, a near-mocking snort. Beecham turned

45

a glare in her direction. Falconetti tensed and rolled her eyes with a muttered, "Oh, God."

Jennifer's neck burned with a mixture of anger and embarrassment. Beecham was supposed to be on her side. They were a team and heaven knew they'd worked that tactic before. Now, the rules had changed and no one had given Jennifer the revised copy.

It royally pissed her off.

She returned Beecham's narrow-eyed stare. He looked away first, returning his attention to Tick Calvert. "I need you to trust me."

"If we were working a case together, in a heartbeat," Calvert replied. "This is different. This is family."

"Cait?" Beecham slid an entreating glance in Falconetti's direction. "Help me out here."

"Sorry, Beech." She lifted one shoulder. "For better or worse, putting him before everyone else, all that jazz. You're on your own, I'm afraid."

With a rough sigh, Beecham rubbed a hand over his nape before he pulled a card from his credentials case. "Listen, I'll be here a couple of days. This has my cell number if you change your mind—"

The cell phone in question rang, cutting him off. He tugged it from his belt and glanced at the display. "Excuse me. Beecham." He listened, his face tightening. "You're sure? Absolutely positive? Yeah. I hear you."

Unease shivered along Jennifer's spine.

"Yeah. Thanks for letting me know. Keep us updated." He snapped the phone closed and returned it to his belt. He flicked a look at Jennifer before meeting Calvert's inscrutable gaze. "That was Weston, our supervising agent. He'll have my ass in a sling for telling you this without clearance, but you need to know. The agents who've been shadowing Stephen Chason lost contact with him. Supposedly he was checked into a hotel in Virginia Beach and supposedly they'd verified his presence, but now no one seems to know where he is."

With his words, Jennifer's unease flared into downright dread. Calvert's face tightened, darkened. "So he knows Ruthie's gone and y'all have no idea where he is."

Beecham planted his palms on the table and leaned forward. "But you know where she is, don't you, Tick? We can keep her safe—"

"Like we kept Tessa Marlow safe?"

Beecham recoiled slightly, stiffening as if in response to a physical blow. "That was different."

"No. This is different. This is my sister and no way in hell am I letting the Bureau use her as freakin' bait to draw Chason out."

"That's not our intent—"

"That's not *your* intent, Beech. But we both know how it works. I've been there, remember?"

"Damn it, Tick. He's going to look here first."

"Of course he is." Calvert shrugged. "Let him look. He won't find anything more than you have."

Beecham's frustration manifested in his inarticulate growl. Jennifer held her fisted hands in her lap. The futility of this was making her crazy.

"Beecham?" Falconetti spoke, her husky voice quiet and intent. "What do you know about Chason?"

Beecham looked at Jennifer with a you-handle-this-one expression. She shifted, leaning forward. "He's all about control. His business dealings, the house, the children, his wife. When you look at the man, you never know what he's thinking. Hides his emotions well."

Falconetti nodded and turned to her husband. "Tick? What do you know about him?"

"I've only met the guy a couple of times, Cait, in the entire time Ruthie's been married to him. He was quiet, distant, when I was around him."

"Sounds like him," Beecham said. "When we've tried to get to him in social situations, engaging him in a conversation is damned near impossible."

A frown drew Falconetti's elegant brows together. "Did it feel like social incompetence or removal?"

"Removal."

"Why are we having this conversation?" Jennifer asked, a trace of her earlier pique twisting through her in a painful spiral. She was missing something and she didn't like being the outsider in the shorthand conversation taking place. She met Calvert's unreadable gaze dead-on. "All you have to do is help us and we can help her."

Beecham didn't move his eyes from Falconetti's, but waved a silencing hand in Jennifer's direction. She snapped her mouth shut and subsided, arms crossed over her chest. Intensity vibrated from his body and he leaned forward. "What is he going to do, Cait?"

"I don't know enough." Annoyance colored her words. "You have to give me more. What happens when he loses control of a situation? Even a small one? Is he a shouter? A hitter? What?"

The memory filtered through Jennifer, bringing with it the lingering nausea. The single time she'd seen Ruthie Chason attempt to stand up for herself, the dark rage on Stephen Chason's face, icily controlled, his words not audible to Jennifer's ears from her vantage point on their adjacent patio, but his actions speaking loud and clear. "He crushes."

Falconetti's attentive gaze flickered to her. "What?"

"A couple of months ago, there was a little stray dog that tried to take up at their house. I think Ruthie wanted to keep it. She fed it, watered it. Chason was...furious." Jennifer shuddered. "He doesn't let the anger control him, though. He killed it. In front of her, with his bare hands. Crushed its skull."

A sick expression twisting his face, Calvert muttered a pithy oath and looked away.

Beecham stared at her. "You didn't tell me that."

She swallowed, remembering still, recalling how she hadn't wanted to relive the experience by verbalizing it. "At the time, it didn't seem relevant to what we were doing."

Bleak realization haunted Falconetti's eyes. "Tick...maybe

you should talk to them."

His own lips formed a taut line. "Cait—"

"I don't think he'll look for her at your mother's first, like Ruthie said." Falconetti caught his hand, intensity trembling in her voice. "He'll want control of the situation. Control doesn't involve him looking for her. Control means making her do what he wants, which is to—"

"Come out of hiding," Jennifer finished for her, queasy awareness settling in her belly.

Calvert jumped to his feet. "How long has he been unaccounted for, Beecham?"

Beecham's face distorted. "Six to eight hours."

"He could already be here," Falconetti murmured.

"We don't know that he knows she's gone," Beecham said.

Falconetti and Calvert exchanged a glance. Calvert nodded sharply. "He knows." He rubbed a hand over his mouth. "Shit, shit, *shit.*"

Beecham shook his head. "Cait, what do you think he's—"

"He wants her to come out," Jennifer said quietly. "What's the best way to do that?"

Falconetti's gaze met Jennifer's, respect shimmering in the dark green depths. "Target her family. Probably the member he'd see as most vulnerable or the one Ruthie would be most attached to."

"Fuck." Beecham closed his eyes on the whisper.

"Call your mother, Tick." Falconetti's command vibrated with urgency. "Have you talked to her today?"

"This morning, after...after. I called and explained, asked her to be careful." He pulled his cell from his belt, his face pale beneath his tan. Phone at his ear, he listened, expression growing grimmer with each second. He slapped the phone closed. "She's not answering. And it's Wednesday. Damn it, Cait, she has Lee, remember?"

Chapter Three

Tick glanced at his watch and tried to stifle a wash of rising panic. Six twenty-three. His mother not answering the phone didn't necessarily mean something was wrong. She could be in the yard with Lee, as she was wont to do even with the shorter days. She could be on the porch, visiting with his aunt or another visitor, where she couldn't hear the phone inside. She could have gone to run errands.

Damn it, he was going to buy her a new cell phone and insist she carry it for sure this time.

"Tick." Caitlin's voice held a nearly imperceptible tremor, one he was pretty sure only he picked up. Seeing traces of his own fear in her expression didn't help.

He straightened, calling up the years of training, letting his cop instincts take over for his father and son roles. "I'm going to run out there, make sure everything's okay."

"I'm going with you." His wife was on her feet instantly. He opened his mouth to argue, but she forestalled him with a look. "Don't even try."

Urgency pounded under his skin with increasing intensity and he wasn't going to waste time. "Let's go."

Beecham took a step toward the door. "Do you want us—?"

"Don't care, but I'm not waiting on you to decide."

Outside, Caitlin's cell phone rang as they hurried down the department steps. She lifted it to her ear, keeping stride with him across the small parking lot. "Hello?"

She stopped short, listening, and he turned, his impatience slithering into something darker at the look on her face. "Did you hear from her today? When?"

He tossed out his hands and mouthed "What?" at her. She shook her head and held up a palm. Over her shoulder, he caught a glimpse of Beecham and Settles climbing into their car. He jerked a hand through his hair. "Cait, damn it—"

"No, Tick and I are going out there now. We'll call you. Yes, I'm sure. Let us go, okay?"

"What is going on?" he demanded as she ended the call. She stepped toward him and touched his arm. Apprehension settled harder in his gut.

"That was Deanne. She still has Lee." The graceful line of Caitlin's throat moved in a swallow. "Your mom never came and picked him up, and Deanne hasn't heard from her since this morning. She's called around and no one else has either."

"Shit." He spun and headed for his truck at a near run. Dire possibilities pulsed in his head in a sickening slide show. "Goddammit."

"I'm driving." Caitlin made a grab for his keys at the driver's door. "I don't think you need to."

He didn't argue, but clenched the keys and jerked the door open with his other hand. "Get in."

She gave him one searching look and did so without further comment, sliding over to buckle her seat belt as he fired the engine. The normally twelve-minute drive took him eight, but they had to be some of the longest minutes of his life. He handled the truck like a patrol car, driving with both hands, taking the curves of the rural highway as tightly as he could at high speeds. Caitlin laid her hand on his thigh, the familiar touch a welcome, comforting weight.

Beecham and Settles pulled into the long driveway mere moments after his truck slid to a stop behind his mother's car. Twilight had fallen for sure now, but the security lights around the house illuminated the yard in the dimness.

The house itself was dark and the side door stood partially

open. Any hope he'd held flickered out. He stepped from the pickup, his stomach in knots, his lungs refusing to cooperate. Nausea trembled in his throat. Caitlin met him at the hood, catching his arm again.

Beecham's brakes whined as he parked next to Tick's truck. Caitlin's easy hold on his arm turned restraining. He started to shake her off, but she grasped tighter, forcing him to turn his attention to her. Loving concern glinted in her eyes. "Settles and I will check the house. Stay here with Beecham."

He glanced toward the house and tried to shake off her grip. "That's my mother—"

"Exactly. Which is why you're staying here." Her fingers dug into him, but her voice softened. "Let me do this for you."

He nodded and she looked beyond his shoulder. "Beech, keep him here until we come out."

She rummaged behind the seat of his truck for his flashlight then signaled to Settles and both women pulled gleaming Sig semi-automatics as they approached the house. They swept the outside first before meeting back up at the side door and slipping inside. Tick stared at his childhood home, a weird buzzing at his ears to match the way his pulse tingled under his skin. The beam of light bounced from window to window, upstairs and down, the interminable minutes stretching into an agonizing eternity. Beecham didn't speak, something for which Tick was entirely grateful. All his concentration was focused on that house, on what Caitlin might find.

Why the holy hell had he let her talk him into staying outside? He needed to be in there, needed to *know* for himself what—

Caitlin appeared through the door, phone at her ear, Settles on her heels with the heavy MagLite in hand. His wife's grim expression didn't induce relaxation; instead he tensed further. A physical throb ran through his shoulders, neck and head as she approached.

"Just hurry, Cookie." Caitlin closed the phone and stopped before him, laying both hands on his arms, holding his gaze.

"She's not here. The house is empty—"

"Holy hell." His knees weakened and he closed his eyes.

"Look at me, Tick. Listen." Caitlin held him tighter and he obeyed, trying to keep his legs under him. "There are signs of a struggle downstairs, a small bloodstain in the hallway, but there's nothing to indicate she's...that she's—"

"Dead," Tick finished grimly. Oh Lord, not Mama too. He'd never really gotten over his father's too-early death.

"Yes. Cookie's on his way and he's calling out the crime scene unit from Moultrie. There'll be leads, Tick, and we'll find her—"

"That son of a bitch is dead. I mean it, Cait, when we find him and she's safe..." His voice cracked and Caitlin pulled him close, wrapping her arms about him. He held on while the fury and fear roiled through him and left tremors in their wake. "When she's safe, I'll kill him for this."

"Hush," Caitlin whispered near his ear. She tightened her embrace and stroked the tense muscles in his back. "It's going to be all right. We'll find her, I promise. We will."

"Looks like the last person to have contact with her was Tori, around eleven this morning." Investigator Mark Cook's face was as taut with stress as his deep whisper. Jennifer stood just inside the kitchen doorway, listening as Calvert's partner talked with Falconetti while the GBI's crime scene technicians went over Lenora Calvert's home with the proverbial fine-tooth comb. "And that's not good."

Falconetti, her expression troubled, glanced toward the living room, where her husband watched every move the CSU guys made. "No. That's more than seven hours and the statistics are—"

"Yeah." Cook ran a hand over his mouth. "Maybe he wants to use her as collateral or bait, something to draw Ruthie out."

"Unless it's about revenge," Falconetti murmured. "Punishing her for leaving, for defying him."

"You could tell us." Jennifer stepped forward, drawing their attention. She held Falconetti's gaze. "You know where she is, don't you? You're Bureau, one of us. Why won't you cooperate?"

The agent shook her head, her expression oddly gentle. "I may be 'one of you', but he matters more." She tilted her head toward the living room, in Calvert's direction. "You think I'm going to undercut him, especially now?"

The impotent frustration scratched at Jennifer. Before she could speak though, the "him" under discussion strode into the room with Beecham close behind. Falconetti moved to Calvert's side instantly.

He jerked a hand through his already disheveled hair. "We got nothing. No prints outside, no tire tracks, nothing." His voice verged on cracking. "God, Cait, how are we going to find her?"

"Stanton's spreading the net." Falconetti ran a soothing palm down his spine. "He's called in every available deputy, they're setting up roadblocks and he's mobilizing search parties." She continued stroking his back in a calming up-and-down sweep. "There's nothing you can do here right now. Why don't we meet Stanton back at the station and you'll know everything that's going on?"

Eyes closed, he pinched the bridge of his nose. "But what if a call comes in here—"

"I'll be here until the crime scene unit finishes," Cook said. "Longer if you need me to be."

A distracted air settling on him, Calvert nodded and allowed Falconetti to pull him outside. Cook disappeared into the living room, leaving Jennifer alone with Beecham. Her lingering irritation and the feeling of exclusion dogged her, and she made sure her voice was cool when he turned to her, his face tense and weary.

She shrugged. "So what do we do now?"

He tucked his hands in his pockets lightly. "Weston wants us to stay here. He thinks it's likely Chason is behind Mrs. Calvert's disappearance, and that given the time frame, he's probably still in the area."

She'd figured as much on her own. Silence settled around them. She looked everywhere but at him and eyed the technicians moving through the hallway and living room.

"Jen?" He'd stepped closer, but not too close, his voice near her ear. "What's wrong?"

Hands planted on her hips, she turned. His calm blue gaze made her want to scream, to rail at him, and she didn't even know why or for what reason, except that when Ruthie had run away, everything had changed. "What was that earlier at the sheriff's department?"

"What was what?"

"That whole..." she waved an irritable hand in his direction, "...*thing* with you and Falconetti and Calvert."

"When I kissed her?" His expression cleared. "That was nothing, it never was, except Calvert's been crazy for her since we were all at Quantico together and I've been trying to throw them together for years—"

"I am not talking about that kiss," she scoffed. "Of course *it* was nothing. I'm talking about what went on in that conference room, when you decided you were going to change sides, change all the rules."

"Jen, honey." He stepped forward and laid easy hands on her shoulders. "It wasn't like that—"

"Don't touch me." She shrugged away from his relaxed grasp. His demeanor and actions reeked too much of her false husband. She lowered her voice and cast a quick look at the rooms beyond. "And don't call me honey. It's not necessary now."

He held his palms aloft in a gesture of surrender. "I'm just trying to figure out what's eating you."

"Forget it, okay?" Suddenly the whole thing seemed stupid and she didn't want to talk about it anymore. "It's nothing. It's been a crazy day and I'm tired."

Hands in his pockets again, he studied her and didn't say anything. She refused to shift under his scrutiny.

"So, we should do what we can to help while we're here,"

she said, grateful that her voice sounded even and normal. "Falconetti said something about search teams?"

His head moved in a slow nod. "Stanton Reed, the sheriff, is working on that now. I already told him I'd help."

So it was *I*, now. She could deal with that. Posture squared, she bobbed her head. "You know what, I think while you're involved with that, I'm going back to the hotel and see if I can get in touch with Brookman. I want to know what all they have on Chason's movements in the last couple of days."

"All right." The stiff silence pulsed between them for a couple of long beats. "I'll drop you off on my way to the sheriff's department."

He was socially retarded.

Chris stood on the small porch, watching the bay waters, silvered by moonlight, lap against the stone shore. That had to be the answer. Okay, "retarded" wasn't PC, so maybe he was socially disabled.

Ruthie's voice carried from the open windows as she settled the children into bed. He frowned. At work, he got along fine with his fellow deputies. He had friends among his colleagues, even if Troy Lee's constant chatter got on his nerves sometimes. He didn't have trouble interacting with other men. Guess he was only socially disabled where women were concerned.

Big surprise there.

It hadn't really bothered him before, but being unable to carry on a decent conversation with Ruthie got under his skin. Bad.

"You didn't have to do the dishes."

He jumped, his skin crawling. She stood right behind him. Blowing out a slow breath, he forced his body to relax. She wasn't a threat to him; he didn't need the fight-or-flight reflexes with her.

Turning, he smiled. Maybe she couldn't see how artificial it was. "You cooked. You didn't think I'd expect you to clean up too, did you?"

Her little laugh emerged harsh and a tad put-on itself. She stepped up beside him and wrapped both hands around the weathered railing. "I never know what to think anymore."

He eyed the elegant line of her nape, exposed by her loose topknot. There was something vulnerable about that sweet curve of skin.

"You were right," he said suddenly, before he'd even thought about speaking. "About being good at cooking. Dinner was excellent."

Another small laugh bloomed between them, more genuine this time. "Dinner was a simple throw-together, not excellent."

He grasped the railing as well. "Don't knock it. I eat a lot of frozen meals. I know good cooking when I taste it."

"I should be good," she muttered, "even if I'm out of practice."

He pulled in another breath and salt air lingered on his tongue. "Why is that?"

"I trained at Le Cordon Bleu." A huff of sound escaped with the words, almost as though she mocked herself. "After I attended the Culinary Institute of America in New York."

"Wow."

"Don't sound so impressed." A wry tone invaded her sultry voice. "The training only counts if you do something with it."

He studied her, fine features highlighted by the moonlight and shadows. "You didn't?"

"No. I married Stephen Chason and let him take over my life."

What was he supposed to say to that? He swallowed. "I'm sorry."

"So am I." She spoke so softly he almost missed the words. Then she straightened, and this time, her voice was stronger. "No, I'm not. Sorry I let him break me? Sure. Sorry I married him and ended up with those three in there? No. I'd never be sorry for having them."

The pleasant memory of their wild squeals on the beach that afternoon echoed in his ears. "They're good kids."

"Too good. But I'm going to change that."

Damn, she was strong. He had no doubt she'd turn her life around now that she was free. Ruthie Chason definitely had what it took to survive.

And prosper.

With a sudden, sharp movement that made him jump, she turned and leaned against the railing. He felt the prickle of her steady gaze on him. "So, tell me about Chris Parker. Did you always want to be a cop?"

"Yeah. As long as I can remember."

She scraped a fingernail along the wood. "Have you been at Chandler County long?"

"Three years. I was with the Tifton PD before that."

Silence fell between them, broken only by the distant lap of waves and the occasional rise and fall of voices from the direction of the village. Ruthie's quiet sigh washed over him. "It's really nice here."

"Yeah." A fall of warm memories tumbled over him—fishing, crabbing, boating, all with his father's steady presence. "It was my dad's getaway."

Her cotton T-shirt rustled against the wood as she glanced up at him. "Was?"

"He died right after I graduated from college. He'd sold the house in Tifton and moved over here fulltime by then."

"What about your mother?"

The familiar cold shadow tried to settle on his shoulders, but he sloughed it off out of habit. No sense dwelling on that. "She took off when I was three. It was just me and my old man. He raised me."

"That had to be hard for you."

"It was okay. Lots of kids survive with just one parent."

"They do. My mother did a great job after my father died, but it was still hard, for all of us. I hope..." Doubt entered her voice as it trailed away and he sensed her squaring those slender shoulders. "I hope I do as well."

"You will." He touched her hand before he thought about what he was doing. The tips of his fingers tingled and he jerked away. Shit. What was he doing? He cleared his throat. "I mean, you're great with them and I'm sure you'll...they'll be fine."

"Thank you." A smile lingered in her voice and this time, she brushed her fingers across the back of his wrist. God, he was too aware of that light touch, too aware of her. This was not good. He had to get away before he went and did something totally stupid, something Troy-Lee-Farr stupid. The possibilities for foolhardy idiocy concerning this woman appeared endless.

Again, he cleared his throat, which felt like he'd swallowed finely ground glass. "I'm going to go give Tick a call, let him know we arrived all right and everyone is okay."

He escaped inside, nerves jittering the whole way, and retrieved his cell from the kitchen counter, where he'd plugged it in to charge earlier.

"Calvert." Terse and distracted, Tick answered on the second ring.

"It's Chris." He closed the bedroom door behind him and dropped onto the narrow bed. "Thought you'd want to know everything is all right on this end."

"Yeah, thanks." Something in Tick's tight voice raised the fine hairs along Chris's nape.

He frowned. "What's up?"

"The Feds lost Chason this morning. At least, that's when they *think* they lost him." Tick's anger vibrated over the line. "And Mama's missing."

"What?" Chris swore and rubbed a hand over his jaw, stubble rough against his palm and fingers.

"Yeah, since sometime after eleven and we got nothing, except that it makes sense that Chason is involved."

"Shit, Tick, I hate that." Damned if Chris knew what else to say. Family held utmost importance in Tick Calvert's life and his mother topped that list after his wife and son. "What do you want me to do? Tell Ruthie?"

"I don't..." Tick exhaled, a rough, shaky breath. "Not yet. I

59

don't...I want to see if the son of a bitch tries to contact us. I don't have a clue where he is or what he has planned, but Cait seems to think he's trying to draw Ruthie out. If you tell her, she's going to insist on coming back here and I don't want her or the kids in further danger."

"Yeah." It didn't feel right, though. Seemed like this was something Ruthie deserved to know. Seemed like any decisions made should have her say.

"Just hang tight and watch over them. I'll call you."

Hours later, his shoes and slacks damp almost to his knees from slogging through miles of riverfront underbrush, Harrell trudged toward his down-and-out room at the small hotel. With exhaustion and self-recriminations dogging him, he'd wanted to check in with Jennifer, see what she'd learned about Chason's movements before he headed back out. Even though it neared midnight, the search continued in full force; the sheer numbers of volunteers spoke volumes about Lenora Calvert's standing in the community. Probably Tick's too, and his siblings. The local people wanted this mother and grandmother found, quickly.

A light rain pattered on the pavement and he shook off the drops that hit his hair. However, he couldn't shake the feeling that somehow he shared in the responsibility for Lenora Calvert's disappearance, for the ragged pain and fear so naked on Tick's face. If he hadn't screwed up, had realized Ruthie was preparing to run, maybe things would be different.

My God, it was Tessa Marlow all over again.

He shuddered and stopped on the sidewalk to pull his key card from his wallet. Clutching it, he eyed Jennifer's room next door, her light burning through a thin space between the blinds. His intent had been to call from his room, but he found himself standing before her door instead, hand raised to knock.

The door swung inward, revealing Jennifer still fully dressed.

"Hi." Her hazel gaze flicked over him, once more leaving the impression that she was pissed off at him. It made him nervous. Quietly angry wasn't Jennifer's style. He'd rather she just gave it to him with both barrels for whatever he'd done that afternoon. "Any luck?"

He shook his head and gestured at his feet. "Need to change my shoes, then I'm heading back out. What about you?"

"Tried to call your cell earlier." Jennifer turned and walked back into the room. He followed, closing the door behind him. Her room was a mirrored twin to his—two queens, dresser, television, table, two chairs. Standard impersonal hotel rooms found all over the country. God only knew how many they'd seen over the years. Her suitcase stood open on one bed; her laptop and notepad lay on the table. "Couldn't get through."

"This place has cellular black holes everywhere." In the past, he'd have dropped onto one of the beds without thought and stretched out while they talked, but once more there was the sensation that things had shifted, changed. He felt unwelcome, too formal with her.

"Get this." Jennifer picked up her notepad. "Chason is back in Charleston."

Shock slammed into him, shifting into a cold, slithering apprehension. "What? When?"

She nodded, a seemingly satisfied smile crossing her face at his surprise. "About two hours ago. Upon arriving home, he promptly called the police and reported his wife and children missing."

"Holy shit," he breathed. Maybe they'd underestimated Chason for real.

"He claims they've been having marital problems and he believes Ruthie took the children as retaliation because he told her he'd planned to file for divorce." Distaste twisted Jennifer's pretty mouth. "Slimy bastard."

"Yeah." Mentally, he tallied the hours Chason had been out of sight. He'd have been cutting it close, but there was definitely time for him to have traveled between Virginia and Georgia and back to Charleston. "So what's the word from the Charleston PD?"

"They, surprisingly enough, are reluctant to cooperate with

us." Irony lurked in her words. "I don't think they're terribly happy that the Bureau was working a major undercover operation in their city without sharing that info."

On a rough exhale, Harrell rolled his eyes. Why did the locals always have to go territorial?

"Weston is flying into Charleston in the morning. I'm going to meet him there."

Harrell's gaze jerked to hers. "Not we?"

Avoiding his eyes, she shook her head. "No."

His sense of being off-kilter flowed through him once more, like a weird form of emotional vertigo. "Jen—"

"Don't you need to let Calvert and Falconetti know what's going on with Chason? I'm pretty sure he'd want to know."

"Yeah, I'm going to head back out in a few but I'd like to—"

"While I'm in South Carolina, I'm going to talk to Weston about assigning us new partners." She delivered the quiet bombshell with deadly calm. The words and their reality exploded in Harrell's consciousness. She was planning to leave him?

"What the hell?" He stepped toward her. His chest throbbed, his lungs struggling to get oxygen in. Shit, he was overreacting. He'd lost partners before and this shouldn't hurt so damn much.

"I don't think this whole undercover gig was a good idea." She lifted her chin to a challenging angle. "The pretending-to-be-married changed things."

"Yeah, I know. It was bound to." He tried to clear his brain, to really think about what she was saying. And not saying. "But I don't want a new partner, Jen. I don't want anyone but you. We're a good team."

"We used to be a good team. Today, I realized we're not anymore." She folded her arms beneath her breasts, a distinctly self-protective gesture. Harrell made another step in her direction.

"Jen, babe, listen, I know things are different. And I'm not real sure what exactly bothered you this afternoon, but—"

"Don't call me babe. I'm not your wife. I'm not...I'm not... Just stop with the endearments, would you?"

"We can find our way back to how things used to be." He swallowed hard. "We can."

"I don't want to go back." Her soft voice held a slight tremor. "That's the problem, Beech."

"I don't understand."

"I can't be your partner anymore. I can't be objective about you."

"Don't talk to Weston yet. Give me a couple of days to show you—"

"It won't change anything." She threw her hands out, frustration crackling in her voice. "Don't you get that, Beech? It won't change this."

In two quick strides, she closed the distance between them, and with her hand at his nape, she pulled his mouth down to hers, kissing him hard. Not one of the fake social kisses they'd traded during their operation, but a real honest-to-God kiss, her lips moving on his, the tip of her tongue teasing him. His stunned surprise rendered him immobile and lasted all of three seconds. He folded one arm around her waist and another along her shoulders, lifting her to him while he changed the angle of his head to fit their lips more closely together.

She moaned and pressed nearer, her short neat fingernails digging into his scalp. When she opened her mouth to him, he dipped his tongue inside, sipping, tasting, relishing the smooth texture and dark mint of her taste. She wasn't shy, holding his head, her tongue taking his mouth in return. Tugging him closer, she stepped back, and when they collided with the bed directly behind her, she tumbled down and took him with her.

Her body accepted his weight, her height making them a good fit—mouths fused, chests and abdomens pressed together, his pelvis cradled by her lower belly, legs intertwined. Arousal speared through his groin and he swallowed a groan, afraid to move, afraid to do more than let this kiss go on and on.

She obviously didn't share his fear and allowed her hands

to roam over his neck and shoulders and upper back, firm sweeping caresses that penetrated his cotton dress shirt and the T-shirt he wore beneath. No words, just the whisper and sigh of kiss after kiss, her hands on him, the heat of her body beneath him, and the slight teasing tilt of her hips into his.

The necessity for oxygen, for sanity, finally infiltrated his brain. Unable to fully abandon the wonder of kissing her, he slipped his arms from about her slender form and rested on his elbows, letting himself have the freedom of burying his fingers in the sweet golden silk of her hair while he softened the kiss to a series of the briefest brushes of lips against lips.

He rested his mouth against the corner of hers, his eyes closed as self-recrimination flooded in. If everything hadn't changed before, it sure as hell had now.

He'd screwed this up, screwed them up, by giving in to what he wanted instead of what they needed, of what she needed—

"Stop it." Her mouth moved under his and her hold on him tightened. "Look at me, Beech."

He obeyed, lifting his head. Her gaze remained steady and calm. She framed his face with her palms. "I wanted this, or I wouldn't have kissed you. This is why I can't be just your partner, Beech. I don't *want* to be just your partner. It's not enough any longer."

"I don't want to lose you," he whispered. "Not as my partner, not as my friend, not as…"

Getting the words out was just too damn hard.

"Not as…?" She stroked a fingertip over his temple. "Tell me. Talk to me."

"Not as a woman." The syllables threatened to choke him. Shit, now he'd done it for sure.

A slow, very sexy, very female smile spread over her kiss-swollen lips. She linked her fingers behind his head and gave a slight wriggling stretch beneath him, a movement that shot desire through him. "What took you so long, Agent Beecham?"

He fought the urge to give in and grin at her playfulness.

"There's too much to lose here, Jen."

She stilled, a frown tugging her neat brows together. "What do you mean?"

"Think about it." He levered up to a seated position, breaking her easy hold. "We're partners, friends. Are you willing to risk all that?"

Sitting up, she pulled her knees to her chest and linked her arms around them, a pose he'd seen her take dozens of times. With her bottom lip caught between her teeth, he knew she was thinking hard, formulating an argument. "I prefer to think about what we stand to gain."

A frustrated growl tickled his throat. "Be realistic, would you?"

Eyes narrowed to glittering slits, she shook her head. "You think it would inevitably end, don't you? In your head, there's absolutely no way we could make a go of a personal relationship in the long term."

"It always ends." The words were out before he realized he'd even thought them. Shit, was he still carrying that old baggage around with him?

"Does it really?" She tilted her head to one side, watching him, assessing him. "What about your friends Calvert and Falconetti? They seem pretty connected. How long do you think they'll last before that ends?"

"That's different." He waved, a dismissive gesture. He cleared his throat. "What time is your flight?"

"Stop trying to change the subject." She leaned forward and he caught a whiff of her—no perfume, just the soft blend of soap and shampoo and Jennifer. He'd become intimately acquainted with that smell over the last few months. "How long do you think they'll last?"

"Hell, I don't know." He shot up from the bed and rubbed his palm over his hair. The answer was easy enough. "With those two? Until it's time to lay one of them in the ground."

Jennifer hadn't moved from her position on the bed. She rocked in a slight back and forth rhythm, watching him with a considering expression on her face. "So you do believe there are long-term successful relationships."

"Yeah, I guess." Hell, she'd obviously paid a lot of attention during her training in interrogation techniques. She was steadily pinning him down, cornering him, working him. "Why are we having this conversation?"

She wiggled her bare toes against the mattress. "Because you've turned into the emotional equivalent of an alien with two heads, you gave me an opening and I'm trying to figure you out."

"Great." Skin crawling, he turned toward the door.

"Walk out that door before this conversation is over, Beech, and I tell Weston to get me a new partner, pronto."

Her steady voice brought him up short. He turned to glare at her. "That's blackmail."

"Technically, it's extortion." She shrugged. "And you're such a pessimist. I prefer to think of it as fighting for what I want."

He threw out his hands. "What exactly is it that you *do* want, Jen?"

"It's simple really, Beecham. I want you, and I'm not willing to give you up without a fight."

Chapter Four

"Chris?" Ruthie paused in the doorway between the minuscule kitchen and the small living room. She'd stayed outside for almost half an hour after he'd disappeared inside, breathing in the sea air, enjoying the alien sense of freedom. She frowned, watching him pace between the door and the couch, from there to the window, in a tight triangle. "Is everything all right?"

He stopped at the window. "Fine."

His stance, the rigid line of his back, whispered of tense deception. The hair on her arms lifted, a wave of goose flesh traveling up her skin with a tiny chill. "What did Tick say?"

"Not much." He'd paused too long, the brief stutter almost imperceptible, but Stephen had made her an expert at watching men, gauging their reactions. Her apprehension deepened.

She stepped into the room, glancing quickly at the room where her children slept. She crossed to his side. "What's happened?"

"Nothing. You're—"

"Stop lying." She grasped his arm, just above the elbow. The muscles tightened dangerously under her urgent hold.

"Don't touch me." His fingers closed on her wrist with near-bruising intensity and he put her away from him, moving so quickly that he was halfway across the room before she realized it. A deep anger trembled in his voice and the incredible tension in his body spoke of fear.

Fear? How absurd. He had nothing to be afraid of, least of all her.

She took a half-step toward him and stopped. "I'm sorry. I didn't mean to—"

"That's fine." He shook his head, but his chest moved with uneven breaths. "I shouldn't have snapped."

"But you are lying to me." She examined him, studying the way he avoided looking directly at her. "Chris, what aren't you telling me?"

He lifted his ice-blue gaze to hers, discomfort flashing over his face. "Ruthie, I..." A shuddery breath escaped him and he rolled his neck, snapping his fingers. "I don't know how to explain to you the situation. Tick asked me to... I'm supposed to watch over you and the kids, keep you safe."

"And not tell me what's going on." Mentally, she kicked herself. Yes, Tick was the best option in terms of helping her, but how had she forgotten his tendency to attempt control of all situations?

"Yeah." One corner of Chris's mouth hitched up in a wry smile.

"Do you agree with him, that I shouldn't know what's going on?"

He shook his head, a soft negative motion. "No, I don't."

"Then why don't you simply tell me what's happened?"

"Hard to explain." He shrugged. "He's my SO."

She fixed him with an inquiring look. "SO?"

"Superior officer." Another loose roll of the neck. "And my friend."

Muted frustration trickled through her. She had nothing to play against that. "At least tell me this—is Stephen in the state?"

He cut his eyes away from her. "I don't know."

"Okay." This was getting them nowhere fast. Her shoulders aching with renewed tension, she reached up to release her hair from its loose knot. She pushed both hands through it. "Tell you what. We'll sleep on it. In the morning, if you still feel like you can't tell me, I'll acquiesce and not ask again, all right?"

He nodded. She turned away, but before she reached the bedroom she would share with the children, his torn voice stopped her. "Ruthie?"

She glanced at him over her shoulder. "Yes?"

"I'm sorry."

"So am I. Good night, Chris."

In the bedroom, she closed the door behind her with a quiet snick.

She'd failed. He'd walked out on her.

The stunned surprise lingered with Jennifer, attempting to distract her from the job at hand.

Needing to get out of her hotel room, with its memories of that kiss, she'd sought refuge at the Chandler County Sheriff's Department, where a command center for the search had been set up in the adjacent parking lot. Being there let her keep her finger on the search's pulse and she'd hoped it would provide her with something to think about *other* than the bleak expression on Beecham's face before he'd turned and left the hotel room.

How the hell could he have done that? Angry hurt washed through Jennifer's veins, poisoning her with bitterness. Damn it, he wasn't leaving her any choices. This wasn't the way things were supposed to be.

She busied herself handing out cups of hot beverages and bagged sandwiches to an incoming wave of weary volunteers. Their grim expressions made it plain that there'd been no positive progress in the hunt for Lenora Calvert.

Their rental car pulled to a stop before the sheriff's department building, mere seconds behind Calvert's dusty pickup. Calvert was out of the vehicle and running up the steps, a taller man unfolding from the passenger seat and moving toward the officer in charge of the command center. Beecham left the sedan and scanned the parking lot, his shuttered gaze finally settling on her. He jogged toward her and nervous excitement warred with a bone-deep disappointment. She cast a quick look around. She didn't want to talk to him with so many others nearby. Setting the cups she held aside, she hurried to meet him.

Damned if she wouldn't look him straight in the eye, either. He might not want to take a chance on them—no way he could deny wanting her, not after that kiss and his admission—but she wouldn't let him see how badly she hurt over that. She wouldn't let him see her confusion.

When she reached the sidewalk, she tilted her head toward the sheriff's department. "What's up?"

"They're suspending the search for a couple of hours."

"Why?"

"For one, the area along that river is hazardous in daylight. It won't help anybody if we lose someone to those waters in the dark." He cleared his throat and tugged his FBI-emblazoned cap lower on his brow. "For another, dispatch here just got a call from an emergency room in Perry in response to the APB they have out on Calvert's mom. They have a Jane Doe brought in tonight, found abandoned behind a motel up there. Unconscious, head trauma, meets her description."

Jennifer tucked her hands in her back pockets. "So you're going with him?"

Beecham nodded. "He has a friend with a small plane and a pilot's license. We can fly up in about a half the time it would take to drive. If it's her, I want to be there when he talks to her."

"Sounds good." Unhappiness shivered through Jennifer in a cold frisson, but she refused to wrap her arms around herself. Already, they were separate, with the ease of partnership between them no longer. What if she hadn't kissed him, hadn't told him how she felt?

Hell, she'd probably have lost him anyway. Maybe it was inevitable, just as he said. Maybe the end had been coming ever since the first day she'd put on that ring and entered a sham marriage with him. What was that old verse? A house built on sand couldn't stand.

She compelled a bright smile to her lips, still a little swollen and tender from his hard kiss. "Maybe by morning you'll have something Weston and I can use with Chason."

"Maybe." Behind him, the glass door to the department shot open and Calvert clattered down the steps.

"Is Falconetti going with you?" Jennifer strove for an even tone.

He shook his head. "Plane's a four-seater and Calvert's brother wants to go. She's seeing to their little boy."

The small talk bordered on painful and she was almost glad when Calvert called his name, a note of impatience in his deep drawl.

Jennifer cupped her hands around her elbows. "Call me when you know something."

He gave a sharp nod, still not meeting her eyes. "Will do. Here, you'll need the keys to the rental."

She accepted them, clutching the metal until its ragged edge cut into her palm, and watched as he left with Calvert without looking back. She glanced over her shoulder at the command center, where a few straggling groups of volunteers remained. Really no reason for her to stay here.

The fact she felt completely lost made no sense and didn't sit well. She straightened her shoulders and lifted her chin. Did he think she'd give up simply because he'd turned away? She wasn't a quitter. Damn if she'd quit on Harrell Beecham.

Their hushed footsteps sighed on the tiled floor of the hospital's nearly deserted emergency waiting area. Harrell hung slightly back as Tick and his brother Del approached the intake desk. The nurse tapped a few keys at a computer there, frowned, then looked up. "I'll find Dr. Taylor for you."

She disappeared through the doorway behind the desk. Del waited, drumming a finger on the Formica countertop, while Tick paced a short back-and-forth path before the counter with tense, tight strides. The waiting had to be hell, maybe even worse than the not-knowing they'd experienced most of the night.

Dr. Taylor appeared, a pretty petite blonde in a turquoise scrubs under a white lab coat. "Investigator Calvert?"

"Yes, ma'am." Tick stopped pacing and stepped forward, Del on his heels.

"She's sleeping. She was quite distraught when she regained consciousness, which can only be normal in a situation like this. We have her under observation—"

"How is she? Can we see her?"

"Is it our mother?"

The brothers spoke together and the doctor's expression softened. "She did identify herself as Lenora Calvert when I talked with her and she fits your description, so I have every reason to believe that yes, she is your mother. She's stable, in good condition other than an elevated temperature, with only minor contusions and lacerations in addition to the head injury. She's understandably agitated, and we're watching her for signs of concussion."

"Contusions and lacerations?" Tick asked, his voice hard. His jaw tightened, a nerve flicking in his cheek.

Dr. Taylor nodded. "Some defensive wounds to her hands, mostly around her knuckles, what looks like gravel scrapes on her palms and knees—"

"As if she'd been pushed from a car," Harrell theorized. The doctor's curious gaze shifted to him.

Tick tilted his head in Harrell's direction. "Agent Harrell Beecham, FBI."

Dr. Taylor acknowledged him with a quick bob of her head. "Yes, you can see her tonight. I'd like to hold her until morning, just to monitor her condition, but I don't foresee any complications at this time."

Del closed his eyes on a whispered prayer of thanks. Tick rested his hands at his waist. "Did she say anything? Tell you what happened? Say who'd done this to her?"

"No," she replied, her tone regretful. "I'm afraid she appears to be suffering from retrograde amnesia at this point."

Del's head jerked up, his eyes flying open. "What does that mean?"

"It means that as far as we can tell, her last cognizant memory is of getting ready for bed last night. She's apparently lost several hours of her recall, which can be quite common with a head injury, even a minor one, not to mention the possible overdose of scopolamine." The doctor's voice gentled. "Please don't think it's a cause for alarm."

Harrell frowned. "Do people with this...retrograde amnesia?" The doctor nodded at him. "Do they often regain those memories?"

"I'm sorry, but usually the memory of the lost hours doesn't return."

"Scopolamine overdose?" Tick's voice emerged with the harshness of ground glass.

"Yes. We ran a tox screen and turned up nearly three times the dosage in her bloodstream."

"Son of a—" Tick bit off the words and flexed both hands, fisting then relaxing. No tension drained from his posture.

Del's brows dipped. "What is scopolamine?"

"It's normally prescribed for relief of motion sickness," Doctor Taylor replied. "The patient indicated it wasn't one of her prescriptions, so I can only assume her attacker administered it."

"Why?"

"It interferes with memory creation." Tick jerked a hand through his hair. "Criminals use it to spike tourists' drinks in some South American countries, and every so often, you'll see it turn up in date-rape drugs."

"The CIA investigated it as a truth serum too." Harrell expelled a breath. "No conclusive evidence that it worked, but if he turned up that little tidbit on Wikipedia, he might have thought he could use it to get Ruthie's whereabouts out of your mother. Interestingly enough, our background data on Chason included the info he suffers from extreme motion sickness when flying and guess what *was* one of his prescriptions?"

"Scopolamine."

Harrell caught Tick's gaze and saw his frustration mirrored there. If she didn't remember what happened and Chason was back in South Carolina...twenty bucks said he'd already covered his tracks. The knot of tension gripping the base of Harrell's neck grew tighter.

Damn it.

"You can see her now," the doctor was saying and Harrell shook himself back to reality. "But only for ten minutes."

Tick cast an earnest look at Harrell. "Would you give the department a call, let them know it's her? And Cait?"

"Will do." Harrell watched Tick and his brother follow the doctor beyond the door marked *No Admittance.* A sign forbidding cell phone usage in the hospital loomed over the counter, so he walked into the cool night air outside. He followed a quick call to the dispatcher with a slightly longer one to Caitlin, her relief palpable over the line. Once she'd hung up, he rubbed his fingers over the edges of his phone.

He needed to call Jennifer.

Why the hell was that so damn hard? Talking to her face to face had been difficult enough earlier. Hell, he hadn't been able to look at her, afraid he'd give in, tell her he'd do whatever she wanted, be whatever she wanted if she'd just give him a chance—

A nauseous shudder worked its way over him, and a cold lump settled in his gut. Where had he heard all of that before? Oh yeah, she wanted him now, wanted him physically, that was for damn sure. But what about later, when her lust and attraction to him wore off?

His mother hadn't raised a fool. He knew from cold, hard experience how that worked.

I want you, and I'm not willing to give you up without a fight.

Jennifer's earnest words sent another tremor over him. Once upon a time, Gina had wanted him too. But that's all it had been—wanting.

He straightened, stiffened his backbone, physically and metaphorically. Let Jennifer find a new partner. Damn if he'd beg. He keyed in the speed dial for her number.

Four rings passed before she answered, her voice weary and a little choked. "Yes?"

"It's her." He glanced back at the tall hospital behind him, its rows of windows a random pattern of light and dim and dark. "Calvert's in with her now."

"So was it Chason? Did she say?" The words seemed torn from duty, holding none of Jennifer's usual case-related blend of excitement and enthusiasm.

"She doesn't remember anything. Doctor says that's pretty normal following a head injury or traumatic event. Not to mention someone gave her an overdose of scopolamine."

"So she can't help us with Chason." Jennifer's frustrated groan carried over the line. "Great. Just fabulous."

"Chason doesn't have to know that," Harrell pointed out. "When you and Weston—"

"He wants you there." The bald statement dropped between them.

Harrell blinked. "What?"

"Weston wants you in Charleston. The flight I'd booked was full, so I rescheduled. We fly out of Albany at nine."

"Okay." He rubbed a hand across his jaw. "I'm not sure how long we'll be here tonight, but I'll see you in the morning. How about if I meet you at that diner down from the sheriff's department?"

"Fine." She disconnected without further words. Harrell stared at the slim black device in his hand. No goodbye. Yeah, that was familiar too.

"Mama?" The nearly inaudible whisper slid past Tick's lips as he leaned over his mother on the narrow bed. Her eyes closed, her face pale beneath the dark salt-and-pepper of her hair, the lines of her features smooth, younger looking in sleep. A smudge of dust darkened one cheekbone and below that, a scrape and bruise marred her chin. A bandage at her hairline hid the stitched wound. He took her hand, her fingers hot and limp in his. A convulsive shiver moved over him. Lord, this could have been so much worse.

Cloth rustled as Del joined him at the bedside, opposite, taking their mother's other hand. Tick flicked a glance at him, his own relief and bottled rage mirrored in Del's eyes. Tick clenched his jaw until it ached. "The son of a bitch will pay for this. And Ruthie."

Wordlessly, Del nodded. He rubbed his thumb across the back of their mother's frail-looking knuckles.

Her eyelids flickered, lashes lifting to reveal brown eyes clouded with pain and confusion. She blinked once, twice, and a tremulous smile curved her lips. Her fingers tightened around Tick's; he was sure she held Del with equal firmness. "My boys."

"Hey, Mama." Del leaned forward to brush a kiss over her uninjured cheek.

She blinked, her eyes glittering with a sudden wash of tears as she focused on Tick. She shook her head, disheveled hair rustling on the starched pillowcase. "I don't remember anything. Why don't I remember what happened?"

"It's all right, Mama," Tick murmured, stroking her wrist in a soothing rhythmic caress. "You're safe and everything's okay. No one's going to hurt you again."

He forced the hard notes of anger and hatred out of his voice. Those emotions didn't belong here, in this room, with her. He smoothed his thumb over the soft crepe-like skin of her arm. "I'm going to take care of it, Mama, I promise."

Del darted a look at him, a narrow-eyed, watchful expression, before he bent down, caressing her hair not covered by the bandage. "You need to rest. I'll be right here, down the hall."

She nodded, squeezing her eyes closed, but a couple of tears escaped, trickling down into the wrinkles near her eyes. Tick caught one on his fingers, taking it away. The anger sizzled in him, made stronger by her distress.

A nurse appeared at the door, tapping her wristwatch, and Tick brushed a kiss over his mother's brow. "Our time's up, Mama, but we'll be close by."

Outside, in the hallway, Del caught his arm. "I want to know everything you know. And I want you to swear to me you're not going to go off half-cocked and do something stupid."

Tick grimaced. "Like what? Kill the bastard? Don't worry, Del, I'll let the system work."

Del jerked his chin toward the room where their mother lay. "Does Ruthie know about this?"

With a harsh exhale, Tick ran a hand through his hair. "No."

Del closed his eyes on a sharp curse. "Don't you think she needs to?"

"I don't know what to do anymore. Don't know whether to tell her, not tell her." He couldn't figure out exactly what Chason was up to—taking their mother, abandoning her, returning to South Carolina to report Ruthie missing, swearing Ruthie had taken the children to get back at him. He obviously wanted to flush Ruthie out of hiding. Was this the psychological warfare she'd lived with the last few years? "I want her safe from him, Del. I hate that she was going through this and she didn't feel like she could come to me—"

"To us," Del said, his voice quiet. "Any of us. I guess on some level, we all failed her. But I think not telling her now is a way of failing her again. She has a right to know what's going on, so she can make her own decisions about what to do, don't you think, Tick?"

Tick fixed his brother, younger by little more than a year, with a steady look. "You think we should tell her."

Del nodded. "I do. Wouldn't you want to know?"

"She's going to want to come back here."

"Yes, she is."

"That's what Chason wants, I think."

"Probably." Del's expression hardened. "I believe between you, me and Chuck, we can keep her safe. We won't let the son of a bitch hurt her anymore. I promise you that."

Jennifer settled into a booth at the small storefront diner and reached for a laminated menu, her eyes gritty and bleary from lack of sleep. She hadn't gone to bed until almost four and once there, she'd tossed around, unable to get her mind to slow down long enough for sleep to take her.

A waitress, her blonde hair piled in a loose knot, approached with a broad smile. "Can I get you some coffee or juice while you decide, hon?"

Jennifer smoothed a finger over the menu. "Coffee would be great. The stronger the better."

"You got it. Be back in a sec."

Perusing the breakfast offerings—what the heck was "breakfast in a cup" anyway?—Jennifer wished she could focus on the case facts, on what needed to be done. She'd never struggled with that before. In the past, putting the job before all else had been so easy.

Damn Harrell Beecham.

"Good morning, Agent Settles." Caitlin Falconetti's husky voice pulled her from the reverie of recriminations. Jennifer glanced up to find the woman standing by the table, clad in impeccable tweed slacks and a wrap-front blouse. The dark-haired baby on her hip made a grab for the stylish beads at her throat. Catching his hand in hers, Falconetti graced Jennifer with a small, polished smile. "May we join you?"

"Of course." Jennifer indicated the booth opposite with a negligent gesture. Why did Falconetti want to join her?

"Here you go." The waitress arrived with Jennifer's coffee in one hand and a wooden high chair in the other. The smile she directed at Falconetti was more of a feral bearing of teeth. "Mornin', Miz *Calvert*." The expression turned more genuine as she shifted her attention to the baby Falconetti settled in the high chair. "Looks more like his daddy every day, doesn't he?"

"Good morning, Shanna." Humor lurked in Falconetti's

husky voice. "That he does."

Shanna straightened. "What can I get you?"

"Coffee and a glass of milk, please." Falconetti slid into the booth opposite Jennifer and watched Shanna walk away. "I'll get the grounds. Just watch."

Jennifer lifted an eyebrow at the droll resignation. She cast a quick look at the waitress, who'd stopped at a table full of farmers. "She doesn't like you?"

"Not very much."

"Why?"

"I took Tick off the market when she was interested in him. Then I had the nerve not to take his last name, which somehow compounded the sin of marrying him. Small towns are strange places. Lee, chew on this instead."

She removed the metal spoon from Lee's death grip and replaced it with a little stuffed octopus with various chewy textures at the ends of its tentacles. Jennifer studied the raven-haired, chocolate-eyed little boy. He gave her a charming grin around the teething toy, his eyes sparkling. "He does look like Calvert, though. She's right about that."

"From day one." An affectionate smile, completely removed from the cool Bureau one she'd given Jennifer earlier, curved Falconetti's lips. "Acts like him too. Stubborn as hell. I figure his terrible twos will be really fun."

Shanna returned with coffee and milk, and they ordered quickly. Falconetti poured the milk into a sipper cup emblazoned with sailboats and handed it to Lee. "Tick and Beecham should be here soon. I wanted Lee to see his daddy before I dropped him at daycare."

Lee lowered the cup with a gurgled "dada" and something that sounded like "here". Falconetti nodded at him and reached over to smooth his bangs with her fingertips. "That's right. Daddy. He's coming soon."

Jennifer eyed the light sparkling off Falconetti's wedding rings. So Beecham could believe in forever for her and Calvert, but not for Jennifer and himself. What was up with that?

She pinned on a bright, interested smile. "Were you and Calvert partners when he was with the Bureau?"

With a reminiscent grin, Falconetti shook her head. "I'm a Behavioral Science Unit agent. He was Organized Crime." She lifted one shoulder in an elegant shrug. "We were at Quantico together. Beecham was too."

Jennifer sipped at her coffee, grimacing a little at the bite. Definitely strong. "So how did you two end up together?"

Falconetti's open expression closed. "It's a long story. I helped prep him for an undercover assignment. Later, we worked a case here that brought us back together."

Not meeting Falconetti's astute gaze, Jennifer rubbed a finger around the rim of her mug. "So you've known Beecham a long time, then."

"Thirteen years. He's a good friend."

Jennifer remained silent. Who knew what answers Falconetti could provide? But asking her seemed like an act of weakness, although Jennifer couldn't say why.

"Agent Settles?"

With a sigh, Jennifer looked up. She laughed, a short, self-deprecating release of hurt tension. "I don't understand him."

"He can be a difficult puzzle to figure out." Genuine affection filled Falconetti's soft voice. "A puzzle with more layers than you'd ever expect."

"Were you two ever...?" The idea made her uncomfortable, but with the memory of Beecham sweeping the other agent into a kiss pricking her with insecure jealousy, Jennifer gestured between them.

"No. Definitely not." A tiny spasm of grief contorted Falconetti's face. "He was—"

"Hey, Leebo." Calvert's deep drawl cut between them and Jennifer closed her eyes for a split second. Calvert lifted his son into a hug, his face drawn and weary. "How's my boy?"

The baby gave an excited squeal and wrapped his tiny, pudgy arms around his father's neck. Calvert held him close, eyes shut, as though being soothed by the warm contact. After a moment, he returned the little boy to the high chair and bent to brush his mouth over Falconetti's upturned lips. "Hey, precious. Lord, I'm glad to see you."

Falconetti stroked his arm and slid over to make room for him. "How's your mother?"

"She seems to be okay." He lifted their joined hands to his mouth, feathering a kiss over her knuckles. "Still doesn't remember anything. The doctor wanted to keep her a little while longer today; Del's going to rent a car and bring her home."

Bothered by the feeling she was spying on an intimate exchange, Jennifer looked away. Her gaze collided with Beecham's and she realized he'd been with Calvert the whole time, standing behind him, watching her.

Oh God, how much of her conversation with Falconetti had he been privy to?

She lifted her chin as she eased to the inside of the booth, giving him space to sit if he chose to do so. Before last night, she wouldn't have thought twice about it. Neither would he.

The imperceptible pause before he slipped in beside her spoke volumes.

She ignored the heat of him beside her, the way a lingering scent of soap and damp air clung to him. Shanna returned, bearing plates and fawning a little over Calvert, asking after his mother before taking his and Beecham's orders, coming back with fresh coffee for both men.

Jennifer focused her attention on Calvert. "So you didn't learn anything?"

"No." He tapped his thumb and forefinger on the tabletop in a jittery rhythm. "I'm hoping you and Beech will be able to get somewhere with Chason today. But considering how his recent actions don't make sense...I'm not really hopeful."

Lifting his coffee cup, Beecham gave an affirmative grunt of agreement. Shanna returned with plates and the men ate, although Calvert did more picking at his food than consuming.

Finally, Calvert rotated his wrist to check his watch. He blew out a long breath, as if in dread of some unsavory task. "I need to go make a couple of phone calls."

Falconetti nudged him. "We'll walk out with you. I need to get going as well." While Calvert extricated their son from the high chair and wiped the baby's face, Falconetti enfolded Beecham in a quick embrace. "Don't be a stranger."

"Pretty sure he's going to be around for a while, Cait." Calvert tugged his wallet from his pocket with his free hand. Juggling Lee and the billfold, he pulled a twenty free and tucked it beneath his empty coffee cup.

When they were gone, Jennifer waited to see how quickly Beecham would move to the opposite side of the booth. To her surprise, he remained next to her, spinning his half-empty mug in a slow circle. Silence hovered over them, broken only by Shanna's arrival to take Falconetti and Calvert's ticket with the twenty and refill coffee cups before whisking away the empty plates.

After a long sip, he continued to rotate the cup in that slow, maddening revolution until Jennifer, nerves already stretched and jangling, wanted to scream at him to stop. "Do you still intend to ask Weston to assign you a new partner?"

She rubbed damp palms over her knees. "Do you want me to?"

He turned a fierce stare on her, his eyes blazing. "What do you think?"

"I think I don't get you."

He glared at his coffee. "What does that mean?"

"It means I thought I knew you." Sadness left her feeling small and cold even this close to him. "But it seems like every time I turn around, I realize how very little I do know you."

"That's crazy, Jen." He shifted, a tight, uncomfortable gesture. Like he felt trapped. She swallowed a sigh. "You're my partner. Of course you know me."

"As an agent." She took a final swallow of her coffee, hoping the warmth of the strong brew would alleviate some of the ice around her heart. She'd *failed* with him and there was nothing about this conversation to give her hope, either. "Give me any situation with you as my partner, and except for yesterday in that conference room, I'd know exactly what you were going to do or say."

"See?"

"But I don't know you as a man." She cringed from the hint of pain that made it into her quiet voice. "You won't let me."

He closed his eyes. "Jen—"

"You know what I don't get, Beech?" She waited for him to raise his lashes. "How you can have so much faith and belief in them." She indicated the vinyl seat Falconetti and Calvert had shared. "And so little in what we could have."

"What exactly is it you think we could have, Jen?" Beneath the rough exasperation lay a hint of entreaty. She grabbed on to that whispered emotion.

"A future." She held his gaze. "A partnership like the one we have professionally, on a personal level. Don't you feel that too?"

He looked away without answering.

"You could give me a chance, Beech. Talk to me." She traced a pattern on the back of his hand. He drew it into a fist but didn't pull away. "Why don't you believe in me?"

"That's the problem." He did tug free then and rose to draw his wallet from the inside pocket of his jacket. His withdrawal, emotional and physical, hurt. He laid a bill on their ticket, and when he finally met her gaze, the cold bleakness had taken root in his eyes again. "I believe in you, babe. It's me I don't have any faith in."

Ruthie set small bowls of bananas mixed with strawberry yogurt and sprinkled with graham teddy bears before the children. John Robert and Camille chattered excitedly to one another and Ainsley about their time at the beach the day before and what might lie before them today, but she only half-listened. Her being seemed focused on Chris Parker, her ears attuned to the muffled movements in the small bathroom as he showered.

She needed him on her side. Keenly aware that *something* had happened back in Chandler County, she needed him to trust her enough to tell her with a desperation that frightened her. Being in the proverbial dark was almost as bad as being at the mercy of Stephen's whims.

She really wanted to know what lay behind that bizarre overreaction of his last night as well. But that answer surely would not be forthcoming any time soon, if ever.

The water stopped in the bathroom, going from full blast to a few loud pattering drops. The metal rings jingled and clattered against the curtain rod. Ruthie, pouring a cup of freshly brewed coffee, faltered as an image flickered in her brain, of Chris's tall broad-shouldered form stepping onto the threadbare rug before the shower, droplets of water trailing down a muscular chest to his narrow waist, sluicing from roped thighs and firm calves as he reached for a towel.

Her face burned and her spoon clinked too hard against the cheap pottery mug. Where had *that* come from? She hadn't even looked at a man with anything remotely like sexual desire in...well, longer than she wanted to think about, let alone fantasized about one naked. That was the last thing she needed in her life right now.

Even if it wasn't, she could surely find better candidates than her brother's rumored-to-be-gay, edgy-around-women colleague. She sucked in a deep, calming breath, centering her thoughts away from the bathroom and its occupant.

The door to that small room scraped open and quiet footsteps creaked on the floorboards in the living room. "Ruthie?"

At Chris's deep voice, she turned, in time to see a flash of firmly delineated abdominal muscles as he pulled a faded T-shirt sporting the logo of a local pub over his head. His short hair, still damp, stuck out in a myriad of directions. She wet her lips and stilled the tiny flutter trying to take up residence low in her belly.

"Yes?"

"Can you step outside with me a second?" He tilted his head toward the kitchen door and the small porch beyond. "We need to talk. I have to tell you something."

Chapter Five

On the small porch, Chris turned to face her, his expression grim. "I've been thinking most of the night and there's no easy way to say this."

Ruthie had been a cop's daughter long enough to realize nothing good ever lay behind those particular words. Grateful he'd given them to her as an opportunity to prepare for whatever blow was coming, she straightened her spine and sucked in a deep breath. "Just tell me, Chris, please."

Hands tucked in the back pockets of his loose, faded jeans, he scuffed a bare foot along the porch floor. Bits of paint flaked under the pressure of his big toe. When he looked up at her, fierce gentleness softened his pale blue gaze. "The FBI has lost your husband."

"What do you mean, the FBI has lost him?"

"You've been... The FBI's Organized Crime Division has had your husband under close surveillance for the past few months. Obviously, his activities weren't as secret as he'd thought."

"The FBI has been watching us. Organized crime." She dug her fingers into the railing. "Did Tick know?"

"I'm pretty sure he didn't."

"And they don't know where Stephen is."

"That's what Tick said."

Oh, Lord. A trembling tidal wave of fear slammed her. Her lungs cramped and a sick weight lodged in her belly. If the Bureau didn't know where he was, did he know where she was?

Fighting off the alarm, she looked back at the children, spooning up their favorite breakfast, still chattering happily among themselves, the familiar strain absent from their smooth features. What would Stephen do when he found them?

"There's more." Chris's tentative statement deepened her dread. With trepidation vibrating beneath her skin, stretching her nerves, she waited in silence, clinging to his gaze. His throat moved in a hard swallow. "Your mother is missing."

"Missing?" Her voice quavered, almost breaking over the word. All sorts of possibilities flashed in her head. Like the night of her sister Tori's rape, when they hadn't been able to find her. Like news reports of "missing" women, their battered, bruised bodies found days, weeks, months later. "What do you mean, *missing?*"

"Her whereabouts are unaccounted for since early yesterday. When Tick went to the house, there were signs of a struggle." The imprecise police jargon made her want to scream at him. This wasn't another alleged victim he was talking about here. This was her *mother.* God, not knowing where Stephen was seemed bad enough—

The reality slithered into her brain with an icy hiss, coiling around all of her thoughts.

"Oh my God." She covered her mouth, fingers trembling. She stared at Chris. "Do you think Stephen...?"

It was too awful to contemplate. Would he punish her escape by harming her mother? Was he that big of a monster? The image of a panting, wriggling pup in his large hands pulsed in her brain, making her want to vomit with the remembered sound of a startled yelp lost in the crunching of a tiny skull.

"It's certainly possible," Chris said, his voice quiet with sympathy. "Under the circumstances, he'd be my first person of interest."

Her thoughts bounced in a wild array. Fingers pressed to her temples, she tried to think, to focus. If it was Stephen, he'd done this because of her, made her mother a pawn, just like he had with Ruthie's babies. He had no qualms about using the ones she loved most as simply another means of controlling her.

The fear and dislike flared into something stronger, truer—a hatred as intense as her original passion for him had been.

"I need to go home." The unexpected words slipped past numb lips.

Startled surprise flickered in Chris's eyes. "To Charleston?"

"No." She shook her head. "*Home*, to Chandler County. If she's gone, it's because of him, because of what I did."

"Are you sure that's a good idea?"

Through the screen, the shrill ring of his cell phone, plugged in and charging on the counter, forestalled her reply. He moved toward the door. "Let me get that. I'll be right back."

Aware of his low voice as he spoke to the children and answered his phone, she stared at the bay, visible between two other cottages. Oh please, let Mama be all right. Let it be a mistake, a misunderstanding. Let her be with a friend, someone, *anyone* but Stephen.

"She already knows." Chris returned, phone at his ear, and Ruthie searched his impassive face for clues. "Yeah, I know what you said. I thought she needed to be aware of what was—" A grimace twisted his sharp features. "Yeah, yeah, I know—midnights for a year. Whatever makes you happy, Tick. She's right here.

"Your mom's okay." At his words, relief cascaded through her. He extended the cell phone. "Tick wants to talk to you."

Her fingers brushed his as she took the device.

"How *dare* you not tell me Mama was missing," she said without preamble. Tick's deep, harsh sigh and mumbled "Ruthie" didn't deter her. The frightened anger steamrolled ahead of everything else. "Damn it, I had a right to know that when it was happening, especially since it's because of me. It is, isn't it?"

"Not *because* of you—"

"Is she really all right?" Her voice quivered, tears burning her eyes.

"Yes. Del's going to bring her home later today." Tick cleared his throat. "Ruthie, Chason is back in Charleston. He's filed a missing-persons report on you and the kids, claims you've taken them as retaliation because he told you he was filing for a divorce."

"He *what?*" The nausea trembled in her once more. What wouldn't he stoop to? Nothing. The answer came quickly, automatically. When it came to dominating her, punishing her, Stephen had no boundaries. Oh God, what to do now? She pressed her forehead, unable to blink back the tears any longer. They slid down her cheeks unchecked. *Think, Ruthie girl. Think!* The situation teetered totally out of her control, constantly shifting around her. "I want to come home. I need...I need to be there."

She couldn't explain why, but the urge was too strong to ignore.

"I think that's a good idea," Tick said. "There'll be an Amber Alert on the children and if you're here...well, we just have more control over the situation then. Let me talk to Chris."

Brushing at her wet cheeks with one hand, she passed the phone back to Chris. His expression intent, he listened. She stared over his shoulder at the tableau visible beyond the kitchen window—John Robert putting dishes in the sink, Camille wiping up Ainsley's face, all of them so well-behaved still it hurt, but with a lightness to them she'd never seen before. She would *not* let Stephen take that away from them. She simply refused to let that happen.

She swallowed a sob, her shoulders shaking with the effort to contain her fear and grief.

"Okay. Yeah. See you in a few hours." Chris closed the phone with a quiet click. "Are you all right?"

Wiping at her cheeks again, she nodded, but her chest hurt with the sobs clawing and fighting for freedom.

"Hey, don't cry." Hard arms came around her with infinite care and she found herself enfolded against a solid chest. Something about the sense of safety and refuge so long missing from her life made the tears flow harder. She bunched her fists under her chin, clamped her mouth shut and breathed through her nose, desperate for control. His clean, freshly showered scent enveloped her and he rubbed an awkward hand over her shoulders. "It'll all work out, you'll see. Don't cry. It'll be okay."

She nodded, trying to pull herself together, her brow rubbing against the soft cotton of his oft-washed T-shirt. She couldn't let the children see her like this.

"Ruthie, you have to stop crying." He slid his hand up to smooth her hair. "I may not have mentioned this, but weeping women tend to scare the hell out of me."

She laughed at that, choking a little, but the tears began to slow, surely what he'd intended. His arms remained around her, and because she liked them being there a little too much, she straightened and stepped back.

"Thanks," she said, running shaking fingertips over her wet cheeks. "But I doubt there's much that scares the hell out of you, Deputy Parker."

His face froze, his mouth twisting. "You'd be surprised."

She remembered, then, that odd trembling fear in him the night before. He was already withdrawing, arms crossed over his chest. His gaze darted away from hers, his jaw set, a muscle flickering in his cheek.

"We need to get moving if we're heading back." He jerked his chin toward the cottage. The icily controlled cop was back in full force. "Get the kids ready while I load up the Jeep."

The Calvert clan descended in full force on the matriarchal home for Lenora's and Ruthie's returns. Chris had been exposed to them in bits and pieces on multiple occasions, but he supposed this was pretty much what it was like to be caught up in the rush of a small tsunami—loud, overwhelming, constantly moving.

They made him nervous. Hell, he was an only late-life child raised by a crotchety older man thrust unwillingly into the role of single parent in his early fifties. The touchy-feely, lovey-dovey stuff displayed in Lenora Calvert's home was beyond his experience.

He leaned against the wall by the kitchen door. For the most part, the children were all outdoors, shrieking and laughing as they played on the back lawn. The adults had gathered around Lenora's huge kitchen table. Ainsley dozed on Ruthie's lap, and Tori clung to Ruthie's hand. Chris didn't think she'd stopped touching her sister since Ruthie had stepped from his Jeep earlier and Tori had run lightly down the steps to embrace her, silent tears trickling down both women's faces.

There'd been more weeping as Ruthie went into her mother's arms and Lenora Calvert, pale but moving under her own steam, had held her daughter close to her heart, rocking her from side to side and whispering into Ruthie's ear.

Once there'd been hugs and kisses all around and a general catching up, Lenora's sons had begun attempting to convince her to stay somewhere other than her home.

"Mama, please." His voice patient, Tick tried again. He leaned forward, one hand curved around his coffee cup, tapping the index finger of his other on the tabletop. "Cait and I have room, Del and Barb have room—"

"Lamar." Lenora shook her head, the white bandage at her hairline snowy against her hair. "The discussion is closed and that's final."

Frustration flashed over Tick's face and Chris hid a grin in a low cough behind his cupped hand. He'd followed enough of Tick's orders over the years to enjoy watching the guy's mom put him in his place.

Lenora reached over to pat Ruthie's knee. "We will be just fine."

A long-suffering look passed between Tick and his brothers. Chris could almost see Tick swallowing a reminder that his mother had recently been everything but "just fine". Tick lifted his hand and waved at his brothers, an eyebrow lifted in inquiry. "I guess we can take turns over here?"

Chris cleared his throat. "I can stay, if you need me to."

The words were out before he'd even thought them through.

All eyes swung to him, and he tried not to cringe. Damn, but they were a crew. He caught Tick's gaze and shrugged. "I'm not on the schedule at the department until next week anyway, right?"

Tick nodded. "Right."

"I'm not going to drive all the way back to the coast. No problem for me to be here until...well, until." Hell, did they have to stare at him? Except for Ruthie, who seemed intent on pleating the hem of Ainsley's dress between her fingers. He looked at Lenora. "If that's all right with you, ma'am."

A slow, sweet smile curved her mouth. "I think that's a wonderful idea."

Over the next hour or so, the crowd dwindled as Ruthie's brothers Chuck and Del took their wives and children home. While Ruthie remained in the kitchen with her mother and sister, Chris unloaded the Jeep with Tick's help.

"I appreciate this, Chris," Tick said as they returned downstairs after depositing the last of the bags in the bedrooms Ruthie and the children would use. "I know you didn't have to offer."

"Yeah, well, she's had a raw deal and your mom didn't deserve all this crap either."

A familiar female voice drifted from the kitchen, the words indistinct. Chris frowned. "Is that Autry Reed?"

"Yeah. She's agreed to represent Ruthie's interests. Figured it made sense, her being in family law now but having the criminal-law background."

"Makes a lot of sense."

Tick tilted his head toward the door. "I'm going to round up Cait and Lee and take off. Beecham called earlier. He and Settles are coming back down to talk with Ruthie tomorrow. They'll be here tonight and we're going to meet with them over dinner." He slapped Chris on the back. "Thanks again."

Chris nodded. Other than the quiet conversation going on in the kitchen, the big old house lay still and quiet. He rubbed the slight pounding at his temples. Ruthie Chason and her children were not his responsibility. Nor was Lenora Calvert. He must have been temporarily insane, offering to stay here like this.

What the hell had he let himself in for?

Ruthie placed the last of the soup bowls in the dishwasher and swung it closed. She wrung out the dishrag and paused, soaking in the sweetness of her mother's voice from the living room. With the children around, very little persuasion had been necessary to convince Mama to rest on the couch and read to them from the *Big Book of Children's Bible Stories.* If Ruthie wasn't mistaken, they were halfway through Noah and the flood.

Footsteps full of quiet authority sounded behind her. "Ainsley's passed out."

She smiled at Chris's words and attacked the spotless countertop with the damp rag. "Reading aloud does it every time. Camille will nod off next."

From the corner of her eye, she glimpsed him rest his shoulder against the jamb. "What about John Robert?"

She rubbed at a nonexistent stain on the grout. "He won't miss a word. He loves books too much to fall asleep during one."

"I could see that. He was all over the bookshelf in there earlier, pulling out ones he hadn't read yet."

She could only imagine. "That's my boy."

"Do you read?"

The question was aimless, nothing but friendly small talk, but it slammed into her regardless. "Not anymore. Stephen doesn't—"

"I'm sorry." Chris cut her off. His voice reeked of discomfort. "I didn't mean to—"

"It's okay." She slapped the rag into the sink and scrubbed. "That's over."

"That's right. It's over." Certainty rang in his words, as if he believed. "You can read whatever you want to, do whatever you want to, and he can't—" His cell phone jangled to life. She glanced over her shoulder to find him peering at the display. He grimaced. "Excuse me."

He lifted it to his ear. "Parker. Yeah. What do you want?"

A laughing male voice was audible even to her, although the words were jumbled and indistinguishable. Chris rubbed a finger over his temple. "Yeah, I'm back already. No, I can't meet you in the morning. Because. Damn it, Troy Lee, I know you have a life that doesn't involve me, so go...ah, Jesus, you didn't just say that. Shut up, would you?"

Her neck hot, Ruthie turned back to the sink. His boyfriend, maybe? Someone who would mind his staying here. Her shoulders slumped. The last thing she wanted was to make trouble for him, even if having him here made her feel safe for the first time in forever.

"Good night, Troy Lee." His voice ringing with finality, Chris smacked the phone closed. He laughed and pressed the thin rectangle to his forehead. "God help me."

Ruthie folded the dishcloth across the sink divider and turned to him. "You don't have to stay. I don't want us to interfere with—"

"Please don't start that." He returned the phone to his belt and leaned on the counter, one foot propped over the other. "So what are you going to read first?"

Sweet complicity unfolded between them and a desire to laugh from sheer joy burbled in her. "I don't know. What do you suggest?"

His eyes widened, a hint of deer-in-the-headlights in them. "I'm not sure we'd have the same reading taste, Ruthie."

"Oh, come on, Chris Parker, what was the last great book you read?"

"A training manual on drug interdiction."

"You're kidding."

"No. Before that I read a couple of biographies and I'm waiting on Tick to finish *Friday Night Lights* so I can read his

copy. What did you read"—discomfort twisted his face—
"before?"

"I loved du Maurier and Agatha Christie. Maybe Mama's got
some of my old ones around here."

"Sounds like John Robert won't be the only one raiding the
bookshelf."

"I guess not." She dropped her gaze from the intensity of
his.

He cleared his throat. "Well, I'm going to hit the shower. If
you need help with the kids, just holler."

"I'll be fine." She folded her hands around the edge of the
countertop, trying to dodge the images of him in the shower.
"But thank you. Goodnight, Chris."

He straightened, his gaze falling away from hers.
"Goodnight."

It had been one long hell of a day, and Jennifer needed a
drink.

Maybe four.

Maybe the whole damn bottle.

Maybe what she needed to do was fuck Harrell Beecham
until he came to his goddamn senses.

The absolute last thing she needed was to have to play nice
over dinner with Beecham's friends Calvert and Falconetti, with
their happy little marriage and their happy little secret-code-
word friendship with her partner.

"Jen?" He rapped on the connecting door between their
rooms.

Jennifer jammed her feet into her shoes and stalked over to
swing her door open. "What?"

He blinked, obviously taken aback. "I was just seeing if you
were ready to go."

She narrowed her eyes in her harshest glare. "Don't talk to
me."

A puff of surprised laughter emerged from his lips. "What?"

"You heard me." Spinning away, she dug in her suitcase for her earrings. "I'm pissed off at you. Don't talk to me."

"You're not wearing that, are you?"

She glared at his shirt and tie. Mr. Bureau Dress Code Poster Boy, all buttoned up, clean shaven, his close-trimmed auburn waves neatly combed.

"Yes, I'm wearing this. We're not technically working tonight." She swept a hand up and down to indicate her black skirt and aqua halter top. "What's the problem?"

"Don't you think the back of that top is a little revealing?"

Considering she'd bought the thing because the chain detail on the back was cute and revealing? Yeah, it was a tad on the side that belonged to visual teasing. She tapped one foot while threading her earrings through her pierced ears. "It's fine. Besides, your buddy Calvert obviously has eyes only for one woman and that's not me. Nobody else is going to be looking."

"I'll be looking," he muttered.

"You don't count."

"Damn it, Jennifer." The words emerged as a veritable growl. "Don't do this."

She propped a hand on one hip. "Don't do what?"

"Don't be this way."

"I warned you. Told you not to talk to me. You started it."

"Jen. You're being a bitch."

Fully dressed, she crossed to stand before him, tilting her head back slightly to meet his blue gaze, gleaming with frustration. She tapped his chest with one finger, hard. "How do you want me to be, partner?"

"I want you to be yourself."

"This is me."

"No, it's not. I don't know what's—"

"What's the matter, Beecham?" She turned away with a halfhearted shrug. "Afraid I'll embarrass you with your friends if I'm not the perfect little FBI agent? You know, I'm a real person. I have a real life and a *personality* separate from the goddamn

Bureau."

"Yeah, whatever." He rolled his eyes and threw up his hands in a gesture of defeat. "Let's go. Maybe you'll get beyond the maturity level of a twelve-year-old before we get there."

She snatched up her clutch, big enough to carry her creds, and tossed her badge folder in, gracing him with a withering look while she did so. He gazed back at her, steadily, as though dealing with a recalcitrant child. Her skin buzzed with annoyance under that expression.

"Oh fuck you, Beech."

One second she was adjusting her thigh holster, the next her back was against the wall, wrists pinned by her head, and she stared into blue eyes ablaze with fury. Her stomach turned over, a visceral reaction to the tension crackling between them. Feminine satisfaction curled through her.

She'd finally succeeded in ruffling cool, calm Special Agent Harrell S. Beecham.

"Jen." A deep, shaky breath heaved his chest and he rested his forehead on the wall next to her, releasing her hands as he did so. "Enough."

He was too close, close enough to touch, but too far away, somewhere she'd never be able to reach him. She could rattle that control of his, but she couldn't break it.

She levered her hands between them to flatten against his chest and ease him away. "Let's go."

"Jennifer." His voice held a quiet plea she didn't quite understand. Didn't matter anyway, did it? More and more, it seemed she was fighting a battle she couldn't win.

She didn't look at him, focusing at her thigh, on the holster she could adjust by touch alone. Once she felt more together, she straightened to meet his shuttered gaze head on. "I'll behave myself, okay? I promise."

A harsh sigh rumbled through him. "Jen..."

"Just..." She waved in terse dismissal. Too bad it wasn't a magic wand. She wanted this night over and done. "Let's *go*."

The silence stayed wrapped around them during the ten-minute drive. Jennifer stared out at the rural countryside, shrouded in the shadows of early nighttime. Her chest quivered with uneven breaths. With shaking fingers, she smoothed the hem of her skirt. She was going to have to ask Weston to assign her a new partner for real. She simply couldn't work with Beecham anymore.

God, this sucked.

Beecham slowed to turn into a long gravel drive that opened up beside a large white farmhouse sheltered by a stand of tall pines. He parked behind a now-familiar white Z71, a Volvo to its side. The interior light flashed on when he opened his door and Jennifer sucked in one last deep, calming breath. Time to get her game face on.

She met him at the edge of the red brick pathway leading to the wide porch running along the back of the house and opening up to a generous sundeck. Solar lights spilled little pools of golden light along the way and ceiling fans with soothingly dimmed lights turned in lazy circles on the porch. Jennifer looked everywhere but at Beecham while he knocked at the back door. It was a nice place, well-landscaped with a mixture of old plants and new, rockers and an antique church pew gracing the porch, chaise lounges and an outdoor dining set complementing a large gas grill on the deck.

It spoke of home and family and happiness, and any other night, she would probably have enjoyed the aspect of a friendly dinner there.

The door swung inward and around Beecham's arm, Jennifer caught a glimpse of Calvert, casually dressed in jeans, a steel blue golf shirt and leather boat-and-deck shoes. His shirt bore a handful of small damp spots and an aroma of baby shampoo wafted from him as he shook Beecham's hand.

"Hey, Beech, good to see you. Settles." He nodded in Jennifer's direction and stepped back. "Come on in. Cait's putting Lee down"—he indicated the front of his shirt with a rueful grin—"since I did bath duty. I need to fire up the grill and get those steaks going. Y'all make yourselves at home, grab something to drink from the fridge and come out to the deck."

The inside of the house was as inviting as the exterior, but Jennifer didn't, couldn't, relax. Frowning, she studied Calvert as he pulled a platter of steaks and a container of vegetable skewers from the refrigerator. Something was different, something she couldn't put her finger on. The guy seemed almost human.

Relaxed. That was it. This was the first time she'd not seen him carrying a hard edge of tension, as he chuckled at some offhand comment of Beecham's. Hell, even Beecham seemed to be unwinding in Calvert's presence.

So she'd be the only one wound tighter than her nephew's ancient jack-in-the-box. Wasn't that fucking wonderful?

She needed that drink all over again. Filled with gratitude, she accepted Calvert's offer of a beer before the investigator went out to the deck. She cast a spurious look at Beecham's glass of sweet iced tea. Hope that worked for him.

With the cold longneck in hand, she wandered along the interior wall of the keeping room, lined with photos in neat arrangements. It could have been her mother's wall of photographic fame—family groupings, weddings, birthdays, graduations, special moments. There were almost as many baby photos as her mother displayed proudly.

At least no one here would tell her she should find a man and add a couple of babies to the pictorial infant-fest or remind her she was facing thirty head on with no prospects of the former or the latter.

The coffee table in the comfortable living area held haphazard stacks of snapshots and a set of open, waiting photograph storage boxes. These people were photo crazy; her mother would love them. Tipping up her bottle, Jennifer took a draw, the icy, bitter liquid tickling down her throat with a warm sense of afterburn. God, maybe that would help take her edge off.

Fat chance, since every nerve in her body sang with the knowledge that Beecham remained at the kitchen island behind her, silent, watching. Silent was good. She had nothing more to say to him.

"Feel free to look through those if you like." Falconetti's husky voice cut through the tension. "It's not like I've even started organizing them. Hey, Beech."

Affection warmed her tone and Jennifer's ears picked up the rustle of cloth and the tinkle of ice in a glass being set aside. Aw, a hug. Wasn't that just all warm and fuzzy?

Tilting her bottle up for another slug, she sank onto the couch and lifted a photo from a stack. Falconetti was right—there was no rhyme or reason here, baby shots of Lee jumbled in with wedding photos. A beach wedding, Calvert in a tux and bare feet, his arms wrapped around Falconetti from behind, a wide grin on his face, her face without its icy Bureau set as she looked up at him. Gorgeous dress, a white silk slip-style—simple, sleek, elegant. Nothing like the hideously expensive, hideously poufy gowns her sisters had chosen for their nuptials.

Fishing expedition. Honeymoon pics. Calvert's bachelor party, maybe? More baby photos. Lee was a cute kid, all big dark eyes and wide grin, black hair sticking out from his head. Between the beer and the mindless activity of peering into someone else's life, Jennifer's inner tension loosened. As long as Beecham stayed on his side of the room and kept his mouth shut, she'd be just fine.

Christmas party. Graduation shots of a tall dark-haired youth. Jennifer flipped that one over and there it was, staring up at her, the implications slamming whatever calm she'd gained right out of her.

Beecham and Falconetti, wearing stupid glittery New Year's Eve hats. And to his right, in the curve of his arm, a stunning redhead whom he looked at with what appeared to be good old-fashioned passionate love.

Jennifer blinked.

The image didn't change, and Beecham's blue gaze remained filled with a mingled tenderness and longing that turned her stomach. She closed her eyes. A deep breath did little to center her. Behind her the door opened and closed, and the sounds of someone moving about the kitchen, liquid splashing, wafted over her. Let that be Falconetti. Let Beecham have gone outside to indulge in some basic male bonding with Calvert over charring decaying animal flesh.

Just give her a freaking break. Just one.

"I'd planned on putting those in albums." Falconetti's voice came from somewhere above and to Jennifer's right. "You see how far I got with that."

Jennifer opened her eyes in time to see her fellow agent sink onto the ottoman before the plush leather chair. She lifted her beer. "At least you have the photos. Mine are still on my digital camera." She laughed, cringing as the sound came out shaky and bitter. "It makes my mother crazy."

Falconetti nodded and Jennifer burned under her scrutiny. God, this had been a mistake. She should have refused to come, should have told Beecham he could handle this. All they were going to do was talk anyway, damn it. He didn't need her for that.

He didn't need her for anything, obviously.

She tapped a fingertip against one of the wedding photos and smiled, the expression so brittle it hurt her face. "Great dress."

"Thanks." Sweet reminiscence colored Falconetti's tone and she tucked a loose strand of black hair behind her ear. She lifted a small stack of the glossy photographs. "You know, I think there's one of Beecham and Tick at our reception."

She didn't want to talk about him. She just wanted—

"Here it is." Falconetti laid it on the table. Jennifer gave it an unwilling perusal. It was a good shot, fairly close, both men laughing and relaxed. She flexed a hand against her knee and sipped at her beer. An impish smile lit Falconetti's face and she held another snapshot aloft. "And here we have Beecham crashing my bachelorette party."

Dutifully, Jennifer glanced at it. She paused, frowning. His eyes were different in that photo. He grinned, on the verge of a laugh, one arm slung around Falconetti's shoulders in friendly camaraderie, but the light glowing in his eyes in the New Year's Eve photograph was gone.

Well, the redhead hadn't been apparent in his life the last two and a half years, so obviously she was gone too.

She darted one more quick look at the photo of Beecham and the redhead. Falconetti picked it up, the tiny spasm of grief she'd worn in the diner darting over her face again. She tapped the picture against her palm. "My partner."

Oh holy cripes, did the woman live *here*? Was that why Beecham was acting so damn weird? Holy shit.

With her luck, gorgeous redhead was invited to dinner.

"She was killed a few months before I married Tick." Falconetti laid the photo aside, her green eyes dark and wistful. She straightened, pinning on a bright smile. "I'm sorry. Not great dinner conversation, is it? Tell me about—"

"I'm sorry." The shocked words finally made their way past Jennifer's numb lips. My God, the woman was *dead*. She was dead and Beecham had obviously loved her. And Jennifer had never known, even with all the late-night conversations they'd shared. Her heart ached for him, but at the same time, a few of the painful pangs belonged to her. Another example of how little she really knew about him beyond the day-to-day working relationship. "That must have been horrible for you."

"It was bad." Falconetti moved a shoulder in an elegant, albeit uncomfortable shrug, as though she wanted to leave the topic behind. "So where are you from?"

"Tennessee. Um, outside of Nashville." Jennifer tried to pull her frenzied thoughts together enough to make coherent small talk.

Falconetti's perfect-hostess expression made an appearance. "It's a nice city."

The door swung open and Calvert's deep laugh preceded the men into the house. Jennifer finished off her beer and patted her thigh with one damp palm. She couldn't look at her partner. How could she want to hug and comfort him over what had to be a devastating loss and want to get as far away from him as possible at the same time?

The busyness of settling at the dinner table saved her,

giving her time and purposeful movement to pull everything together. She even managed to distance herself from the exquisite torture of sitting at Beecham's side as Calvert outlined for them the plans for his sister, offering her something tangible and real to focus on. After dinner, he gifted her again, bringing out a manila folder packed with scanned copies of handwritten ledger pages.

Stephen Chason's ledgers.

Ruthie had possession of Chason's ledgers. And now they had copies of them. With reverent fingers, Jennifer paged through the file, her excitement growing with each column, each digit, each page. Here was something real, something in black and white she could make sense of. Pure, unbelievably profitable money laundering. None of the chimerical puzzles that made up Harrell Beecham here.

This she could deal with.

This explained why Stephen Chason had seemed so edgy in South Carolina, why he'd been so eager to find his wife and children. He didn't want Ruthie back. He wanted what she had in her possession. A frisson of unease trickled down Jennifer's spine as she recalled Chason's hands engulfing the stray puppy's head, how he'd squeezed and twisted. What would he do to Ruthie for defying him this way, putting him at risk for prosecution?

"Jennifer?" Beecham's terse tone pulled her from the morass of memories. One hand in his pocket, he jingled the rental keys. "Are you ready?"

She flushed and darted a glance at Calvert. She held the folder close to her chest. "May I keep these?"

He nodded, his eyes dark with renewed tension as unspoken understanding flashed between them. He wanted Ruthie safe more than she did, was willing to do whatever it took to make that happen. She could almost like the guy.

Almost.

Like she could almost love Harrell Beecham, if only things were different.

She was quiet. Harrell glanced sideways at Jennifer, Tick's folder neatly aligned on her thighs, her posture straight and perfect, hands folded over one another atop the file. She stared straight ahead, her face set in impassive lines, filtered moonlight occasionally flitted across her features. She was too quiet, her earlier fit of pique seemingly forgotten and gone for good.

He almost preferred her riled and needling him. There was something so real and passionate and alive about her when she was giving him what-for that he wasn't sorry for letting her beneath his skin.

Hell, all he wanted was a happy medium, not her tense and frustrated anger causing her to strike out at him with sarcasm nor this cold, emotionless silence. He wanted his partner back. No, he wanted *Jennifer* back. He tightened his hands on the wheel and negotiated the sharp double "S" curve.

"You loved her, didn't you." The quiet statement came out of nowhere, startling him. "Falconetti's partner, I mean."

The car swerved once and he quickly brought it back to center. He darted a look at Jennifer, who continued to gaze ahead. How the hell did she know about Gina?

"I..." He shook his head, trying to clear his mind and gather his thoughts. "I thought I did."

She didn't respond and he clutched the wheel. His chest tightened and he swallowed. "I guess I loved what I thought she was."

Jennifer didn't turn in his direction, didn't move at all. "What do you mean?"

"She...she simply wasn't the person I believed her to be. So I can't honestly say I was in love with *her*." Maybe the explanation would satisfy her. He wasn't going to get into all the ways Gina hadn't been what he thought. She was dead and he wanted her memory to rest in peace. She deserved that at least.

"I can understand that." Her soft voice filled the dimness around them. She tapped her thumb once atop her other hand.

"It would be hard to love an idea instead of a flesh-and-blood person."

"Yeah." The edges of the town of Coney opened up around them, a handful of houses, a convenience store, a small restaurant under a huge oak tree. She shifted against the seat, wrapped her arms over her midriff, and turned her face to the window. Braking for a traffic light, he glanced at her profile, outlined by the garish lights of a used car lot.

She'd said she wanted him, was willing to fight for him. She'd insisted they could have something together, but it seemed all the fight had drained out of her.

Because of him. Because of his goddamn fear.

He rested an elbow on the door and pinched the bridge of his nose. All that sarcastic anger in her earlier, her quiet withdrawal now—she was hurting. No. That didn't cover it.

He was hurting *her*.

"The light's green." Her hushed, weary voice washed over him. He straightened and drove on, taking a left at the next intersection.

I believe in you.

His words came back to taunt him. Belief. That involved trust. He'd lied when he told her he believed in her, that he didn't believe in himself. He wasn't convinced he was capable of maintaining a long-term relationship, but that wasn't the real issue was it? The real issue was trusting someone enough, believing she'd never let him go, never let him fall.

But he was letting her fall, standing back, doing nothing, because of the risk to himself. And the hell of it was, he wasn't saving himself. He hurt so damn bad at the idea of losing her, worse than he ever had over Gina walking away from him, worse even than knowing Gina was dead, that all his second chances there were over and done. He pulled into the lot at the small motel and drew to a stop before their adjacent down-and-out rooms. Shifting into park, he stared at the nondescript stucco wall before him.

"Good night." With Tick's folder clutched to her chest,

Jennifer pushed open the door and slipped from the car. Killing the engine, he watched her walk to her room, the smooth muscles in her bare back moving in supple grace as she unlocked the door and went inside.

Damn it, there had to be a way to fix this. Cool, moist night air wrapped around him as he locked up the car and walked to his own door. His entire body ached, each muscle taut and singing with invisible tension. He let himself inside, tossed his keys on the dresser, toed out of his shoes.

The connecting doors remained open between their rooms. Acting on a rare impulse, he walked to that doorway, loosening his tie as he went. Barefoot, she stood on the other side, one hand on her door in preparation to close it. Their gazes caught, clung, her eyes damp and glittering. His throat closed, his lungs tightening. She lifted her chin to a defiant angle and didn't look away.

He held on to the edge of the door, digging his fingers into the hard surface. "Jen, I don't know how to say this—"

"I think we've said enough." She shrugged, her bare shoulders slumped. "I'm tired, Harrell."

She made to shut the door and he caught the slab before she could do so. "Jennifer."

"No." She blinked, the moist shine in her eyes intensifying. "No more."

"Listen to me, please." He shook his head, desperation coiling in him in a wild frenzy. "I thought I loved Gina, that's true, but what I felt, what she meant...it's jack shit compared to what I feel about you, what you mean to me."

Her lips parted on a harsh breath. "Beech—"

"You have to help me, Jen." His heart thudded, trying to come out of his chest, his palms went damp, hell, his knees wanted to buckle under him. "I'm in love with you and it fucking scares me to death."

Chapter Six

The house sat dark and silent, but Ruthie found the shadowy quiet both familiar and comforting. With the children sleeping in the rooms her sister and brothers had used, she slipped along the hall to check on her mother, then tiptoed down the stairs.

The kitchen light cast a golden glow into the hallway. Her bare feet padded on the polished hardwood. Lord, it was so good to be home. As she passed the living room, a looming shadow at the picture window moved and she jolted against the hallway wall. Her pulse kicked into a wild pace. A scream rose in her throat, unable to find release.

Oh, God. *Stephen.* He'd come for her.

"It's me." Chris's calm voice slid across her jangling nerves, and she slowly relaxed, hand over her heart.

"What are you *doing*?" she whispered as he stepped into the dim light. "You scared me to death."

"Couldn't sleep." He came closer, his tall form lean and lithe in a faded T-shirt and pajama pants. "Used to town sounds, I guess. It's too quiet out here."

She crossed her arms over her abdomen, the warmth of home pulsing in her. "I like it."

He circled one shoulder in an exaggerated shrug and rubbed at the muscles there, as though it pained him. He gazed down at her, but she couldn't read the expression in the murky hall. "What are you doing up?"

"Couldn't sleep." She tipped her head toward the kitchen.

"How does hot chocolate sound?"

"If it's that powdered stuff, really, really gross."

"Bite your tongue, Chris Parker. I said hot chocolate, the real thing."

"Then it sounds pretty damn good."

In the kitchen, she busied herself with the preparation. Something about his presence made the huge room with its high ceiling and old-fashioned cabinets seem small and intimate. He didn't watch her but studied her now and then, his steady scrutiny on her like a whispery touch before he turned it away again.

Finally, she joined him at the scarred oak table, placing a steaming mug before each of them. One foot tucked beneath her, she rubbed her fingers into a smooth gash on the wood. The table had been in her family for generations; each mark held a distinctive memory.

He cradled his mug and sipped, wincing a little, probably at the heat, before pleasure warmed his eyes. A slow, satisfied smile curled his mouth, softening the hard line of his bottom lip. Her stomach fluttered. "This borders on sinful."

Somehow, she didn't need that word from him, simply because it sent another shiver through her. She cupped her palms around her own mug but didn't drink yet. Warmth seeped into her skin. "Thanks."

His attention dropped to the rich liquid for a moment. When he lifted his head, he studied her, a speculative gleam in those ice-blue eyes. "So what are you going to do with all that fancy chef's training of yours now?"

She blinked. "What do you mean?"

His fingers tapped a slow, steady rhythm against the heavy pottery. "Your husband isn't around to stop you from using it. Cooking obviously meant enough that you went after the best training you could find. What are you doing to do with it?"

"I…" With a wry laugh, she shook her head. "I haven't really thought about it."

His face closed with the swiftness she'd grown used to over

the past two days, and he dropped his gaze. "Not a lot of time for that yet, I guess. I'm sorry, I shouldn't have—"

"No." On impulse, she laid her hand on his wrist. He jerked slightly at the light contact. "Don't be sorry." She laughed again, a rich happiness curling through her. She would be able to cook now. The possibilities danced before her. "You've given me something fantastic to think about. To dream about, maybe."

He darted a look at her, one corner of his mouth quirking, his features slowly relaxing.

Ruthie leaned forward, wanting to ease the final vestiges of tension from his face and body. "Probably not too much demand for a gourmet chef in Coney, Georgia, huh?"

"Don't know about that. The hunting plantations put on some fancy meals. There're a couple of really nice restaurants in Albany. Bet there's a catering market down here too."

She bit her lip on an excited smile. Her fingers practically itched with the need to take up a knife, to flip a sauté pan, to... Oh, he was right. The options could be endless.

He lifted his mug. "Looks like serious contemplation there."

"It's..." Words failed her and she waved an airy circle. "It's hard to explain."

"It's like getting a whole new life," he said. "Like being reborn, almost."

"Yes. Exactly." How did he know how to articulate what she was feeling, what she hadn't been able to put into words herself? She tightened her hold on his wrist for a second, an affectionate squeeze, and released him. "I'm glad you're here."

Surprise flashed over his features. A laugh rumbled from his chest and he leaned back. "Why is that?"

"Because you've made this whole mess so much easier. Because for some reason, you seem to understand how I feel and because, well, because I trust you."

"You've known me two days, Ruthie." He drained his cocoa, his face set in a frown that reeked of discomfort. "That's not enough time to know you can trust someone."

"Actions say a lot." She trailed a fingertip along the rim of her mostly untouched mug. "I've had a lot of time the last few years to realize that, to see in retrospect the warning signs I should have recognized and didn't. Or maybe I did see them and simply talked myself into not believing them."

His lashes shadowed his cheekbones. He spun the empty mug in a slow circle. "That happens, more than you might think."

"Have you been hanging out with my sister?"

"What?"

She shook her head. "Tori said the same thing. It's odd, having my baby sister try to be my crisis counselor. I'm sure she means well, but—"

"It makes you uncomfortable."

"Yes." With a light laugh that felt faked and forced, she indicated her cocoa. "Do you want this? I don't think it's what I wanted. I've barely touched it."

"Yeah, I would." With a sheepish grin, he reached for it. "What can I say? I'm used to the microwaved powder stuff and this is the best damn hot chocolate I've ever had."

Warmth spread through her veins with his praise. She'd gotten little of that, if any, over the years with Stephen. "I promise I don't have cooties."

A chuckle rumbled in his throat. "Funny."

Comfortable silence wrapped around them as he savored the chocolaty concoction.

When he finished, he carried the mugs to the sink and rinsed them, setting them on the sideboard. "I'm going to have to pay you to teach me how to make that." He snapped his fingers. "Hey, there's an idea for you. Private cooking lessons. Cookie would love it if you started with your sister."

Eyebrows lifted, she looked at him askance while she gathered her cocoa-making materials and put them away. "If my mother couldn't teach Tori to cook, no one can."

"She likes the status quo, I think. He does all the cooking and probably the dishes too." A small grin playing around his mouth, he used a dishrag to wipe down the counter. "He's tried to teach her, but she ain't having any of that."

The sadness filtered through her all over again. He knew more about her family than she did. She frowned, blinking away a rush of tears. God, she hated that, hated the weak desire to bawl. She should be looking forward, thinking about forging stronger relationships and not missing anything else where her family was concerned.

She should be grateful that she had her life back.

"Hey, don't look like that." He smoothed the area between her eyebrows. "Everything's going to be better."

Startled, she looked up at him. He was closer than she'd realized and once more his uncanny ability to know what she was thinking surprised her.

He dropped his hand, a sweet half-curve to his mouth. "It's gonna be good. You'll see."

"This is why I like having you here." She touched his arm just above his elbow, the biceps strong and rounded under her palm. A different warmth curled through her, one she'd forgotten herself capable of feeling.

One step closer and she was in his circle of heat, one movement—she wasn't sure who shifted first—and their lips met. His mouth danced over hers, a mingling of breath and emotion. Sensation cascaded through her—the shifting of skin and muscle under her palm, the supple movement of his lips against hers, the sweet flicker of attraction she'd long ago lost. There'd been no soft, sweet kisses with Stephen after the first few months of their marriage, only control and humiliation, only his attempts to steal her soul. There was none of that in this kiss, just a tender sharing that made her hungry for more of him. She smoothed his jaw, a hint of stubble abrading her fingertips.

He lifted his head, took a step back. His tongue made a quick foray over his bottom lip. Stunned reaction lingered in his gaze. "We shouldn't. This is a bad idea."

"I know." Her body hummed with a new awareness, his scent on her fingers, the taste of him on her mouth. She clutched her hands into small fists, digging her nails into her palms to cut the urge to reach for him.

A grimace puckered his brows together. "You're married."

"Legally. Not in my heart. Not where it counts."

"Tick would kill me."

"No. Don't use him as an excuse." She shook her head. "Be honest."

"I've got so much crap in my past...I'm no good for you. For any woman."

"I don't believe that."

"Hell, it's only been two days." He jerked a hand over his nape, still glowering. "You don't feel like this after two days. It's not smart."

"I know." A small purely feminine smile curled the corners of her lip. It might be a bad idea, but he'd wanted it as much as she had, that was obvious. Mere inches separated them. "But you're still standing here."

"Crazy, isn't it?" His lashes fell to brush his cheekbones and he blew out a long, unsteady breath. "I must be insane."

"It's a plain old-fashioned kiss, not a lifetime commitment, Chris." She dared to touch his tight jaw, and he turned preoccupied blue eyes on her. "It's a simple attraction with what feels like a dash of friendship thrown in."

"You sound awful happy about that."

A muted giddiness bubbled in her. "I thought...I thought he'd killed everything inside. Yes, I feel something for you, and yes, that makes me happy."

"Ah, damn it, Ruthie." He closed his eyes again. "This is not good."

"Listen, neither of us wants a romantic entanglement, obviously." She waited for him to look at her. "But you're a good man and one thing I could really use right now is a good friend."

"Just one problem with that." An ironic expression twisted his mouth. "I don't go around kissing my friends, Ruthie. They're all guys. And I definitely don't think about...never mind."

And her brother thought he was gay? The laugh burst from her before she could help it and she clapped a hand across her lips. His brows went upward once more. "What?"

"I'm sorry." Her fingers muffled the words, her giggles still attempting to choke her. "I really am. I shouldn't laugh, but—"

"But what?" He rested his hands at his hips, just below the waistband of his pajama pants, and looked at her in quizzical confusion. When she didn't answer, merely shook her head, her shoulders trembling with suppressed mirth, he rolled his gaze heavenward. His exhale reeked of exasperation. "Ruthie."

"Later. I'll tell you later, I promise." She sighed. "I can't remember the last time I enjoyed an evening this much."

His face softened. "All right. Here's the deal. We're friends. No kissing, no fooling around. Just friends."

She could handle that. Shoot, that was all she could handle right now. The last thing she needed was to get wrapped up in another man before she fixed everything Stephen had damaged or destroyed. She held out her right hand. "Deal."

He eyed her a moment before his large hand surrounded hers. "Deal. Now go get some sleep."

He'd lost his mind. That was the only explanation.

Agreeing to be Ruthie's friend? He'd lost it for sure. He didn't have female friends, even avoided dealing with the wives or girlfriends of his male friends and colleagues. He could handle Tori in limited doses, because of her serene calmness, could spend an evening with Troy Lee and his fiancée Angel because of Angel's open honesty, but Caitlin Falconetti with her quiet, icy control set him on edge. He didn't date anymore either, not since his disastrous early efforts after Kimberly, when he'd been so damn determined to be normal again.

The only problem was he wasn't normal. He'd never be. How could he?

Sitting on the side of the narrow bed, he rested his head in his hands and blew out a harsh breath. Damn it. He shouldn't have gone downstairs in the first place. It was just a nightmare, not reality, and he'd let it drive him out of bed. He shouldn't have let her draw him in with sinful cocoa, easy conversation and her sweet smile, either. And Jiminy Cricket, he shouldn't have kissed her.

Or had she kissed him? He still wasn't sure and it didn't matter anyway. It had happened, it was a bad idea, it was over, it was done.

They were friends. He'd actually agreed to be her *friend*.

God help him.

"Don't say that." Jennifer stared at Beecham. She clutched the door, as much to keep from falling as to prevent herself from reaching for him. "Don't say that to me unless you mean it."

A deep breath shook his frame. He still looked as though he might throw up. "I wouldn't say it unless I did."

"Oh my God." Jennifer let go of the wooden slab and covered her mouth. Harrell Beecham telling her he loved her, and goddamn it, she didn't have a clue how to handle it. She continued to stare at him, her pulse jumping under her skin.

His hold on the door tightened, knuckles glowing white. "I shouldn't have—"

"No." She stepped forward, laid her palm over his heart. His lids lifted and he regarded her with wariness and something more. She'd have almost called it desire, except it went deeper. Yes, he *wanted* her, but he also wanted *her*. She moistened her lips with the very tip of her tongue and moved even closer. The sharp, clean scent of him wrapped around her. "I mean, yes, you should have."

Under her hand, some of the tension drained out of him. She flexed her fingers, stroking a little at the tight muscle of his pectorals. She lifted her other hand to touch him, palms flat on his chest, and held his gaze for a long drawn-out second.

From the room next door, canned laughter from a sitcom filtered through the wall. Jennifer slid her fingers up his chest, to his shoulder, to curve around his nape. One more step brought her almost into direct contact with him, little more than a breath between them.

"Tell me again."

A pained frown brought his brows down and together; the wariness in his eyes ratcheted up to very real fear. "Jen—"

"Please." On tiptoe, she brushed her lips over his. "Say it again."

He moved then to touch her, sifting his fingers through her hair, cradling the back of her head. "I love you."

She slid her caress from his nape to his jaw. The sudden freedom to touch him thrilled her almost as much as his declaration. "And that scares you."

He nodded, the smooth warmth of his clean-shaven cheek gliding against her gentle touch.

"Do you think I'd hurt you?" She whispered the question along his lips. "Or let you fall? Haven't I always had your back, Beech?"

Turning his head, he pressed a fierce kiss into her palm. "Told you, Jen, it's not you. It's *me*."

She wanted to catch that kiss, hold on to it, keep it forever. She feathered her lips along his cheek. "Do you trust me?"

He pulled his head back, far enough to meet her gaze. "Implicitly."

"Then let yourself love me." She cradled his face in both hands. "Let me love you."

His fingers came up to wrap around her wrists. "It's not that easy—"

"Ssh." She rubbed one thumb across his mouth, the silencing caress turning to an exploration of his lower lip. "It can be that easy." She wrapped her arms around his shoulders and pressed close, determined to ease that fear, to take him through it. "Let me show you."

Holding him, she took his mouth in a slow kiss, tangling her tongue with his, thrilling to the mingled textures of smooth and rough, the clean blending of mint and sweet tea and saltiness. He groaned deep in his throat and slid his hands to her hips, lifting her against him, deepening the exchange.

How long they stood in the doorway, wrapped around one another, the kiss going on and on, she wasn't sure, lost in him, in the slow swirl of passion and desire. He settled his hands on her back, his fingers and palms tracing an unhurried path along the exposed length of her spine.

Twirling her tongue around his, scraping the edges of his teeth, she freed his tie and let it hang, unbuttoned his shirt and parted it, almost moaning in frustration when she discovered a soft white undershirt rather than bare skin.

"You wear too many clothes," she murmured into his mouth, tugging the undershirt free of his waistband, affording her access to his leanly muscled abdomen.

"You don't wear enough." He dropped his lips to her bare shoulder and she felt his smile there. "Makes us even."

Squirming a little in his embrace, she pushed his shirt from his shoulders and down his arms in a rustle of starched cotton. It fell to the floor and she gripped his undershirt to strip it over his head.

She'd seen him naked from the waist up before, plenty of times during that undercover assignment in South Carolina and even before that, after he'd been swimming or while they'd talked over case details in a dozen different nondescript hotel rooms just like this one.

This was different. This time he was hers and she could see him, touch him, taste him, however she liked. She didn't intend to waste a second of it and refused to rush. Instead, she would savor every inch of him.

She rubbed her palms up and down his biceps, unable to resist the smile pulling at her mouth. "You're beautiful."

Surprise flared in his eyes and he laughed, a rusty sound that rumbled from deep in his chest and reverberated under her touch. He shifted, a tight movement that whispered of a man discomfited by her words. "Women are beautiful. I'm not—"

She stopped him with a single fingertip. "But you are."

Her gaze traveled over defined shoulders, tight pectorals, a trim waist and delineated abdomen. The body of a man who was serious about his health and his training. The body of a man who claimed to love her. She ran questing fingers along the lines, the planes and angles and shadowed indentations of those muscles, relishing the play of skin and movement beneath her touch.

He hissed in a sharp breath as she rubbed along the contours of his flat belly. "What are you doing?"

She caught her tongue between playful teeth. "Loving the feel of you."

"I think you're playing with fire, Settles."

She leaned in toward him, ran her tongue along his lower lip. "I think I'm setting a fire, Beecham."

His hand dipped to rub at the small of her back, laid bare by her halter top. "What if it gets out of control?"

"I want it to," she whispered, their lips touching with the words. She pushed into him, breasts to his chest, abdomens flat together. "I want you to burn me all over."

This time he took her mouth, but there was nothing slow about this kiss, his tongue slipping past her teeth, invading her mouth in a steady rhythm that set desire pulsing in her veins. Without breaking contact, he backed them into his room, continuing to caress the line of her spine in sweeping strokes that tingled and sizzled through her.

Finally lifting his head, he nuzzled her ear and danced his tongue around the shell. Her knees threatened to buckle as sheer sensation zapped along every synapse she possessed. He stroked her shoulder. "Still want me to make you burn?"

"Yes," she murmured, digging her fingers into the thick springy waves of his hair.

He stepped back and the way he looked at her burned along the line of her body, set off a deep, fluttering ache low in her belly, a stinging need to have him fill her completely.

Trailing a finger along her shoulder and arm, he walked around her in a small semicircle, until he stood at her back. She caught a glimpse of them in the mirror over the low bureau, found herself drawn to the way the low light gilded his bare torso, to the way her body seemed to vibrate visibly at his proximity.

He traced the back of his index finger down her biceps, the simple touch bringing all awareness to those few inches of skin. He kissed the curve of her shoulder. "Where do you want me to begin?"

"I don't care." That maddening finger feathered over the sensitive inside of her elbow and along her forearm, and the tender throbbing between her thighs pulsed harder. She swallowed, fighting not to close her eyes. "Anywhere."

"Anywhere?" He dragged the lightest of touches over her wrist and to her palm. She'd wanted him to burn her, but this felt more like...she didn't know. She felt swollen and sensitized all over, as though her body was ripe for this man and whatever he chose to do to her.

"Yes." Her head fell back, resting in the curve between his neck and shoulder while he traced a maddening circle on her palm. Heaviness settled inside her, flushing her. How could such a simple touch make her feel like she was going to come apart? "Anywhere you want."

He cupped her other shoulder, sliding his thumb against her skin there. Pushing her hair to lie over that shoulder, he unclasped the hook holding her halter in place and swept the straps apart.

The thin fabric pooled at her waist and she couldn't tear her gaze from the mirror, from the picture they made, her skin a shade darker than his, golden tanned against his ruddy tone, the agonizingly slow sweep of his hands along the length of her arms, the curve of her breasts, nipples furling into hard, red peaks of excitement.

She moistened dry lips. She needed him to touch her *there*, to shape and heft her breasts, to tease and torment her. In the mirror, she caught his gaze and the smile that spread over his face. She'd told him she wanted him to make her burn and something told her he was going to do so in typical methodical Harrell Beecham style.

He palmed her rib cage, thumbs scarcely brushing the undersides of her breasts, and she hissed in a sharp breath as that barest of touches arced straight to the heart of her swollen sex. A rough chuckle growled from his throat and he flattened those wonderful, torturous hands on her abdomen, where desire fluttered and ached for him. Easing strong fingers inside the band of her skirt, he teased the sensitive area where her thighs joined her pelvis.

She caught his wrists, a shaky laugh rushing from her. "My knees are weak."

Her zipper rasped, the material sliding down her legs to the floor in a swish, leaving her wearing only the briefest of panties. "I'll hold you up."

"That's supposed to be my line." Was that breathless whisper hers? And when had everything shifted, so that he was in control and she was hanging on edge with everything he did?

She swung around in his arms and reached to curl her fingers in his waistband. He grabbed her forearms and used her momentum to spin them both to the bed, where she ended up on her back with him leaning over her, a roguish glint in his eyes.

"You said you wanted me to make you burn," he whispered.

"I didn't think that meant I didn't get to touch you."

"Time for that later." He lowered his head, nuzzling along her throat, nipping and sucking. He grasped her wrists and pushed them over her head, fingers dancing along the sensitive inner skin. "Do you know how long I've wanted to touch you?"

"How long?" Her voice broke slightly as he nibbled at her collarbone, the wall of his chest rubbing against her sensitized breasts.

"Honestly?" His nose brushed the delicate curve of her underarm and he dropped a kiss on the far upper side of her breast. She resisted the urge to squirm under him, to lift her hips and push against his pelvis.

"Honestly." She fully expected to hear him say South Carolina, when they'd first begun living together as a sham couple, when she'd found herself wanting his touch, wanting him.

He pressed open-mouth kisses down her sternum, tasting and teasing. "Since Arkansas," he mumbled.

"Arkansas?" The surprise squeaked in her voice. "That long?"

His lips moved against her navel and he cradled her hips in his hands. "Yeah. That long."

The admission shot a thrill of warm emotion through her. Over a year. She stirred then, tangling her fingers in his hair, caressing his nape. He glanced up at her, wickedness shining in his gaze while he peeled away her panties. He curved his hands around her thighs, separating them with a gentle push. A different thrill, one of liquid, wanton desire, traveled over her nerve endings. He dipped his head and she tightened in anticipation.

The first swipe of his tongue over her swollen clit almost did her in. She moaned, and he chuckled, the deep sound vibrating all the way through her, increasing her arousal. She was wet and open already, she could feel it, and the dance of his mouth on her had tension and electricity stinging through her.

She arched, fingers digging into his hair, the heat of his touch separating her further for his marauding tongue. Slowly, he pushed first one, then two fingers inside her, creating a rhythm in sync with the magical ministrations that were turning her inside out, pushing the pressure higher, expanding the swollen feeling in her lower belly until she was shattering, clutching at his hair and pressing her hips upwards, until a low, keening cry ripped from her lips.

Gasping, she stared at the ceiling, trying to put all the pieces back together and catch her breath all at the same time. He turned his head and pressed a kiss to her thigh.

"Beautiful," he murmured and levered himself away.

Her eyes slid closed while she attempted to regulate her breathing. Metal clinked, a zipper rasped and cloth rustled before the bed dipped and those fabulously tormenting hands framed her hips. She felt the brush of his body between her thighs a split second before he closed his mouth around one taut nipple.

The sensation arced straight to her too-sensitive sex and she smothered another soft cry. He rolled the tight flesh between his teeth, rubbing the rough surface of his tongue against it, and the swollen pressure in her belly unfolded again, unfurling, curling another urgent ache through her.

"Beech," she whispered as he moved his attentions to her other breast. "Too much."

"No," he murmured, his voice muffled against her skin. He cradled her rib cage, rubbing his thumbs over her. "Just enough to make you burn." He nipped her, lightly enough to tease, hard enough to send pleasure tingling alive again. "And it's Harrell when we're in bed."

He made it sound like it would be a regular occurrence, and she stroked his hair before giving herself over to the magic of his touch. She brought up her knees, hugging his solid thighs with her own, and bowed up into him as he continued to tug and tease her already aroused nipple.

His thumbs kept up a cadenced stroking on her lower rib cage, the only touch other than the sinful attention he paid to her breasts. She didn't need anything else to make her crazy for him—the warm brush of his naked body against hers, the soft rhythm of his thumbs on her skin, the hard suckle of his mouth and teeth and tongue—all had desire twisting through her in a heavy, pulsing sting in her belly and between her legs. There, she felt swollen and heavy and full yet empty, waiting for the thick hardness of him.

One of his hands left her torso, sliding down her stomach, muscles flickering beneath his easy touch, sifting through the curls at her mons, flicking at her clit, delving between the lips of her vulva. She bit her lip on a muffled moan.

"You're wet for me." He licked along the upper curve of her breast, dropping a kiss or two along the way.

"Yes." The syllable emerged on a breathy gasp and she clutched at his shoulders, tightened her knees around his hips.

His heavy erection bobbed against her. "I want you inside me, now."

He reared up on his elbows, his eyes hot and stormy yet serious at the same time. "You're sure? There's no going back from there, Jen."

"Yes, I'm sure." Her body reacted like an addict in the first throes of withdrawal, craving his touch once it ceased so suddenly. "Please, Harrell." She lifted her head to bring their mouths together. "Take me. Make me burn."

Taking her hand, he drew it down to his groin. "You take me, Jen. Make *me* burn."

Fisting his hard-on, she shifted beneath him on the bed, perfecting the angle. He winced and sucked in a scratchy breath as she rubbed her hand up and down his length, once, twice. He caught her hand and eased back. "Condom."

He grabbed his slacks and plastic crinkled moments before he returned to her arms. Holding his gaze, she curled her fingers about his erection, placed the head at her vagina and pushed up against him, meeting his first deep thrust so he was firmly, completely seated in her. Abrasive pleasure seared her with the pressure, her body adjusting and stretching around him.

"God," he groaned, eyes squeezed shut, his face set in severe lines, his arms trembling. "Hell, babe, you're so tight."

She reached up to cradle his face, fan her fingers over his cheekbones. She brushed his lashes, and he lifted them, staring into her eyes, his own dilated with pained satisfaction. She smiled, a giggle bubbling up from deep within, and an answering smile relaxed his face before he moved, withdrawing to push home once more and beginning a deep, steady, rhythm.

With her hands linked behind his neck, she sighed. "Oh, that's...perfect."

His rough laugh growled over her ears. "You're perfect."

"*We're* perfect." She tilted her hips and wrapped her calves around his thighs to change the angle, taking him deeper with each penetration, and he groaned through another laugh.

He lowered to rest on his forearms, his chest along hers, so they touched at every possible spot. Maintaining those satisfying hard thrusts, he sifted his fingers through her hair, stroked her throat and shoulders.

"Jen," he whispered, lips moving at her jaw, and the pure, raw emotion in his voice speared through her, intensifying the compelling heaviness building in her belly, her sex, her body again. "Jennifer."

She slipped her hands to his shoulders, nails digging at him faintly, and she pushed higher against him, wanting him deeper, harder, all the way, however she could have him. He gasped her name near her ear, followed by words of love, and she let go, let the exquisite buildup of pressure and weight and tingling excitement take her in a wild crushing flow as she came, his name leaving her mouth on a harsh cry.

She was still trembling and spasming around him when he stiffened above her, lunging into her with two, three harder thrusts, a throaty shout drowning her gasping sighs. A fierce sense of possession curled through her. He was *hers.*

He slumped in her easy hold, collapsing against her, his face buried in the curve between her neck and shoulder, murmuring her name over and over as he regained his breath. Jennifer ran her hands over his neck and back, tracing his spine, feathering along his shoulders, as warmth and well-being suffused her body.

Could life get any better?

With a low groan, he rolled away onto his back, an arm thrown over his eyes. Something about the quality of that groan snuffed a little of her giddy afterglow. Something about that small growl spoke of regret. Eyes narrowed, Jennifer lifted up on an elbow and studied her lover. She could literally see the tension seeping into his muscles with each second.

Oh, hell, he was going to make this hard and it didn't have to be. And damned if she was going to let him crawl back into the protection of his fear. She rested a hand on his flat abdomen and he jerked in reaction. Lowering his arm, he sighed and met her gaze, and sure enough, his was troubled and tinged with regret. His Adam's apple bobbed with a hard swallow. Jennifer lifted her eyebrows at him and waited.

He moistened his lips. "You realize we just changed everything?"

Chapter Seven

"You know what? I'm hungry." Jennifer stretched, lean muscles shifting under her golden skin, the lovely curve of her breasts bouncing. Harrell tried to still the nervousness jumping inside him, tried to quell the renewed desire to touch her. Renewed? Hell, who was he kidding?

Making love to her had only deepened the jones.

He scowled. "Did you hear what I said?"

"I did." She shrugged and scooted to the end of the bed. Small red marks highlighted her breasts, tiny little love bites he didn't remember leaving. He'd been too lost in the sensations of her. She bent to retrieve her skirt and top, giving him an excellent view of her tight, luscious ass. She straightened them and laid them over the back of the desk chair. "I wonder if there's an all-night diner here. Pancakes would be awesome."

Irritation gathered under his skin. "Jennifer."

She turned to face him, seemingly unconcerned with her gloriously nude state. "What?"

"I asked you a question."

"I know." She shook back her tangled sheet of shining hair. Picking up his clothing next, she tugged the second condom from his wallet and folded the slacks and shirt onto the opposite bed.

He had the distinct sensation that he'd seriously lost control of this situation. Reality tilted under him. "Is there a reason you're ignoring it?"

"Yes." Crossing to the bed, she took his hand and pulled him to his feet. Fingers wrapped around his, she tugged him toward the bathroom.

He balked at the doorway and she released him. The loss of her touch filtered through him immediately. She swept the shower curtain aside and turned on the water, adjusting the temperature and flow. He rested his forearm along the doorjamb.

"And that reason would be...?"

She glanced at him over her shoulder, and the determined set of her chin sent foreboding sliding through him. Straightening, she turned and walked to stand before him, mere inches away.

With a serene smile, she looped her arms around his neck, bare breasts brushing his chest. "Because you're trying to backpedal and I refuse to let you." She tapped his nose with her forefinger. "You have issues. We're going to deal with them." She leaned up, her gaze fixed on his. "But I am not letting you go now and I am not letting you screw this up for us with your fear. We're going to face it and handle it, together. Got that?"

A blend of warmth and unease shivered through him. "But—"

She covered his mouth with a hand, their mingled scents filling his nostrils. "No buts. That's the way it's going to be."

"Yes, ma'am," he mumbled against her palm, and she smiled, the serene, regal smile of a princess accustomed to getting her way. His princess.

"Good." She stepped away and took his hand, drawing him after her to the shower, sending him under the warm spray first. She ducked inside and pulled the curtain closed after them. She pushed him against the tiled wall and curled against his chest with an impish grin. "Because after our shower, we're going to find a place that serves pancakes. But first..." She trailed a finger along the center of his abdomen and his gut tightened, muscles jumping beneath that soft teasing caress. Her smile widened, her hazel eyes slumberous and glowing. "But first it's my turn to make you burn."

✧

Morning brought sanity with it.

Ruthie dawdled through getting the children up and dressed, dreading what waited downstairs, dreading facing Chris after their midnight interlude. What was worse, kissing him, bullying him into agreeing to be her friend, or having to push him into that simple relationship?

He had to think she was crazy.

And he was right. She made herself slide the comb slowly through Ainsley's silky hair, although her hands jittered. She didn't look at him the way she did her friends. She didn't go around kissing her male friends.

Well, if she had any friends, male or female.

That part of what she'd told him had been true. She needed a friend right now, with a desperation that frightened her. She couldn't remember the last time she'd had someone to confide in, to share warmth and closeness with, but despite their agreement, sealed with a handshake or not, she didn't think she could be Chris Parker's *friend.*

"Mama, I'm hungry." John Robert, dressed and lying along the foot of the bed, rolled restlessly from side to side, jostling her as she attempted to subdue Ainsley's fine hair in a braid.

Ruthie opened her mouth to tell him to be still while he waited and smacked it shut instead. What was she doing? They weren't in Charleston anymore. She didn't have to keep him and Camille here until she had all three children dressed. That had been Stephen's dictate.

Why was she still following it? She suppressed a shudder.

Still working on Ainsley's tresses, she smiled at John Robert, then at Camille, who was peeking at her through the scrollwork of the iron footboard. "Would you like to go downstairs where Grandma is? I smell breakfast."

John Robert paused in mid-roll and levered up on his elbows. He eyed her with suspicious incredulity. "Without you?"

"Yes, without me." She twisted a ponytail holder around the end of Ainsley's hair. "Grandma won't mind, she'll be glad to see you and there's really no reason why you have to wait for me."

Camille's dark velvet eyes flickered to meet her gaze. "Daddy wouldn't like it."

Ruthie straightened her spine, but made sure her voice and smile were reassuring. "But Daddy's not here, sweetheart. If you're hungry, it's fine to go downstairs."

John Robert glanced at his sister and bobbed his head in a sharp bob. "All right, Cammie." He slid from the bed and held out his hand. "I'll take you. Come on, it's okay. We'll find Grandma."

Tears prickled at Ruthie's eyes. He was already so strong and gentle at the same time. Pride swelled in her as the pair slipped into the hallway, John Robert's calm voice fading once they reached the stairs. Ruthie hugged Ainsley close, and her daughter giggled, patting her arm.

"Ainsley, girl, what did we do with your shoes?"

Scrambling free, Ainsley shook her head, perfect little teeth displayed in a grin. She held her hands out wide. "I don't know, Mama."

Ruthie covered her mouth. "Are they under the bed?"

Eyes twinkling with glee at the simple game, Ainsley dropped to peer under the tall old bed. "No, not here."

"Maybe they're in the closet."

From below, the muffled squeak of the side door sounded, followed by a quiet rumble of male voices.

Voices, plural. Ruthie paused, one eye on Ainsley as she searched the closet, and listened. She relaxed. Tick's deep drawl, joined by another low male tone, slow and resonant.

A rich *woof* followed them. She frowned. A dog, in her mother's house? That was on par with learning her neighbors, the couple living next door, were really undercover FBI agents.

"Mama, where could they be?" Ainsley pouted a little, hands at her hips. Ruthie leaned down to kiss her daughter's nose.

"I bet they're in your go-bag." She tapped a light finger on her daughter's cheek. "Check there."

In short order, Ainsley was shod and they descended the stairs, Ruthie holding Ainsley's hand. Scents of coffee and scrambled eggs wafted down the hall, blending with a quietly raucous mingling of adult male voices and childish giggles. She smiled. Gosh, that was good to hear.

She stopped at the doorway and stared. There wasn't only a dog in her mother's house, it was in her mother's *kitchen.* And the German Shepherd was huge, a large mass of brown and black fur, limpid eyes, enormous lolling pink tongue.

Not to mention, it was licking her child, delving that colossal tongue between John Robert's outstretched fingers. Camille, eyes shining with excitement, watched from her chair next to her grandmother at the kitchen table. Nerves jumping in her stomach, Ruthie stepped forward.

And stopped.

Chris knelt by the big dog, one hand on its neck, the other on John Robert's shoulder. John Robert giggled. "Does he like bacon?"

"He'd love bacon, if we let him try it. But he's only supposed to have his special food and treats. So we can't feed him from the table, okay?"

Biting his lip, John Robert nodded. "Can I pet him?"

"You stroke him." Chris ran a hand over the dog's massive head and down his neck and shoulders. "See? Like that."

His expression set in earnest lines, John Robert followed Chris's instructions. The dog seemed to sigh with bliss, appearing to melt into her son's easy patting.

"That's right." Chris grinned in tacit approval and simple joy bloomed on John Robert's face. "He likes to be touched but we have to be careful with him."

Ruthie's heart lifted and turned over in her chest. Ainsley tightened her hold and pressed closer to her thigh. "That's a big puppy, Mama."

"Yes, it is." She laid a palm on her daughter's shoulder, her cheeks warming as Chris, still crouched by John Robert and the dog, looked up at her with neither his face nor his eyes betraying any emotion.

He shifted his gaze from Ruthie to Ainsley and his expression softened. "Hey, Ains. This is Hound." He rubbed a firm hand across the dog's ruff. "Would you like to meet him?"

Ainsley danced from one foot to the other. She ducked her head. "Does he bite?"

Chris glanced up at Tick and Mark Cook, both in uniform and gathered at the coffee pot. "Only if I tell him to."

With a nervous giggle, Ainsley nibbled on her fingers. "I don't know."

Ruthie leaned down to look into her face. "What if I go with you?"

One last chew on her fingers and Ainsley's small white teeth flashed in a smile. "Okay."

Holding hands, they crossed to the dog. Ruthie knelt opposite Chris and laid Ainsley's little hand in his larger one. As Tick and Mark joined her mother and the older children at the table, Ruthie watched while Chris showed her youngest how to approach the dog, let him get used to her scent and voice and finally stroke him. Every so often, Hound shifted adoring eyes in Chris's direction, ears flicking whenever he spoke.

Ruthie rested her palms on her denim-clad knees. "Is he yours?"

Tick snorted. "Might as well be."

Affection lit Chris's face as he patted Hound's side. "Technically, he's the department's, but Hollowell's boys did a poor job of maintaining his training. He was pretty neglected when the sheriff took over. I've enjoyed getting him back in shape." He gave the dog another solid pat. "He's a great dog. A good partner too."

Their gazes caught and there was that feeling again—as if she had stepped into a private airless space with him, where she couldn't catch her breath, where little else existed.

Oh yes, she could be simply *friends* with this man.

"I figured since I wasn't at the coast, there wasn't much point in him staying at the boarder's." One corner of Chris's mouth curled up as the dog rested his large head on Chris's knee, eyes sliding closed in supreme bliss under Ainsley's tentative stroking. "Your mama said it would be fine if I used the dog kennel down at the pond for him while I was here. I can work on his training. I want to teach him some commands in a different language. German, maybe."

"There's always French," Mark said, his voice as deadpan as his expression.

Tick choked on a swallow of coffee, flushing a fiery red from his open collar all the way to his hairline. The glare he directed at Mark was killing. Shaking her head at an obviously private joke, Ruthie swung her gaze back to Chris, only to find him biting his lower lip, his eyes watering with the laughter he fought to contain.

"I'm going to take him outside to work a little while," he said, the words strangled, his face reddening as he blinked away the glitter at his eyes. He cast a quick glance at the children. "Would you like to come and help?"

He didn't have to ask twice and when he headed out the door, John Robert was on his heels like a shot. The girls followed, hands clasped.

Tick pushed up from the table. "We'll go out too. Help watch the kids and give you and Mama a chance to catch up."

He leaned down to kiss their mother's cheek, brushing the bandage at her hairline. Mark preceded him out the door, Tick's voice filtering through the screened porch. "What the hell was that all about? I can't tell you anything without you holding it over my head."

The screen door slammed shut on his fussing.

Her mama dissolved into laughter, setting her cup aside and resting her face in her hands. Ruthie paused in the act of pulling down a ceramic mug dotted with flowers. Her mother's joyful delight warmed her, bringing with it a sense of home and security.

She reached for the carafe, smiling at the memory of

131

Chris's silent mirth. "Did I miss something?"

Her mother wiped away a stray tear. "Your sister-in-law speaks French very fluently. Obviously, your brother finds that quite attractive. Or maybe stimulating is a better word." She laughed again, shaking her head.

"Oh." Ruthie bit her lip on a laugh of her own. Yes, that would explain Tick's fierce blush. "Mama, how do you know that?"

"I'm sure, judging by his reaction, that I'm not supposed to. But then, I'm not supposed to be aware either that he and Caitlin can't keep their hands off one another or have any understanding of how things can be between a woman and a man, you know." With a saucy wink, she lifted her cup for a long, slow sip and pursed her lips. "As to how I know, Mark can be quite the useful source of information, I've found."

Ruthie joined her mother at the table, shaking her head at Camille's mostly untouched plate. She'd never been much of a breakfast eater, to Ruthie's chagrin. She snagged Camille's abandoned fork and picked at the scrambled eggs, her chin propped on her other hand.

"You like him, don't you? Mark, I mean." She savored the fluffy eggs. "He's a good bit older than Tori, though, isn't he?"

"I do like him. He's a good man and he loves your sister." A soft expression crossed her face. "He's a strong man. He settles her and she definitely keeps him on his toes."

"I'm sure." Tori had spent most of her life keeping various members of her family on their collective toes.

"She'll be here later today. I want to work on those alterations on her gown."

"Mama, you just left the hospital yesterday. Are you sure you should—?"

"Yes. I'm sure." Her mother patted Ruthie's hand. "I'm fine."

"Mama. You were kidnapped, suffered a head injury and don't remember what happened. I don't call that fine."

"Ruth Ann, I assure you I have been through worse things than this incident." Strength vibrated in her mama's voice. "I survived those, and partly how I did so was I kept on doing what had to be done. Just as you are right now."

"Oh, Mama." Ruthie reached for her mug. "If you only knew. I feel like all I'm doing is putting one foot before the other, with no real idea of where I'm going or what I should be doing. I don't know if I know how to make those kinds of plans anymore."

"Of course you do, darling."

She dropped her gaze from her mother's gentle face. "I don't trust myself any longer, Mama. I was so wrong about Stephen and I remember how sure I was that he was the perfect one, how stubborn I was when you tried to tell me I hadn't known him long enough. What if I'm showing the same lack of foresight now?"

"What you are showing is incredible strength and wisdom." Mama covered both of Ruthie's hands with her own, a sweet blanket of love and faith. "I couldn't be prouder of you. You're doing everything you can to make things better for yourself and those babies. What you need to remember is that you don't have to do this alone, darling."

"I wish I knew where to start," Ruthie mumbled. Her mama patted her hand once, twice.

"You start with a new step. You're meeting with Autry Reed later today, aren't you?" At Ruthie's affirmative nod, Mama smiled. "Well, then, that's your next step. And you can spend the morning helping me with altering Tori's wedding gown."

Ruthie rolled her eyes. "I suppose there's no point in arguing with you?"

"None whatsoever."

"Okay. But just remember, I never could stitch a straight line."

A trill of childish laughter drew her to the window. Camille and Ainsley sat on the patio steps, flanking Chris. Tick and Mark had disappeared, and John Robert stood on the grass before the stoop and threw a tennis ball. The German Shepherd raced after it, almost tumbling over in his excitement. He gamboled back to drop the ball at John Robert's feet and gaze with eager eyes and a lolling tongue at her son.

The simple scene, man and children and dog, hurt. This was what life should be, pure and good. She caught a quick flash of Chris's smile in profile, and the pull started all over again. She lifted her mug for a fortifying swallow, struggling with the lump in her throat.

Friends. They were nothing more and she shouldn't go looking at him with her children and thinking of anything else. Even so she couldn't resist the early-morning sunshine, the flash of exhilaration on her children's faces, the circle of warmth surrounding Chris. She set her cup aside and struggled for a nonchalant air.

"Mama, I'm going outside for a bit."

Crisp fall air wrapped around her, tinged with wood smoke and full of memories. Light glittered off the pond, a few sleepy ducks dozing on the bank. At the fall of her footsteps, Chris darted a look up at her. Some indefinable emotion flickered in his eyes before he turned to watch John Robert and the dog once more.

"Looks like y'all are having fun." She settled on the step behind Camille. Ainsley clambered up one tread to nudge into her side, putting her squarely behind Chris.

"Mama." Ainsley leaned in to stage whisper at Ruthie's ear. "The big puppy likes John Robert."

"I can see that." Ruthie trailed her fingertips through the silky fall of Camille's dark hair. She glanced sideways at Chris and caught his gaze on her face. She lowered her lashes. "He's very well trained."

"Like I said, he's a good dog. Usually." A wry note invaded his voice as the dog, overcome with joy, reared up to lick John Robert's face. "Hound, down."

He accompanied the stern command with a downward motion of his index finger. The shepherd complied, dropping to his belly and turning those adoring eyes on Chris. The dog's brow furrowed, ears flicking forward. Camille's quiet giggle rose and she looked up at Chris. "He minds."

"He has to. If he didn't do what I told him when I told him to, someone could get hurt. He could get hurt."

John Robert spun, and suspicion tightened his features. "What do you do if he doesn't?"

Ruthie's breath caught. God only knew what memories cascaded through John Robert's mind. Chris's shoulders tensed, then relaxed. He leaned forward, hands dangling between his knees, his attention focused on her son.

"I correct him." Chris's voice held matter-of-fact reassurance. "He might get a time-out and have to stay in a sit or a down for a while. He might have to go in his kennel. But you know what? If I reward him with some playtime when he does what he's supposed to, I really don't have to correct him all that often."

John Robert eyed him a moment, as if weighing the veracity of his words, his genuineness. After a long pause, he nodded, dark bangs falling forward on his brow. He rubbed his thumb over the tennis ball fuzz. "So it's okay to throw the ball now?"

"Perfectly okay." Chris pushed to his feet. "But how about we give your sisters a turn?"

"All right." John Robert gave a sharp bob of assent with his chin. Camille jumped up; Ainsley pressed closer to Ruthie's side.

Chris grinned down at Camille. "Ready?"

"Yes." She bounded down the steps. Chris glanced back at Ruthie. Their eyes locked.

"Thank you," she mouthed at him. *Thank you for showing my son, my daughters, that a man can be strong and in control yet gentle at the same time, that being in command doesn't make him a monster.*

Pleasure glinted in his blue gaze, more of what she'd glimpsed there the night before. He held her gaze a second longer before Camille took his hand and tugged him toward the boy and dog capering on the lawn. Ruthie wrapped an arm around Ainsley, hugging her close. This had to be an omen for what was to come, a pure and shining future.

135

"I wish I had better news for you." Autry folded her hands together. The polished surface of the long cherry table in the formal dining room reflected back the light glinting off her wedding rings. From the laundry room off the kitchen, Mama's soft conversation with Tori drifted to them, but did little to still the horrible tension tearing into Ruthie. "There's no such thing as a no-fault divorce in South Carolina. And mental cruelty is not a legal reason for dissolving a marriage in that state either."

Ruthie shattered. That was the only way to explain the way she felt—as if she'd splintered into a thousand tiny shards, like someone dropping a sheet of plate glass. God, she'd run, risked their lives, risked her mother's life, for nothing?

"But I'm looking for a way around that. However, I need you to be aware that this probably won't be the average thirty-days-and-you're-done divorce."

Nodding, Ruthie rubbed tight circles at her temples. Her fingertips felt like ice and did little to dull the piercing ache taking up residence there. She'd believed she'd considered every angle of escaping. Why hadn't she thought to look up the damn divorce laws?

Because she'd been desperate. When the opportunity to finally get away had presented itself, she'd snatched it.

"One thing I want to do is establish legal residency for you in Georgia as soon as possible. I'll have some more information on that for you as soon as I can. I'm hoping I can find a loophole that will let you file here, since Georgia does have a no-fault divorce law."

Ruthie nodded again but didn't speak, still trying to process everything Autry was saying.

"Listen, I'm going to go. I have a two o'clock meeting but I'll check back in with you later today. My understanding is that the FBI should have some information for us about what they're going to do with those ledgers by then. Hopefully, we can find a way to make those work for us as well."

"Okay." Ruthie rose and walked her to the door. The movie soundtrack swelled slightly, filtering down the hall. "Thanks, Autry."

"Anytime." Autry touched her arm, a warm, friendly gesture. "I'll call you."

Closing the door and locking it, Ruthie leaned against the solid oak slab, hands over her eyes. When would this nightmare really be over?

"Ruthie?" Chris's quiet voice shivered over her and she cringed, fighting a wave of weak tears. She didn't want him to see her like this. "Are you all right?"

Still concealing her face with trembling hands, she shook her head.

He didn't speak, but moments later, strong arms closed around her and pulled her close to an equally strong chest. He rocked them from side to side. She wrapped her arms about his waist and pressed her face to his shoulder.

His cheek brushed her temple. "Want to talk about it?"

"It keeps getting worse, more complicated, every day." She sighed. "All I wanted was to get away from him, to get my children away from him. I'll never be free of him, not really."

"Yes, you will." He pulled back and cradled her face in his palms, thumbs stroking lightly over her cheekbones. "You will."

A rapid knocking at the door dragged her from his easy hold, a sense of dread rushing through her at the urgent tone of that rapping. A quick glance at Chris's suddenly tight face told her he felt the danger in that summoning. Without speaking, he put her behind him and peered through the peephole. If anything, his posture tautened.

He glanced at her over his shoulder. "It's Autry. She doesn't look happy."

Ruthie's anxiety deepened as he opened the door. Autry gave them a terse smile as she swept inside. Ruthie folded her arms and braced herself. "What's wrong?"

Autry tucked her thick chestnut hair behind her ear. "Tick called my cell as I was pulling out of the drive. Stephen's taken legal action against you for removing the children from South Carolina."

Ruthie took a slight step closer to Chris's sturdy frame. She swallowed, hard. "Legal action?"

"He's trying to force you back up there." Autry's narrowed eyes glittered sharply with a predatory light. "He's sworn out a warrant to have you arrested for interference with custody and extradited back to Charleston."

"Oh, God." Ruthie sagged, grateful for Chris's supporting hands at her elbows. She struggled to breathe, to listen to Autry over the horrible roaring in her ears.

"He's also put in for sole custody of the children."

"No." Ruthie shook her head. "No. He can't. You can't let him do this, Autry."

"Oh, I have no intention of doing so. I'm heading over to the courthouse square now to talk to Judge Barlow about a few injunctions of our own. I just wanted to let you know what was going on."

"Thank you." The words slipped past numb lips and Autry hugged her quickly before breezing out.

Ruthie covered her face. This wasn't happening. This wasn't. It couldn't. Stephen couldn't win, not now. Chris's arms came around her from behind, a strong, silent source of support, and she leaned into him.

Dear God, what was going to happen now?

Chapter Eight

"Chason's up to new tricks."

At Beecham's terse words, Jennifer looked up from packing. Beecham's suitcase waited by the door. "What do you mean?"

"That was Calvert." He frowned, the fine lines on his brow deepening. "Chason has sworn out a warrant for Ruthie and is filing for custody of the children."

"Like he wants them." She tucked her jewelry bag into the carry-on. "Sleazy son of a bitch. He just wants to get back at Ruthie."

"Yeah."

"Maybe he'll change his tune when Weston and Brookman pick him up." They'd scanned and emailed copies of the ledgers to their superior agent that morning. Fierce satisfaction flushed Jennifer's body. They had enough to put Chason away for a very long time. Ruthie would finally be free of him; he wouldn't be able to hurt her any longer.

Her own cell chimed and she picked it up, swallowing a groan as she recognized the number on the caller ID. Rolling her eyes at Beecham, she flipped it open and lifted the slim device to her ear.

"Hi, Mom," she said brightly. Beecham smirked and she considered smacking him alongside the head.

"Jennifer, darling, how are you?" Her mother's cultured drawl slid over her like thick, heavy molasses—sweet and suffocating. She dropped onto the foot of the bed, sure of what would come next. "It's been forever since we talked."

"Only since last week." Not exactly forever, she didn't add. No point in antagonizing her mother and providing her with more ammo.

"I'm just spoiled." Her mother's laugh was a light trill. "Your sisters and I talk every day."

"Guess it's a peril of working for the federal government, Mom. Not being able to call home every day." More like a blessing, maybe? Immediately, guilt slithered through her. In all actuality, she adored her mother, knew her mother loved her. But, God help her, if she had to carry on one of these minefield conversations every single day, she might just eat her own damn gun.

"Well, how are you?" She could picture her mother, not a silver hair out of place on her elegant coif, settling into the wing chair by the fireplace in the formal living room.

"I'm fine." The mattress dipped next to her and Beecham, damn him, rested his face in his hands, shoulders shaking with silent laughter. He'd been privy to enough of these phone interrogations and her resulting after-bitching to know how her skin crawled by this point. "You?"

"Terribly busy. Allison is planning a huge birthday party for Madison and I'm helping Lori redecorate her dining room." At her mother's pause, Jennifer made a noncommittal sound in her throat, which seemed to satisfy. "Trish is chairing the committee for the Junior League charity ball. We're hoping you could come home for that, darling. Your father would love to see you. Oh, and Paul Coleman asked about you the other day. I don't think he has a date for the ball yet—"

"Mother, I can't make plans that far in advance. You know that." She planned to kill that other little seed too. "And I have no interest in going out with Paul Coleman."

"Well, why ever not? Honey, he's an absolutely delicious catch and it's not like you have many prospects—"

"Mother, I'm not interested." She kept her voice firm and level. "Besides, I'm seeing someone."

Beecham lifted his head, eyebrows raised, his shoulders tensing. Jennifer stuck out her tongue at him. Teach him to laugh at her five minutes of hell.

Her mother paused for a solid three seconds. "Really? Who?"

Holding her gaze, Beecham shook his head. Jennifer ignored him. "Beecham, Mother. I'm seeing Beecham."

She had no trouble reading Beecham's silent "shit".

"Your partner? Oh. You're seeing him? Romantically?"

Irritation sparked under Jennifer's skin. "Yes, I am."

"Oh." Her mother recovered quickly. "Who are his people?"

"I have no clue."

"You haven't met them?"

"No, Mother, I haven't." Only his mother, once, for like five minutes, and that didn't count, really.

"When do you intend to do so?"

"Mom?" Jennifer pinched the bridge of her nose. "Do we have to talk about this now?"

"Of course not, it's simply that...Jennifer, you know I want the best for you." A pleading note of affection entered her mother's voice and Jennifer sighed.

"I know. But we have different definitions of that, I think." She was suddenly tired, the lack of sleep and the conversation catching up with her. Besides, the tense set of Beecham's posture left a tight, sick feeling in her stomach. "Mom, I have to go. I need to finish packing."

"Of course, darling. I love you."

"I love you too."

"And don't be such a stranger. Even intrepid FBI agents should call their mothers."

"Yes, Mom." The connection broken, she flopped back on the bed. Why did those maternal talks always leave her exhausted and guilt-ridden?

"You told your mother." Disbelief hovered in Beecham's voice. He hadn't moved, still sitting on the end of the bed. "You

141

told your mother about us."

At least he could admit there was an "us" now. Jennifer closed her eyes, not sure she was ready for a Harrell Beecham go-round so soon after a Letitia Settles go-round. She folded her hands atop her stomach, the muscles there flicking and jumping.

"Yes, I did. She's trying to fix me up again. Do you really think I'm not going to tell her, if for no reason other than to get her off my back about my lack of romantic prospects?"

"I just..." His voice trailed away and the bed shifted, fabric rustling. He was spinning around to look at her, she figured. He sounded a little lost and sympathy spurted through her. "I didn't expect you to tell her, I guess."

She levered up on her elbows and shook back her hair. "I agreed not to tell our colleagues, Beech. I never said anything about not telling my mother."

He rubbed a hand over his nape. "I know."

She frowned as a new thought occurred. "You are going to tell your mother about us, right?"

He straightened, stiffening. He opened his mouth, looked at her, snapped it shut.

She sat bolt upright, hands planted to the mattress. "Harrell."

"I don't talk to my mother about my personal life," he mumbled.

"What?"

A long exhale carried his aggravation with it. "My mother and I don't discuss my personal life."

"Really." The concept boggled the mind. How on earth had he managed to work that? If she tried not talking about her personal life, her mother would resort to...well, the possibilities were endless and horrifying.

"Yes, really."

"Wow." Even in passing, Julia Gruen had seemed like a normal, everyday loving mother, the kind Jennifer equated with her own—the woman who pried details out of her children like a

Chinese torture artist. "So you're keeping me a secret from your mother?"

"I wish you wouldn't put it that way." He scowled. "You make it sound sordid."

"You'll tell her at some point?"

"Yeah, I guess so." He stood, almost leaping to his feet, and strode to pick up his bag. "I'm going to put this in the car. Are you almost ready?"

Surely he didn't think he was getting off that easily. She fixed the back of his head with a look he should be able to feel and rolled to her feet to finish packing. "You really don't intend to tell her, do you?"

"Jen. Can we drop this line of conversation, please?" He stood at the door and watched her, bag slung over his shoulder, looking a little lost once more. "Why is this such a big deal?"

"It's not." She made herself smile at him, but all the while the sense of angry hurt settled in her stomach in a low, tight, cold knot. All she could figure was that either he was ashamed of her or he still believed they had no real chance together.

She was betting on the latter. Glimpses of the future opened before her. Would she be fighting him all the way, trying to hold on to him as he pulled into himself? That wasn't the type of relationship she wanted by any means.

One night, Jennifer. She was one night in. Patience. She simply needed patience to make this work. Sooner or later, he'd see what they could be, believe in what they were together. As always, and even more imperatively now than it had ever been in Jennifer's life before, failure was not an option.

"You did what?" The quiet fury in Jennifer's voice lifted the hairs along Harrell's arms and raised his own temper further. At her side in the hallway of the justice center, he stared at Senior Agent in Charge Greg Weston.

Weston shrugged as if he might be aware of their anger but

remained unmoved by it. "We cut a deal with Stephen Chason. He rolls on his cronies and we provide protection until any resulting trials, with entry into the Witness Protection Program afterward."

"You offered him immunity." Harrell repeated the idea pounding in his head. Ah hell, Calvert would lay a gold brick when he found out about this. "You offered that bastard a goddamn immunity exchange."

"Careful, Agent Beecham." Distinct warning iced Weston's tone. "Chason is willing to give us everything. Do you know how valuable that is? How many of his higher-level associates we'll be able to prosecute? Hell, this could cripple racketeering in this area of the Southeast."

"What about Ruthie Chason? What about her children?" Jennifer shook her head. "Were you aware he swore out a warrant against her today? That he's trying to take those kids?"

"The situation is regrettable," Weston conceded.

"Regrettable." Jennifer echoed the word, her expression twisting in disgust. "I guess that's one way of putting it."

"Have you put anything in writing yet?" Harrell asked, his mind jumping ahead, looking for some way to alleviate the personal disaster he saw looming.

"Legal's working on it now."

Jennifer glanced up at Harrell, her eyes sharp, and he nodded. He turned back to Weston. "Add a couple of caveats. He drops the custody interference charge against his wife, drops the suit seeking custody and agrees not to contest any divorce proceedings she may instigate."

Weston sighed. "The FBI does not get involved in marital or domestic situations—"

"Sir?" Jennifer stood straighter, her voice vibrating with earnestness. "It's not much to ask, to make those children's lives better. Not to mention, in consideration of what Ruthie Chason provided us with. We wouldn't be standing here now, with this case ready to break wide open, if not for her."

Bearing a frown of consideration, Weston wavered visibly

for several long moments. Finally, he gave a curt nod. "No promises, but I'll see what I can do."

"Thank you, sir." Once Weston disappeared down the hall, Jennifer turned to Harrell, her eyes shining up at him. "And thank you."

"I didn't do anything." Damn, but he liked it when she looked at him like this. It was a hell of a lot better than the glimmer of hurt she'd turned on him earlier that morning, over whether or not he was going to tell his mother about them.

"You went to bat for her." A wide smiled curved that oh-so-kissable mouth of hers. "That's definitely something."

A pulsing silence fell between them and he cleared his throat to dissipate the charged tension. "We need to clear our stuff out of the house."

She darted a look down the hall. "I can pack up for both of us. I'd really rather you stayed here to see what Weston comes up with."

The plan made sense. "Sounds good."

"I'll meet you back here in a couple of hours." She held out a hand. "Keys."

When he laid them in her palm, she wrapped her fingers around his, sliding her fingertips from his wrist and along his hand, leaving tingling awareness in her wake. She gave him a saucy wink and walked away. He swallowed a surprised laugh and turned to seek out their supervising agent.

Less than an hour later, Weston had managed to have a small team of federal lawyers pound out the details of Chason's immunity agreement, which gave Harrell the supreme pleasure of tagging along as said agreement was presented to Chason and his attorney.

In the cramped conference room, Harrell leaned against the wall and studied Chason. The man didn't look like a criminal, but then in Harrell's experience, the white-collar-crime guys never did.

Of average height, his dark hair and goatee neatly trimmed, Chason sat with his attorney, supercilious eyes darting over the men in the room. The lousy son of a bitch didn't look dangerous. Harrell didn't doubt for a minute that he was. Something about the guy raised Harrell's gut instincts to screaming level.

Shit, even if Chason went into federal witness protection, with a new name and a new location, Ruthie would still have to live her life looking over her shoulder. Chason wouldn't simply let her go that easily and sure as hell he was smart enough to manipulate the situation to allow him to get at her.

Chason's gaze flicked to his, distaste and something akin to hatred flaring there. Harrell stared back at him, not batting a lash, not letting his expression change in any way. He didn't intend giving the little rat the satisfaction of a reaction to that revulsion.

Harrell watched Chason's posture and expression change as Weston outlined the terms of the agreement. Halfway though the SAIC's spiel, Chason began shaking his head and leaned over to whisper to his attorney.

Weston ceased speaking and lifted his eyebrows. "A problem, gentlemen?"

Chason's attorney, a prissy little man with a balding head and crooked glasses perched on his nose, folded his hands on the table. "Mr. Chason is not willing to surrender custody of his children. Nor does he wish to agree to a divorce."

Weston shrugged and flipped the file folder closed. "Then he can spend several years in a federal prison."

Chason's mouth tightened. His attorney pulled a handkerchief from his pocket and dabbed at his brow. "Surely the FBI has no interest in the personal family affairs of my client—"

"You know, I'm positive the IRS would be keenly interested in seeing those ledgers," Weston said, rubbing a thumb along the edge of the manila folder. "Lots of income Mr. Chason obviously didn't pay taxes on. Don't you think the boys over there would be ready to jump right on that, Agent Beecham?"

Both Chason and his attorney blanched and Harrell fought a grin. "Definitely. You know how they are about anybody cheating them out of a dollar or two."

Still dabbing at his forehead, the attorney leaned in to confer with Chason in subdued whispers. Finally, Chason slumped back in his chair and directed an icy glower in Harrell's direction.

The attorney folded his hands again. "Mr. Chason is willing to agree to the terms and cooperate fully."

Harrell narrowed his eyes. Maybe he'd agree and maybe he'd cooperate, but something told him that "fully" was nothing more than a goddamn lie.

Once the papers were signed and Chason was in protective custody, Harrell listened as Weston outlined his plan for Chason's security detail. Harrell nodded but inside, his nerves were crawling. Jennifer would have a fit once she heard this plan.

At the door, he shook Weston's hand. "Sir, I'm going to help Settles finish clearing our things from the house here. I'll fill her in as well. We should be back in Atlanta tonight."

Weston nodded. "Very good. The two of you take the weekend and I'll expect you in my office Monday morning."

"Yes, sir. Thank you, sir."

Jennifer didn't answer her cell and the phone had already been disconnected at the Charleston house. Harrell caught a cab and was relieved to see their rental car still in the drive before the massive brick Tudor. The downstairs was empty and he jogged up the stairs, muted anticipation jingling under his skin.

He found her in the master bedroom's huge walk-in closet, moving clothing to open suitcases. She hadn't heard him and he momentarily considered walking up behind her and sliding his arms around her, trailing his hands up her stomach to her breasts, nibbling at her neck. His dick stirred to life at the mental images. Then he remembered how much she didn't like being startled and how good she was at takedown techniques, decided he really didn't want to end up flat on his back and reconsidered.

He leaned a shoulder against the doorjamb. "Hey."

At his voice, she glanced around and a pleased smile spread over her face. "Hi. I thought I was meeting you back at the justice center."

"I got through first and there really wasn't any reason for me to hang around over there. Thought I'd come see if you needed help."

"I'm almost finished." She waved at the near-empty closet. "But you can definitely help load the car. There was more here than I thought."

"Because you're obsessed with clothes."

She sent him a look of mock outrage. "I am not. Well, maybe just a little."

"Maybe just a lot."

"Load the car, Beech."

He chuckled and hefted two of the cases to do as he was told. When he returned, she was zipping up the final suitcase. He paused in the doorway. "Chason agreed to Weston's terms."

Her head came up, eyes lighting up. "Really?"

"The warrant's already been vacated."

"Thank God for that." Fingers curled around the countertop, she leaned against the island in the center of the closet. "Does Ruthie know yet?"

"No. Weston and I thought you might like to tell her."

"I would. Thanks."

"Chason's gone into protective custody. They'll move him to a safe house in north Georgia tonight." Harrell cleared his throat and rubbed a hand over his mouth. "We're half of his security team. We'll swap out duty with Edgewood and Banning."

A moue of distaste twisted her features. "You mean we have to live with the bastard?"

"We're on a forty-eight-hour rotation."

"Great." She threw up her hands. "I can't wait."

"There is good news, though."

She fixed him with a wry look. "Really? Do tell."

"We're off until Monday." He rested a shoulder against the jamb.

"Okay, that marginally makes up for having to spend time with that son of a bitch." Her exaggerated pout struck him with unexpected humor and he chuckled. Her expression relaxed into a grin. "What's so damn funny?"

"You are." He made himself stay where he was, made his body stay relaxed, despite the way he seemed to damn near buzz with awareness in her presence. Before had been bad enough, but now that he'd made love to her, kissed her and held her in his arms, the absolute need he had to touch her was frigging scary.

Her chin tilted. "So what are we doing this weekend?"

The assumption they'd spend their off time together warmed him and he was damn grateful she'd broached the subject. It had been uppermost in his mind, but letting her see how much he needed her was asking for a swift kick to the nuts later.

He tucked his hands in his pockets. "What do you want to do?"

"Oh, I don't know. Shopping sounds good." She pushed away from the island and approached him with a sultry, rolling walk. Instead of stopping before him, she strolled by him, sliding a finger across his chest as she did so. "I think I'm in need of a little black nightie."

"Really." His body reacting to that mental image, he closed his eyes for a moment before he went after her.

He caught up with her in the bedroom and slid his arms around her from behind. Her back hit his chest and he could feel the vibration of her soft laugh. He nibbled at her neck, easing his palms up her stomach to cup her breasts.

"Do you know what it's been like," he whispered, his gaze trailing to the big king-sized bed, "having to sleep with you in that damn bed and not touch you?"

"Yes." She turned in his embrace, her eyes burning.

Grasping his tie, she backed up and pulled him with her, until the bed hit the backs of her thighs and she sat on the foot, scuffling with his tie. "I don't want slow and lots of foreplay this time, Harrell."

He shrugged out of his jacket, letting it hit the floor. "What do you want, babe?"

"I want you." She tossed his tie aside before hiking her very Bureau black skirt up and shimmying out of a pair of very non-Bureau teal panties. "Hard and inside me, making me come."

Hard he had covered. The other two he fully intended to remedy in short order. He freed the top couple of buttons on his dress shirt and tugged both it and his undershirt over his head. Jennifer slipped out of her blouse, revealing a very brief bra the same teal as the panties she'd discarded.

He reached for his belt and she slid up the bed to rest against the bank of pillows. Her gaze locked on his, she spread her thighs and slipped one hand between her legs, touching and teasing herself.

"Hurry," she murmured, one slender finger circling and dancing over her clit. God, much of this and he'd come out of his skin. He fumbled his belt free, managed to unfasten his slacks and lower his zipper without doing himself bodily damage. She let her head fall back, a moan slipping from her damp lips, and the visual zinged through his brain, along his nerves, straight to his already straining dick.

He shoved slacks and boxers down together, letting them gather around his thighs as he sheathed his erection. Finally, he lowered himself between her wide-spread legs. Moving her hand aside, he ran a finger along her swollen clit and below, testing, finding her already wet and open and ready.

For him.

She moaned again at his touch and shifted her hips in a restless movement. With his free hand, he tugged the lace cups of her bra downward. Drawing one hard nipple between his teeth, he positioned himself and thrust inside her. The hot, wet clasp of her body around his was unbearably tight, unbelievably exquisite. He tensed and stilled, fighting off an urge to plunge toward an early completion.

Fingernails dug into his bare ass.

"Damn it, Harrell, move," she hissed near his ear, and he breathed a laugh, regaining some sense of self-control.

"God, you're bossy," he mumbled around her tight nipple, teal lace scratching his chin. He half-withdrew and thrust again, setting up a hard, driving rhythm. She damn well purred in satisfaction, flexing her fingers on his buttocks, pulling him even deeper. His back ached, protesting the angle of their position, but hell if he'd move, with her sighing and moaning beneath him, arching her hips up into his.

He squeezed his eyes shut, fighting off a looming climax. He needed this to be good for her, needed to—

"Stop thinking so damn much." Her gasp shivered over him, a wave of tiny convulsions rippling through her body, tightening the wet hold around his erection. She bowed on a sharp cry, fingernails digging deeper into his skin. He felt the orgasm travel through her, triggering his.

Moments, hell, maybe light-years later, she shivered under him, laughing. He recovered from his boneless slump, shifting his weight from her body, and nuzzled her ear when she pulled him back. "What?"

She trailed a fingernail down his spine, sending goose bumps over his flesh. "Just thinking maybe I don't need that little black nightie after all."

He smiled against her neck. "Oh, you need one. Believe me. Hell, I'll buy it for you, babe."

"Really?" That teasing finger danced along his buttocks. "Would you go shopping with me? I'd want to make sure I got just the right one. I might have to try them on for you."

His mind took that little scenario and ran with it, picturing the beautiful woman in his arms in an array of provocative scraps of black mesh and lace. He kissed her collarbone. "I think I could be persuaded."

"Oh, fun." She stretched under him and looped her arms around his shoulders. "That's definitely a date."

He dropped a series of light kisses down her chest. "We need to get moving, though."

"Hmm." She rubbed her cheek against his hair. "I know. I want to call Ruthie."

With a swift kiss on her sternum, he rolled away, pleasure still thrumming through him. She slipped from the bed, gathering clothing, and he took one last second to catch his breath before he dressed.

With his tie stuffed in his jacket pocket, he hefted the final two bags and prepared to take them out to the car. Jennifer's gorgeous voice washed over him as she talked to Ruthie and he grinned, suddenly itching to get back to Atlanta.

He couldn't wait to see what else the weekend held in store.

A muffled thud startled Chris from his half-doze. His pulse thumped a sick rhythm in his throat. Shoulder aching, he straightened from his slump on the sofa. The kids were okay— John Robert reading in the armchair, Camille snoozing on the other end of the couch. By his feet, Ainsley sat enraptured by SpongeBob and idly plucking at Chris's shoelaces.

Another hushed bump. He frowned. What the hell was that?

With easy hands, he nudged her aside. "Excuse me, Ainsley."

The house seemed normal enough. Down the hall, Lenora and Tori's voices rose and fell in quiet conversation. A quick glance through the dining room windows revealed no new vehicles in the drive. So not car doors closing.

A third bang drew him to the foyer. A shoebox hit the floor, joining the two already there. A lid tumbled off and a tattered paperback fell out. He rested a hand on the coat closet's open door. "What are you doing?"

"Cleaning off the shelf." Ruthie didn't turn. She stretched higher, reaching for the next precarious stack of shoeboxes.

Chris laid a hand on the top box. "Let me help you with that."

He pulled the containers free and set them next to their counterparts. Only when he turned back to her did their proximity and her glittering tears sink in. She tilted her chin to a defiant angle. "I suppose you want to know why I'm cleaning the closet."

A couple of steps back returned him to a safe distance. "Because you need something to do, something to keep you busy."

The look she slanted in his direction was probably meant to be a glare. The unshed tears and her trembling mouth ruined it. "You're too insightful."

He shrugged. Pointing out he was a cop and therefore pretty much required to be insightful seemed like overkill.

She bent and lifted the book back into its box. "I despise him. You can't *own* another person and that's what he wants, to possess and control me, even from a state away... You can't own another person, Chris."

"I know."

She surveyed the handful of boxes. "I made a mess of things."

"Messes can be cleaned up."

Her disbelieving laugh quivered between them before it morphed into a sob. Two steps and he'd tucked her close. She turned her face into his shoulder.

"I'm so scared." Her torn whisper shook him. He tightened his arms and rested his lips on her hair.

"I know."

"Ruthie?"

Tori's quiet voice tensed every muscle in Chris's body. Oh, hell. Leaning against his chest, Ruthie stiffened as if anticipating yet another blow and anger singed his nerve endings. She didn't deserve this, any of this.

No one did.

Ruthie swiped at her eyes and slipped away from his easy hold. Her shimmering gaze flicked to his before she turned to face her sister.

"I'm sorry." Apology hovered in Tori's rich voice as she held out the cordless phone. "You have a phone call. It's Agent Settles."

"Thanks." Ruthie's face blanched somewhat, but she accepted the phone and lifted it to her ear. "Hello?"

Chris watched as she listened, varying expressions chasing across her features. A prickling sensation slid over him. He glanced sideways to find Tori studying him as he watched. Discomfort settled under his skin.

"Yes, thank you for calling." Ruthie ended the call.

"Good news?" Tori asked.

"I think it's over," Ruthie whispered, her eyes flicking between Chris and her sister. The tension drained from her body visibly as her posture relaxed. "The Bureau worked out a deal with Stephen. Immunity and witness protection in exchange for his testimony, but he agreed to drop the charges against me and his custody suit. And he won't fight the divorce."

Chris stared, a weird blend of relief and disappointment curling through him. He scuffed a palm over his nape and looked away. A deep breath helped center him, helped him bury the disappointment where it belonged. She was right. It was over. Time for him to pack his stuff and go back to his real life. She didn't need his protection anymore.

"That's fabulous news." Tori moved forward to embrace her. She stroked her hand over Ruthie's hair and expelled a trembling exhale. "I'm so glad for you, Ruthie."

"Me too." Even muffled by Tori's hug, Ruthie's voice emerged choked with emotion. Chris shoved his hands in his back pockets. Weird how he felt completely superfluous but unable to walk away, not just yet. Ruthie's shoulders heaved under a broken breath almost like a sob.

Tori pulled back and smoothed Ruthie's tousled hair from her face. "Listen, I have to be back at the center for an appointment, but I'll call you later, okay?"

"Sure." Ruthie passed a knuckle beneath her eyes, catching

the stray tears there.

"I promise, I'll give you a call." Tori brushed a kiss over Ruthie's cheek.

Once she was gone, Chris smiled at Ruthie. "She's right. That's good news."

"I can't tell you how relieved I am." Ruthie leaned against the door, phone pressed to her heart. Her dark eyes shone with a light he hadn't seen there before.

"I can imagine." He remembered too well the hard-won sense of relief when he'd finally extricated himself from Kimberly. He shifted, suddenly uncomfortable. He'd lied to her, when he'd told her she would someday be free of Stephen entirely. That she'd get beyond this, as if drawing from his own experience. Hell if he was free of Kimberly and all her crap. Hell if he'd ever started really dealing with that.

"Guess Hound and I can head on home now, huh?"

She blinked, something like surprise and disappointment sliding over her face. "I guess so."

He jerked a thumb toward the stairs. "I'm going to go pack up then. The kids are still in the living room. There's a SpongeBob marathon going today, I think."

"Chris?" Her quiet voice stopped him within steps. He turned to look at her, the dark depths of her gaze pulling at him hard. "I meant what I said. About us being friends." She smiled, the expression in her eyes far from casual. "Don't be a stranger, okay?"

"I won't." Damn, why did turning away and heading up those stairs take so much effort?

It didn't take long to gather his stuff together and get Hound situated in the Jeep. He made sure he said goodbye to the children before leaving, garnering sweet hugs from Ainsley and a shy smile from Camille. John Robert watched him with big eyes and stuck out a hand, his face solemn as Chris took it in a handshake. Hell, even her kids got to him.

Being home was even worse. The big old ranch-style house he rented, normally a peaceful haven where no one bothered him, seemed too quiet, too empty. After rambling around for an hour or so, he found himself heading to the sheriff's department. Late in the afternoon, the squad room stood quiet and nearly deserted. Mark Cook sat at his desk with Tick kicked back in the chair opposite, both of them reading through incident reports.

Just inside the door, Hound slumped to a sighing heap in his favorite spot in the corner.

The two other men glanced up from reading. Cookie's incisive gray eyes sharpened on Chris's face. "What are you doing here?"

"Nowhere else to be, I guess." With a shrug, Chris fed a couple of quarters into the soda machine and waited for a bright red can to tumble out. He slanted a sideways glance at Tick. "Settles and Beecham called you, right?"

Tick nodded. "Yeah."

Chris popped the top on his Coke and leaned on the long counter running along one wall, where the coffee station and officer mailboxes stood. His own box lay empty. He turned in Tick's direction. "Thought you were off today."

Tick shifted in his chair. "Yeah. I was."

Cookie smirked. "He's in trouble at home and he's avoiding Falconetti's wrath by hanging out here, pretending to work."

"I'm not avoiding anything." A grin full of self-derision quirked at Tick's mouth. "I just know when it's time to go."

Their banter grated. Chris downed half the soda, the sugary carbonated beverage burning his throat in an icy slide. He set the can aside with a thump. Hound lifted his big head.

"You're so whipped it's pitiful." Cookie flipped a folder across the desk at his partner. "Admit it. You pissed her off, probably by being stupid and stubborn, and now you're hiding out here because you know she could kick your ass if she really wanted to."

"That's—"

"Shut up, Cookie." The weird itchy anger simmered under Chris's skin. Damn, he was tired of hearing this kind of crap.

"God, that's so not fucking funny."

He tossed his can in the trash. Hound's hackles lifted, a growl rumbling deep in his throat.

A quick look passed between Tick and Cookie. They glanced at the dog and then at Chris. Tick frowned. "You all right, Chris?"

"I'm fine." Under Hound's watchful gaze, he made a conscious effort to relax and managed to unclench his jaw. Tension lingered at his nape and shoulders. A mild pulsing ache spread up the back of his head.

"You're sure?" Cookie asked.

Shit. Now he'd done it for sure. He'd let the carefully shut-away tension and anger find a chink in his emotional armor. The two men before him, respected colleagues, hell, his superior officers, watched him like he'd sprouted a prehensile tail or something.

"Yeah, I'm sure." He rubbed at his eyes. "More tired than I thought, I guess."

Tick examined him, appearing far from convinced. "Take the rest of the week off like we'd planned. You've been working hard, even before this whole mess with Ruthie."

Chris looked away, refusing to show any physical weakness. His damn stomach spun, a sick afterwave of adrenaline washing through him. "Sure."

He moved toward the door, giving the soft whistle that drew Hound to his side, a sure, steady presence.

"And Chris?" Tick's quiet voice stopped him at the hallway. Chris glanced over his shoulder. "I really appreciate everything you've done for Ruthie."

"Anytime."

Chapter Nine

Chris woke, trying to hold onto an insubstantial dream of hands on his skin, a warm body beneath his own, his name on Ruthie's lips. He wrapped an arm around the pillow, turned his face into the softness. Eyes closed, he let his mind wander through the images and sensations. He was hard, remnants of sleepy desire pulsing in his blood, and he slipped an arm beneath his body, wrapped his fingers around himself, canted his hips to relieve the awkward angle.

Dark hair, all shine and satin, begging him to bury his hands in it. Those big eyes of hers, the way she'd looked at him the other night in her mama's kitchen. The briefest of kisses, richer and sweeter than the hot chocolate had been.

He wanted more, wanted her mouth open under his, tongues stroking together. He wanted her touching him, gliding those pretty tapered fingers along his body. He needed to touch her, to explore skin he knew would be soft and hot and so damn perfect it hurt. He ached to be wrapped up with her, naked, skin on skin, breasts pressed to his chest. Wild, wet open-mouth kisses. Arousal prickled through him, gathering at the base of his spine, tingling up from his balls.

He wanted *her*, wild, wet, open. Needed to press into her, long legs wrapped around his waist, hips tilting into his, faster and harder, the slide of sweaty bodies, the rippling grasp of her around him, his name bursting from her lips, a climax barreling through him.

A rough groan ripped free of his throat. He shuddered and

palmed the head of his dick, catching the spasms of semen. He sagged, face pressed to his arm.

Shit. Fantasizing—*jacking off*—thinking about her, and she was...she was...

Married. Beaten and fragile and...no, not either of those things. Strong and gorgeous and...

Not for him. He wasn't for her, either, wasn't for any woman.

Friends, he'd said. No kissing, no nothing. Just friends. Sealed the bargain with a handshake, and here he was conjuring up all the ways he could take her, how damn good it would be between them, when he was the absolute last thing she needed, would ever need.

He was a dog. No, lower. A worm, maybe? With a rough exhale, he shoved the covers away with his foot and rolled from the bed, grimacing at the sticky residue. Shower. A run with Troy Lee if he hadn't missed him. And then...the day stretched before him, empty and aimless. Wonder if Tick would let him work?

In the bathroom, he washed his hands, relieved himself and brushed his teeth. He stared into his own shadowed eyes while he attacked his teeth and gums. The loneliness crushed in around him and made his chest hurt. Hell, he didn't miss only her either. He'd gotten used to Ainsley's quiet chatter, Camille's shy presence, John Robert's near-worshipful shadow. Damn it, he missed the kids too, and that was insane.

He spit and winced a little at the pink tinge in the sink. He started on his molars again. Maybe not so insane. He'd wanted kids, once upon a time, had even talked about the idea with Kim early on. A shudder worked over him. Thank God she hadn't gotten pregnant. A child, living in that hell.

Three children, living in Ruthie's hell. Three more reasons for him to stay away, to be a merely friendly presence when he did see her. Hadn't he seen the suspicion and fear in John Robert's eyes himself? No telling what they'd seen in that house in South Carolina, and someone didn't get over that just by getting out. They'd need time to heal and that kind of healing took a hell of a long time, if it ever happened at all.

He was living proof of that.

The damp air stung his lungs. Chris concentrated on the run, the terrain, glad Troy Lee was pushing this morning. Maintaining the strenuous pace meant he didn't have to talk. They rounded the edge of Railroad Park and a steady hum of generators and chatter greeted them. Vendors for the Pecan Festival set up booths and readied wares. By ten a.m., the downtown area would be crawling with people. He could hang out at the festival for a while, kill some time that way, although arts and crafts really weren't his thing.

"Think"—if he were with anyone else, the breathless rasp of his voice would be an embarrassment—"we need...someone else working here today?"

Troy Lee snorted. "Hardly. What's gonna happen—some of the old-biddy committee get in a fight over a crocheted throw?"

He sounded anything but winded, and Chris straightened to relieve his own cramping lungs. Troy Lee slanted a searching look at him and Chris glanced away. The next block passed in silence broken only by the rhythm of worn running shoes on the sidewalk and their breathing. Each soundless second ratcheted tighter the tension in Chris's muscles. It wasn't like Troy Lee to be quiet, not when he'd been giving Chris those looks all morning, like he was a particularly interesting math equation begging to be figured out.

"So what's up?" The quiet question came from nowhere.

Chris shrugged, using the pace as an excuse not to answer. The palpable look Troy Lee bounced off him squirmed under his skin. Troy Lee slowed, more of a cool-down jog than a racing tempo.

"Chris, seriously, man. What's with you?"

"Don't know what you're talking about." He swigged from his water bottle.

Troy Lee stopped dead. Surprised, Chris continued a few

strides and turned to face him. Chris spread his hands in silent inquiry. Troy Lee stared back, chin lifted in challenge. Chris shook his head. "This is stupid."

"Well, yeah. You're buzzing like a Taser, have been all morning, and won't talk about it."

"Not all of us have to spill everything, Troy Lee."

"Not all of us internalize every goddamn thing that happens, either." Troy Lee's brows dipped in a frown. "It's not fucking healthy, Chris. Sometimes you gotta talk about it."

"Nothing to talk about." And there wasn't beyond a simple friendship agreement and his own pointless fantasies. Except maybe a woman who, so fast it was terrifying, made him forget every reason he'd chosen solitude as his preferred way of life. "Nothing important, anyway."

"Yeah, sure."

With an index finger, Chris indicated the sidewalk before them. "We gonna run or not?"

For a long moment, Troy Lee studied him with that mathematician's look. "Yeah. We are."

The remainder of their miles passed in companionable, if strained, silence. Back at their vehicles, parked behind the sheriff's department, Chris leaned on his Cherokee and finished off his water. Muscles jumped and quivered in his thighs despite the stretching they'd done earlier.

Troy Lee lifted the hem of his T-shirt to rub his face. "Listen, Chris..."

Whatever he planned to say trailed away in an uncomfortable cough. Chris scrubbed the end of his nose, tingling from the chilly air. "Yeah?"

"You decide you want to talk...you know where I am."

Something about the genuineness of the offer, the easy acceptance, heated Chris's neck, the way his dad's pride had done way back when. He cleared his throat. "Thanks."

They separated on casual plans for several runs during the week. Chris drove home with the day still before him, empty as a rural highway. He chafed his palm over the worn leather of his steering wheel. Maybe he'd find a game to watch on cable. There was that new action film on pay-per-view. If he looked hard enough, a couple of books he hadn't read yet probably existed somewhere in his place.

The bitch of it was that nothing he did would be enough.

Inside, silence smothered. Through the glass doors, he could see Hound snoozing in his kennel. Smart would be digging out something to read, lounging in front of the television. Smart would even be driving back to the coast.

He passed a hand over his jaw. Hell, he wasn't going to be smart, and he might as well just go ahead and acknowledge that fact. No, he was going to take a shower and then give in to the insane pull.

Once the grime and sweat were gone, he was going to see Ruthie. God only knew what he'd say when he got there.

"Mama, maybe this is an omen." Tori's desperation carried down the hallway. "A sign."

"Victoria, you know I don't hold with such nonsense." Maternal impatience lingered in their mother's tone. "Now get the phonebook."

Tori's hefty sigh hinted at long-suffering patience. "Mama, I don't need the huge reception anyway."

Ruthie stepped into the kitchen and her younger sister threw a help-me-here look in her direction before turning back to their mother.

"I know you don't want to admit any weakness, but you have to remember you just suffered a traumatic event and a head injury. You had amnesia, for Pete's sake." Tori's distress built, seeming nowhere near running out of steam. "I simply want to marry Mark and it doesn't matter if we have the catered shindig or a family deal here at the house."

The two women stared at one another in a visual power struggle. Ruthie lifted an eyebrow at them on her way to the coffeepot. The sounds of the children playing in the living room wafted down the hall. Ruthie poured coffee into one of the green lily-patterned mugs. "What's going on?"

"My caterer cancelled. Everyone else locally is booked." Tori rolled her eyes, lips pinched in a frustrated line. "And I'm trying to convince Mama all the trappings don't matter."

With a sip at the rich French roast, Ruthie shrugged. "I can do it."

"What?" Tori shook her head, the single word distracted. Their mama turned sideways in her chair to fix Ruthie with a measuring look layered with maternal pride and approval.

"I said I can do it." Ruthie smiled at her sister's confused expression. "I have catered weddings before, Tor."

She didn't mention that was how she'd met Stephen in the first place. Excitement uncurled within her, the long-forgotten taste of a culinary challenge sweet and seductive. She caught her sister's wary gaze.

"Let me do this for you," she said, hoping how much she needed the opportunity to prove herself all over again didn't show as badly as it felt it did. "You won't be sorry."

"Are you sure?" A hint of doubt remained in Tori's voice.

"I'm positive." She turned her attention to her mother, still studying her face. "Would you mind if I commandeered your kitchen for this?"

A slow pleased smile spread over Mama's face. "Not in the least."

Once Tori had departed and her mother disappeared to putter around the house, Ruthie threw herself into measuring, mixing, baking. The dust of flour on her hands, the feel of batter smoothing out under a wooden spoon, the mingling of vanilla and almond...it was like finding her way back to friends long lost and long missed.

An engine purred into the yard, tires crunching on gravel. She stilled, straining her ears as footsteps thumped up the back steps. From the kitchen window, she caught a glimpse of dark hair and a tall form, and her anxiety shifted into a giddy anticipation. She went through the screened porch to meet him at the back door.

"Hey." Holding the door open with one hip, she tucked a stray hank of hair behind her ear. Pleasure bubbled along her veins. Oh, she was happy to see him.

"Hey. Something smells good."

"I've been baking." She waved him up the steps and into the house. "Come on in."

"Wow." He paused in the kitchen doorway and she looked at it through his eyes. Various bowls sat out on the counters, ingredients gathered in bunches. It wasn't the meticulous way she'd been trained to keep a kitchen, but having been so long denied the pleasure of cooking, she'd thrown herself into it with a visceral thrill that didn't allow for neatness yet. "Baking, huh?"

"Yes, samples for Tori's wedding. Taste this for me." She held out a small hunk of the chocolate amaretto groom's cake she'd been experimenting with half the morning. The warm, moist firmness of his lips brushed her fingers as he obeyed. His eyes slid closed on a muffled grunt of pleasure. An insidious tendril of wanton desire uncurled low in her belly. She wanted to make him sound like that again, without food involved. "What do you think?"

"God, that's good." His lashes lifted, flames flickering in his shuttered gaze. "Sinful."

"Think Mark would like it?"

"He'd be crazy not to." He propped against the counter, one ankle crossed over the other.

"What are you doing here?" A ridiculous level of pleasure flushed her body, just from seeing him. His eyebrows lifted and heat touched her face. She busied her hands with cleaning and putting away her supplies. "I didn't mean that the way it sounded. I meant, I wasn't expecting to see you."

A small smile touched his mouth and he leaned on the counter, watching her. "I can't find Hound's short lead. Thought maybe I'd left it here."

"Oh well, I haven't seen it, but I haven't been looking for it either—"

"Hell, what am I doing? It's not about that damn lead." The smile disappeared. She stopped, wariness invading her. He lowered his head and rubbed a hand over his mouth. "Truth is, I couldn't stay away. Couldn't stay away from you."

His simple words filled her with a bubbling, rushing elation. She leaned against the opposite countertop, hands clenched around the edge to keep herself from reaching for him. "I'm glad you didn't."

He held her gaze for a long second. "This really isn't convenient, is it?"

"Not at all." She shook her head. "But I don't care."

"I'm not—" He bit the words off, frustration sliding over his features. "There are things you don't know, Ruthie. I'm not whole."

It seemed a strange thing for him to say, yet somehow she understood. God only knew what pieces Stephen had slowly chipped away from her. She lifted her shoulders in an easy shrug, unable to keep a rueful smile from her lips. "I don't care."

"But—"

"You know, Chris, we've talked about all the reasons why not. What about the reasons *why*?"

His gaze burned into hers. "I don't know why. I just know I'm drawn to you, to your strength and serenity, and none of the rest, none of the shit that came before, matters. I think all that matters is us, you and me, and the way I feel whenever I'm near you."

"I'm a package deal." She made herself smile, although even she could hear the deadly seriousness in her voice. "A four-for-one deal."

He shrugged. "So am I. Except your package deal doesn't shed everywhere."

She laughed. "I don't know about that. Ainsley is discovering the joy of being messy."

"It doesn't matter," he repeated. "I can't walk away from you, Ruthie. God knows, I tried. I told myself it was done and over, and I needed to just let you move forward. I told myself it was too soon after your marriage. Hell, I told myself a lot of stuff, and the only thing I kept coming back to is that if I walked away, I knew I'd regret it."

She let go of the countertop. Maybe she could let herself reach for him. Maybe if she reached for him, he'd be real and warm and solid, nothing like the mirage Stephen had been. "I'm glad you didn't. Walk away, that is."

"Knew I was right when I said we couldn't be only friends." One corner of his mouth lifted in the lopsided smile that always warmed her.

She took a step toward him, feeling her own version of that draw he talked about. "So where do go from here?"

He watched her advance, a light blazing in his blue gaze. "No clue. But I'm all for slow and easy, Ruthie. Rushing isn't a good idea."

"Slow and easy is good." She tucked her hands into the back pockets of her jeans, remembering too late that she probably still had flour on her palms. "The last time I went rushing into things I ended up with a heap of trouble."

"Been there, done that." His gaze dropped from her eyes to her lips, then to the curve of her breasts, slightly thrust forward by her position, for the briefest of seconds before settling on her mouth once more. She sizzled under that look.

"I want it too," she whispered.

He blinked, as if her words had brought him out of a dream.

Or maybe a fantasy.

"You want what too?" he asked.

Oh, the answers to that question. She wanted him to kiss her. She wanted his hands on her. She wanted...the visions tumbling through her mind brought heat to her cheeks and that long-forgotten thrill of desire to her belly. Naked skin and heated whispers. His long, muscled body taking hers. Her body taking his, making him writhe and groan beneath her.

Her mouth dry, she slipped the tip of her tongue out to

moisten her lips. "I want...I want you to kiss me."

The corners of his mouth hitched up in a warm grin. "I think I can handle that."

With a step forward, he tangled a hand in the hair at her nape and drew her in. His lips met hers, and the tingle of desire and attraction was immediate. Ruthie shifted her hands up, to rest against his hard chest. Tilting her head to one side, she parted her lips and he made a noise of approval deep in his throat. Rather than a rough tangle of tongues, the kiss involved a clinging of mouths, the exchange of warm breath, an exploration of taste and texture. She sucked his bottom lip between hers, the rich tastes of chocolate and amaretto lingering.

Slow, easy, devastating in its intensity.

He released her mouth, a hoarse chuckle rattling from him. Ruthie dared to turn her head, pressing small open-mouthed kisses to his throat and jaw. Again, he rewarded her with that throaty noise of pleasure and linked his arms about her waist, thumbs kneading the small of her back. His long exhale stirred the hair at her temple before he dropped a kiss there.

"Damn, slow and easy is hard with you." Self-deprecating humor colored his whisper.

She smiled into the curve of his neck. "But it has its rewards."

He lifted his head. A new emotion glittered in his blue eyes and squeezed her chest tight. He smiled, his eyes intent on her face. "Oh, yeah. It definitely has its rewards."

Chris let himself in the house, nose still stinging from the cold outside, sweat-dampened T-shirt clinging to him in a clammy mess. He felt good, the endorphins released by the long run he and Troy Lee always scheduled for their shared Sundays off zapping through his system. He caught his reflection in the mirror over the hall table and grinned.

"More than that and you know it," he said aloud. He stripped the shirt over his head. It was more than the exercise high. Wasn't hard to pinpoint the source of his good humor either. The way his brain kept circling back to Ruthie's smile, the way she felt in his arms, the fact she wanted him too? Yeah, that was hard to figure out.

The new-message light blipped on his answering machine and he punched the playback button.

"Chris, it's Ruthie." Her voice held a hushed excitement, an almost breathless note. "Mama suggested we invite you to Sunday dinner, since we effectively ruined your vacation—"

He rolled his eyes. How many times did he have to tell her she hadn't ruined anything?

"—and I don't know if you have plans already, but I'd love to see you, if you wanted to come that is. We're going to eat about one-thirty, but if you wanted to come earlier, that's fine. Um, I guess that's it, then. I hope to see you later. Bye."

The line went dead with a soft click. He hit the button, for the sheer pleasure of hearing her voice once more. A chuckle worked up from his throat. This was sad. He'd given Troy Lee hell for how into Angel he'd been at the beginning—heck, for how into Angel he still was—and now here Chris was playing a message over and over because listening to Ruthie made him feel good.

He scrubbed a hand over his damp hair. He needed a shower, then he needed a way to keep himself from showing up over there way too early.

Somehow, he made himself stay away until one o'clock. Cars filled the parking area near the house and he cringed inwardly. How had he managed to forget this part, that all of Lenora Calvert's children and their families tended to show up for Sunday dinner? Easy answer there—he'd been focused on seeing Ruthie and hadn't thought about how being surrounded by her entire family left him overwhelmed and off-kilter. He blew out a long breath and slid from behind the wheel. He was here now; he'd simply treat it like a nerve-wracking domestic and focus his way through it.

Refusing to swipe his damp palms down his jeans, he crammed both hands in his jacket pockets and strode around to the back door. Ruthie met him there, pushing open the screen before he could knock.

"Hey. You came." She stood one tread above him, her face flushed, although he couldn't know for sure if it was from pleasure or the heat of the kitchen.

"I did." He kept his hands in his pockets. Pulling her into his arms was, for one, moving too fast, and for another, probably not smart when the noise emanating from the rooms beyond the screened porch confirmed that the entire Calvert clan was present.

"I'm glad." She cast a swift glance over her shoulder, and when she looked back at him, her eyes sparkled with the same happiness that curved her mouth. "Rather loud, aren't we?"

"That's one way of putting it." He suppressed a wince as a little-boy yell reverberated through the house. He leaned a shoulder against the doorjamb. "Something tells me that isn't John Robert."

"Probably not. Chuck's youngest, I think." Her smile turned rueful. "Give them time, though, and they'll have him inducted into the noisy-Calvert-boy club."

"I'm sure." He couldn't quite see it, as reserved as John Robert was, but maybe, with enough security and confidence. Silence fell around them, and he lifted his gaze from her mouth to her eyes. The sparkle there shifted, not dimming, but morphing to a slow burn he felt along his nerve endings. He leaned in.

"Mama!" Ainsley's plaintive voice echoed from the kitchen and Ruthie jumped. A blush played over her cheekbones and she smoothed loose strands of dark hair behind her ear.

"I'm being summoned." Her small laugh trembled and she took a step back. "Besides, it's rude of me to keep you on the steps like this and I have to check on the...on the..." She touched her lips and shook her head. "The ham. I don't know where my mind is today..."

She was completely flustered now and probably the most

adorable thing he'd ever seen. He grinned and gestured toward the kitchen, where Ainsley's voice grew louder and more petulant. "Come on."

The female domain of Lenora Calvert's kitchen provided a whole new set of challenges. Ruthie's mother was absent, but the remaining Calvert women filled the room with movement and easy conversation. Inside the door, he tensed, nerves jangling with strain. He was good with Tori, could tolerate Tick's brothers' wives because he really didn't know them, but the quick, cool examination Caitlin Falconetti slid over him set his teeth on edge, just like always.

He darted a glance at the hallway. Maybe finding Tick or Cookie to talk shop would provide an escape. He opened his mouth, intending to excuse himself.

"Did you bring the big puppy?" Ainsley's whispered question forestalled his getaway.

"Not today." He shook his head and her dainty brows dipped into a V. With a disappointed sigh, she grasped his index finger.

"Camille and I are coloring Mama's cookies. Come help."

That was a command if he'd ever heard one. He swallowed a chuckle and let her tug him to the big farm table where Camille knelt on a chair, applying colored icing to a variety of sugar cookies with painstaking care. Ainsley maneuvered him between Camille's chair and her own, then clambered to the wooden seat. He glanced up to find Ruthie watching them from her spot at the oven, her mouth slightly open. He grinned and she bit her lip before a smile lifted the corners of her mouth.

The sudden sense of quiet in the previously chatter-filled room prickled awareness down his spine. He shot a quick study around, the way he would upon arriving on scene, and caught a pointed look passing between Tori and Caitlin. Unease shivered over him, bringing with it the familiar claustrophobia and need for flight. He made himself focus on Camille's low voice offering decorating instructions.

He sucked in a harsh breath. He could do this. Really, he could. So he was surrounded and feeling pushed in a corner.

Wasn't the first time. At least he knew it was all in his head this time around.

With a drowsy sigh, Ainsley rested her head on Ruthie's lap and curled up. Ruthie feathered her fingers through her daughter's hair and set the glider into soft motion. Amazing that Ainsley could doze with the pickup football game going on in the yard, but her lashes fluttered once or twice and she stilled. Her lips parted on quiet snores. The chill of morning had faded under the afternoon sun, making a sweater almost too warm. Ruthie could get used to this though, the laziness of Sunday after dinner, having her family enfolding them all.

In a move Ruthie had witnessed dozens of times at long-ago high school games, Tick faked left to dodge Chuck and Mark to make a pass to Del. Chuck's boys, conveniently forgetting the game was supposed to be two-hand touch, took Tick down in a gleeful tackle seconds after the ball left his hand. Tori, perched on the top patio step with her arms wrapped around her knees, shook her head.

"You know, they're too old to be doing this. Someone's going to get hurt."

"Oh, Tick for sure." In the wooden rocker, Caitlin shifted Lee, who'd finally slipped into slumber, his face resting on her shoulder. "He'll want a backrub later. Same as if he had to wrestle a suspect into the car."

"Well, I can't watch anymore." Tori stood and dusted the seat of her jeans. "I'm going to check on Mama."

She disappeared inside and on the lawn, Tick grimaced and chafed at his shoulder. Caitlin laughed. "Make that a backrub and sympathy later."

Indulgent affection softened her voice and Ruthie glanced at her. "You adore him."

"Absolutely." Caitlin rubbed her palm over Lee's back and pressed her lips to his dark head. "He's honest and upright, loyal and intelligent, loving and steady, a good father...what's not to adore?"

"*Alors, il est un homme bon?*"

Surprise flitted across Caitlin's face before her eyes sparkled with humor. "*Oui.*"

Ruthie stroked her fingertips through Ainsley's tresses again. "I'm glad."

Her gaze wandered to the edge of the yard, where Chris had taken John Robert aside and was demonstrating the fine points of throwing a football. Even at this distance, she couldn't mistake the worshipful gleam in her son's eyes as he drank in every word, every moment of Chris's attention. A rush of warm affection filled her. Chris Parker was *bon* as well.

"Ruthie." Quiet discomfort colored her name on Caitlin's lips. "Maybe I shouldn't say anything, but you have to know...you should understand that you're very vulnerable to transference, to displaced affection right now."

"What?" Ruthie turned to her sister-in-law. Should she be surprised or offended by Caitlin's calm observation?

"Like I have any room to talk about transference." With an ironic laugh, Caitlin kissed Lee's head once more. "I fell in love with a man who was the utter opposite of my father. No surprise in that."

"What are you talking about?"

"I'm talking about the way you look at Parker." Caitlin lifted one shoulder in an easy shrug. "And the way he looks at you."

"We're not...we're not rushing anything." Unable to meet Caitlin's perceptive gaze, Ruthie stared across the lawn. Chris crouched a few feet from John Robert and caught his wobbly throw. A grin flashed over Chris's face and he tousled John Robert's dark hair. She was sure those were words of praise moving his lips, just as she was sure her son was drinking it in like a rain-starved cornstalk.

"I didn't say you were. I simply want you to be aware of the reality that it would be very easy for you to transfer any lingering affection you might hold for your husband onto Parker, especially since he's been in the role of protector—"

"You have no idea what you're talking about." The words

came out a cold, harsh hiss. "Affection? For Stephen? There is none. He killed it, when he threatened to take my children if I didn't obey, when he took every choice I had, when he tried to take my thoughts, when he...when he..." She shuddered, remembering. Her skin crept under the mere idea of his touching her again. "I hold no affection for my husband, and any feelings I have for Chris come out of the fact that he's good and decent, that he understands the difference between being controlled and being controlling, and maybe that my children don't look at him with fear and loathing the way they did their father."

Silence trembled between them for long seconds after her hushed outburst. Caitlin nodded finally. "He is a good guy, but I think he's vulnerable too, Ruthie, beneath that controlled exterior of his. A relationship can be hard enough when one person walks around with emotional scars. But two? I can't begin to imagine."

"Maybe you help one another heal." Chris's quiet laugh tickled her ears as he loped to retrieve the football from John Robert's wild throw.

"Maybe, but you've been hurt enough." Caitlin shot a glance across the grass at Chris and John Robert. "I believe he has too. Just be careful and go into anything with your eyes wide open. If you don't, if you go in deceiving yourself, or him, someone's going to get hurt."

"I've way overstayed my welcome."

Ruthie smiled at Chris's wry murmur. He waited at the bottom of the staircase, one shoulder resting against the wall. It was late, after ten o'clock. Her mother had gone to bed much earlier, but it had taken two episodes of SpongeBob, a handful of bedtime stories, one massive search for Ainsley's bunny, both she and Chris tucking the children in and an act of Congress to get the youngsters, completely wound up from the day's activities, into bed.

"No, you haven't. They enjoyed having you here." She

Linda Winfree

stopped on the second tread. "I enjoyed having you here."

"Even so, I should..." He jerked a thumb at the door.

"Please stay." She didn't reach for him, as much as her hands itched to do so. On the island, he'd jerked away from her sudden touch, and Caitlin's concerns still rang in her head. Vulnerable, her sister-in-law had called him. He looked anything but, tall and strong and still leaning on the wall with that negligent posture, but hadn't she seen the truth of that vulnerability in his eyes herself? "Let me be selfish and keep you to myself for a while."

He only studied her in unsmiling silence for a moment. Feeling that somehow her teasing words had touched some distasteful memory for him, she came down another riser, closer, but not invading his wall of personal space. She found herself wanting to alleviate the strain on his features.

"I won't ask you to watch SpongeBob."

With a quiet laugh, he straightened. "Hey, I like SpongeBob. You wouldn't believe the number of slow nightshifts Troy Lee and I have passed deconstructing the subtext of that cartoon."

"SpongeBob has subtext?" She left the stairs to stand before him.

"Well, you wouldn't think so, except then Troy Lee gets started on Squidward as the modern equivalent of the pretentious Renaissance man and SpongeBob as some sort of Everyman. At that point, it starts making sense, even coming from him." A lazy grin quirked the corners of his mouth and she dared another step closer. "Which is kind of scary in and of itself, Troy Lee making sense about anything but math, I mean..."

His voice trailed away and they stood in the shadowed silence. Awareness trembled between them, vibrating on the still air.

"Kiss me," she whispered, her throat aching and tight, echoing the sensation low in her belly. "Kiss me so I know it's all right to touch you."

174

The quiet pulsed between them a second more, until he moved, until his fingers entwined with hers, until his mouth was on hers. The simple touch of lips flared and became a hungry seeking, a ravenous tasting. Her back collided with the wall, their joined hands on either side of her head. She melted, curves accepting every inch of the hard male body pressed to her own.

"You're dangerous," he gasped near her ear. He dropped a kiss on the side of her neck. "You make me forget."

"I want you to forget. I want to forget." She tightened her fingers around his and tilted her head back the little she could, allowing him access to her neck. He brushed a wet caress along her throat. "Is that wrong, to want to lose it in you?"

She sought his lips, need coiling and beating between them.

"We said slow and easy." He muttered the words into her mouth and used their joined hands to lever mere inches away.

"You think I'm rushing you." She searched his eyes, fiery with desire, shuttered with caution.

He blinked, offering her the impression he was choosing his words. "I don't want to be something you regret later."

"You could never be—"

"Ruthie." His quiet voice rang with finality. He swallowed hard enough to jerk his Adam's apple and looked away. "Shit."

"What?" The frustration emanating from him held no threat, merely the sense he was fighting himself. "Just say it, Chris."

His glittering gaze swung back to hers. "If I say it, I'm going to come off like a bastard."

"Chris." She flexed her fingers within the circle of his. "Say it."

On a muttered curse, he released her and paced a few steps away. He rubbed a hand over his jaw, a visible tremor attacking his fingers. "At the beginning, you didn't think you'd regret him."

"You're not him." The very idea spilled bitter laughter from

175

her lips. "You're so far removed from him it's not funny. Don't you think I see that?"

He rested his hands at his hips and turned his gaze away once more. "I don't...I don't want to regret you later either. The physical stuff, the way I want you, it...clouds things."

"You want me." The idea pleased her, mostly because she knew it went beyond the physical and was tied into the connection that flowed between them. At the same time, she appreciated the veracity of his thoughts.

"Well, yeah." He slanted an ironic look in her direction. "Then you kiss me senseless and I forget how to think. And not thinking? Just letting myself feel? That's dangerous."

"Chris, I..." She rested her palms flat against the cool wall and tried to put her own jumbled ideas into words. "I come from an affectionate family—"

"I never would have noticed that."

A smile touched her mouth at his wry observation. She sobered. "And other than from my children, I've been deprived of the right kind of physical contact for a long time. The way I feel about you, it's hard not to want to touch you, to be close to you."

"I like you touching me too much. Damn it, Ruthie, you make me lose my head." He chafed a hand over his short hair. "I can't afford to be stupid with you. We need a freakin' chaperone."

She glanced heavenward. "We have three sleeping upstairs."

His chuckle held little humor. "Yeah. We might have to keep them around twenty-four-seven."

"I don't think they'd mind." Glad the tension around them was seeping away, she wrapped her arms across her chest. "They like you. A lot."

"I like them too."

"I know. It's obvious." Warmth pulsed in her and she hugged it to herself. "That's the biggest reason I can see you're nothing like him. He *didn't* like them, and they were his."

He nodded, glanced at his feet and a deep breath moved his shoulders. "I really do have to get out of here. Hound needs some run time since he's been kenneled most of the day."

"I understand." She crossed to him and laid a hand on his arm. He didn't flinch away and she lifted her mouth to his. He whispered the softest of kisses over her lips. She touched a light caress to his jaw. "See? We can do slow and easy when we have to."

Chapter Ten

Jennifer hated the subterfuge. She understood the need for it at this point. Like the way traveling to the safe-house location in the airless back of a UPS truck protected both the agents on security detail and the material witness, keeping the relationship between her and Beecham guarded within their partnership insulated him, allowed him a level of comfort with her he wouldn't have had otherwise.

She stretched out her legs and let her head drop back against the wall, the truck's movement jostling her slightly. Weariness filled her, but it was the warm, relaxed tired of returning from a vacation, rejuvenated and filled with memories.

With a sideways glance at Beecham, his head tilted back and eyes closed, she smiled. He did that for her, made her feel that way. But how long would she and Beecham be hiding? Patience. Faith. She'd wait, give it her all and believe that the strength of emotion between them would at some point override his fears and doubts.

Beside her, he didn't move, long lashes shadowing his cheekbones. She nudged his knee with her own. He grunted but didn't lift his lids.

"Tired?" she murmured, aware of the camouflaged agent in a brown UPS uniform behind the wheel.

A small grin crossed his face. "Yeah, but it's a nice kind of tired."

She didn't take his hand as she wanted to, but let her knee

and thigh continue to rest next to his. "I was just thinking the same thing."

The truck leaned into a sudden, sharp turn and she reached out to brace herself, palm against his chest. Once the vehicle steadied, she removed her hand, but his gaze remained trained on hers, a familiar fire smoldering in the blue depths. It should be familiar; she'd seen it often enough over the weekend, especially once they'd discovered the perfect little black nightie and she'd modeled it for him long enough to entice him to remove it. The desire in that look thrilled her. The emotion lurking within the fire took her breath and sent a giddy happiness bubbling through her.

"Almost there." The driver's terse acknowledgement dragged them from the bubble of isolation.

The safe house was an old frame farm home, a nondescript two story in the middle of rolling green pasture fringed by a towering pine forest. They shouldered their bags and stepped from the truck, both of them blinking at the bright sunlight. Beecham exited first, taking her arm for a moment to steady her, and she flashed him a grateful look, warmth tingling up her arm from the simple contact.

She turned toward the house, dread skipping chilly fingers along her spine. The last thing she wanted to do was spend two days here trapped with Stephen Chason.

Inside, the house was clean and sparse, though anything but modern. In the kitchen, Agent Michael Edgewood sat at the stained Formica tabletop, sipping a cup of coffee, his bag waiting by the door. Chason was seated opposite him, also with a coffee, reading a newspaper. A sharp frisson of dislike moved over Jennifer as he lifted dark eyes to her face, then skittered to Beecham. Something about those watchful eyes made her think of a predatory reptile.

Beecham cast a glance toward the shadowy living room beyond the kitchen area. "Where's Banning?"

Edgewood jerked a thumb over his shoulder. "Packing his stuff."

Beecham eyed Edgewood for a long moment. Jennifer knew

179

what he was thinking, simply because she was thinking the same thing. Edgewood was too casual. They should be involved in debriefing, swapping information and insight, out of Chason's range, and Edgewood looked in no hurry to do anything other than sip coffee while Chason enjoyed his newspaper.

Jennifer tamped down a spurt of bad temper. When they got back to Atlanta, they could talk to Weston, possibly have a different set of agents assigned. Having someone too comfortable with a witness like Chason, with any witness really, was trouble waiting to happen. Beecham caught her eye and she shook her head, blowing out a long, calming breath. He nodded, unspoken reassurance in his expression.

The unease didn't go away.

When Chason lifted his gaze to hers again, an indefinable smile gracing his face, it increased. Suddenly the next forty-eight hours stretched like an infinite horizon—a visible end, but one that could never be reached.

Once Edgewood and Banning were gone, with the barest of debriefing conversations, Jennifer left Beecham in the kitchen with Chason while she performed a security sweep of the house. Obviously, the anonymity of the place served to provide the ultimate security, because getting inside the house, if someone really wanted to, would be laughably easy. Regardless, she made sure all the window and door locks were engaged and the outside motion sensor lights worked. A quick scan of the house's layout revealed two bedrooms and a rather rustic bath upstairs, with a larger bedroom and tiny bath downstairs, as well as the large living area, smaller formal dining room and the big square kitchen.

Chason's things were spread over one of the smaller rooms upstairs, although the spreading reeked of meticulous placement. Beecham could have the other upstairs room. She didn't want to sleep on the same floor as Chason, although she and Beecham would be sleeping and trading out guard duty in shifts, one of them always awake.

Another way their partnership would keep them apart, it

seemed.

She paused in the kitchen doorway and listened as Beecham laid out the house rules under their watch. Stephen Chason's face tightened with each dictate and mean satisfaction ran through Jennifer's body. So now he knew just how it felt to be controlled, the way he'd controlled Ruthie and the children.

"Lights out at eleven. You're never without one of us..."

Once he was finished, Beecham stepped into the dim living area with her. Jennifer glanced over his shoulder. Chason had abandoned his newspaper and gripped his cup with white-knuckled hands, his gaze trained beyond the kitchen window.

"He doesn't look happy."

"Too bad. His business associates aren't happy about his cooperation. If he wants to stay alive, he damn well better follow the rules." He raised his voice slightly on the last sentence, and Jennifer bit her lip on a laugh.

She managed to keep her face straight, though, as she turned toward the stairs—she had the sleep-nights-guard-days shift. However, she couldn't resist nudging him with her elbow as she passed. "I really like it when you're bad, Beech."

His dark chuckle followed her down the hall to her room.

In the night, the house lay still and quiet. Harrell had checked in on Chason mere minutes before, assured himself the guy was alive, breathing, sleeping. He didn't want to admit how many times he'd checked, simply because the oily son of a bitch set off every instinct he had.

Now he stood on the narrow porch that ran along the front of the house, gazing into the darkness. No lights from distant homesteads disturbed the deep blackness surrounding the house.

The loneliness of the setting wrapped around him with scary, suffocating tentacles. The deep-down male part of him wanted to go crawl into bed with Jennifer, wrap himself around her. She was his—somehow over the past few days, she'd wound herself deeper and deeper into his emotions, his being, his life.

His mind kept toying with the idea that Jennifer was right—there was no Bureau dictate that forbade a romantic involvement between them. Hell, it definitely wasn't the first time in FBI history that partners found themselves facing something more than friendship and fidelity. Maybe keeping what lay between them a secret was a mistake.

He was still fiddling with that idea when the screen door creaked behind him, followed by Jennifer's quiet "hey".

She joined him at the railing. Her white robe, patterned with green frogs and belted over pink pajamas, glowed a little under the dim stars. Goddamn, she was adorable, hair mussed, her eyes sparkling.

"You're supposed to be asleep." He pitched his voice low.

"I know," she said, her own voice a stage whisper, and he bit back a grin. "I tried. But I miss you. I've gotten used to having you next to me."

He closed his eyes on a smothered groan. God only knew he was going to have the same trouble tomorrow, when it was his turn to catch some zzz's. "Don't say that."

She moved closer and looped her arms around his waist, pressed her cheek against his shoulder with a sigh. "Just hold me a little while and I promise I'll go to sleep."

Unable to resist, he folded her tight against him and rested his face on her shining hair. She murmured in approval and snuggled in. "Hmm, you feel good, Beech."

He turned his head, dropping a kiss on her head. "Jen?"

She made a noncommittal sound in her throat. He opened his mouth to tell her he'd rethought the whole secrecy angle, that he was ready to take that leap of faith, but a sudden clenching fear held him back.

Jennifer lifted her head. "Beech?"

"Nothing," he said, tugging her back against him, chilled. "Never mind. It's not important."

"Are you sure?" A small yawn cracked her voice.

"I'm sure." He stroked her hair, the strands smooth and

incredibly soft under his palm. "Go get some rest."

Over the next day or so, they settled into an easy routine, although Jennifer's nagging unease where Chason was concerned didn't abate. Something about the way he watched them, like a waiting predator, niggled at her, making the forty-eight hours of their rotation the slowest, most nerve-wracking she could remember.

She told Beecham so, the night before their rotation ended, standing on the front porch with the dark quiet surrounding them. "I just don't like it, Beech."

"You don't like him."

"That too, but I feel like he's waiting for some opportunity to...hell, I don't know." She shrugged, unable to articulate the shadowy apprehension.

He leaned on the railing next to her. "Your instincts are good. We'll talk to Banning and Edgewood, make sure they keep a close eye on the guy."

Jennifer snorted. "Come on, Beech. You saw how they were with him. I think we should ask Weston to have another set of agents assigned. They're too relaxed. They don't see him as a flight risk or a threat at all."

"Baby, listen." He rubbed a soothing hand over her shoulder, left bare by the thin straps of her pajama top. "I said your instincts were good. Mine are screaming too, but I don't think he's going to try anything. Hell yeah, the guy wants out of here. Think about it. By taking this deal, Chason has given up control over everything. With a guy like him, it's probably worse than prison. Sure, he's thinking about getting out. But where would he go?" Beecham swung a hand along the black horizon, a fringe of pine trees rising in a dark line against the sky. "We'll talk to Banning and Edgewood. Weston too. It'll be all right. You'll see."

"I hope you're right," she grumbled and he chuckled, the low warm sound that never failed to send an intimate tingle through her.

gentle hand on her arm, he tugged her closer. "I am."

She rested her nose against his shoulder and closed her eyes. She'd be glad when morning came, when they could leave the house and Chason behind them for a couple of days. When they could be normal with one another.

One hand resting lightly at the small of her back, he turned his head and brushed his mouth against her temple. "You need to get some sleep."

Probably, but she didn't want to leave him, didn't want to sleep alone. She moved, pressing her cheek on his smooth shirtfront. She fingered one button.

"Who is Tessa Marlow?" She gave voice to the question that had been bouncing around her mind for days, ever since Tick Calvert had thrown the name at Beecham in tense anger. As on that other day, his body went tight. She lifted her head. "Beech?"

He dropped his hand from her spine and she shivered at the sudden loss of warmth. He swallowed, Adam's apple bobbing with the movement. "Tessa...Tessa was my responsibility. I failed her."

Residual pain vibrated in the quiet, broken words. She waited, sure if she pushed, he'd only close off, retreat into silence. Instead, she stroked one palm over his biceps, a soft, silent show of support.

"About four years ago, OCD sent Calvert into Mississippi on a deep-undercover assignment to infiltrate a pocket of the Dixie Mafia."

She pulled back and frowned. "What? They don't really exist, Beech—"

"They're loosely organized, but yes, they do exist, babe." He rubbed a hand over his mouth. "Anyway, Calvert's job was to get inside this group that was mixed up in a ton of shit—illegal gambling, prostitution, drugs, even a little bootlegging. You name it, these boys were doing it. Tessa had been one of their girls, had worked in one of their brothels since she was fourteen or fifteen. Somehow, she ended up as the mistress of one of the two brothers who ran this particular rat's nest of the Dixie

Mafia, and she ran the brothel in Biloxi."

She rubbed her thumb along the inside bend of his elbow.

"Once we got Calvert in, and goddamn, that was hard enough to do, as closed to outsiders as these people are, they had him working 'security' at the Biloxi whorehouse."

"I'll bet he loved that," Jennifer murmured.

"Yeah. Said it took him a month of showers to wash the grime of that off. For whatever reason, Tessa took a liking to him. She pretty much tended the bar in the house and she'd talk to him most nights. Inadvertently gave him a shitload of information."

And that would have been gold. Jennifer was sure of it.

"Finally, when we were ready to make our move, it was pretty much based on something she'd told Calvert. We raided the brothel during a major drug transaction. Arrested the big guys, played like we were arresting Tick too. The thing was, it didn't take much for the brothers to figure out where our info had come from. Calvert wanted Tessa safe. She was mad as hell, tried to refuse protection, but we talked her into it."

He retreated into silence and Jennifer lifted her head to look at him. The worst was yet to come. She knew it as surely as she knew he had a cute pair of dimples at the base of his spine. "What happened?"

"They put a hit out on her. Got to her before we could finish our plans to move her to a safe location." A deep shudder ran through him. "I have never seen...it wasn't pretty. She didn't die an easy death."

"I'm sorry." She rubbed a comforting hand down his arm.

He shrugged. "So am I."

It made sense, then, Calvert's initial reluctance to trust them to help his sister. He knew firsthand how everything could go pear-shaped in the wrong circumstances. Jennifer brushed her hair, tossed by the light breeze, away from her face.

She only hoped her instincts about Chason proved to be completely off base.

Because if they were right...something whispered there

would be hell to pay.

"You know, this is the first time I've seen you in uniform." Ruthie's voice washed over Chris and sent his heart racing, as much from surprise as a too-intense elation. He straightened from checking the air in his unit tires. Across the hood of the car, she graced him with a cheeky grin. Ainsley clung to her mother's hand and smiled at him shyly. "I think I like it."

"What are you doing here?" His neck heated as he heard the words leave his lips. "I mean—"

"I know what you mean." She smoothed a loose hank of hair behind her ear. The red sweater she wore with jeans set off her dark prettiness and made her glow like some rich, rare jewel under the watery sun. He hadn't seen her since Sunday night, had indulged in just a couple of short phone calls, and the hunger to have her close pulsed to life in him, scary and intense as always. "I had some errands to run before I collect Camille and John Robert from school. I saw you and thought I'd stop to say hi."

"I'm glad you did." Pleasure warmed him. He tossed the tire gauge on the passenger seat and gestured over his shoulder. "I've got about a half hour before I sign on. You want to grab a coffee or something?"

"I'd love it." Her eyes gleamed. She ruffled the ends of Ainsley's dark hair. "What do you say, Ains? Want to spend some time with Chris?"

Biting her lip, Ainsley darted an excited glance at the car. "Is the puppy coming?"

"Not today. He's at the vet, getting a checkup and a good grooming." At his words, disappointment flickered across her little face, and affectionate laughter rumbled up from his chest. "Come on, Ains. The coffee shop does hot chocolate, although it's not nearly as good as your mama's."

With Ainsley's small hands tucked into his and Ruthie's,

they crossed the courthouse alley and made their way toward the coffee house on the corner. Ruthie's gaze traced over him, palpable as a touch, and he could taste her mouth under his again, feel the way her fingers had tightened around his. Ainsley skipped between them, and Ruthie leaned closer over her head to murmur, "I meant what I said about liking the uniform. You're very dashing in it."

"Thanks." He slanted a wry grin in her direction and found himself whispering as well, conscious of little ears. He'd been right about the chaperone idea—it kept them, or at least him, in check. "You look beautiful, but you always do."

At the corner, Ainsley tugged free to ooh and ahh over the pansies still blooming in the concrete planters before the historic building housing the coffee shop and adjacent bookstore. Ruthie caught his hand and took a step closer. "You don't know how badly I want to kiss you."

He stared into eyes deep and dark enough to lose himself in. "I have a pretty good idea. Probably as much as I want to kiss you."

Devilry sparkled in her brown gaze. "So how much trouble would you get in if I planted one on you, right here, right now?"

"Considering the county commission chairman's wife is standing down the sidewalk watching every move we make as we speak? Probably a lot, just as soon as she called the sheriff. Kissing you would be worth every second, though." He tilted his head toward Ainsley. "But us liplocking in front of Ains? Not a good idea."

"No." Her eyes dimming slightly, she cast a look at her daughter. "She's already picking new and improved daddies out of Mama's JCPenney catalog. I don't think we need to add fuel to that fire."

"She—they—will be fine." He smoothed his thumb over her wrist. "Listen, when I was in the third grade, I spent half the year trying to convince Miss Hazelhurst, my teacher, that she wanted to be my new mom."

Ruthie's mouth curved, although her eyes remained solemn. "Did it work?"

"No. Probably a good thing too, since she had something like six cats and my dad was allergic." He maintained a straight face with serious effort. "Not to mention she had to be seventy if she was a day."

The genuine quality of Ruthie's laughter melted into him. Her gaze traveled to Ainsley once more. "I worry about them, about what I let their lives be and if I acted soon enough—"

"Ruthie." He curved his palm to align with hers, nosy chairman's wife or not. "They'll be fine in the long run. I won't lie and say it will be easy, but you're a damn good mother and you have resources."

She brought his knuckles to her lips, her breath puffing over his skin. "You have the best way of doing that, of making me believe everything will be all right."

"Keep looking at me like that, sweetheart, and I'm going to forget that public kissing in front of the kid is a bad idea."

Small fingers wound into the fabric of his slacks and tugged. Startled, he dropped his gaze to tangle with Ainsley's curious one. She rested one hand on her hip and looked up at him. He swallowed a surprised laugh. He'd seen that same body language and expression on her Aunt Tori a time or two. "Are you a daddy?"

Ruthie's strangled gasp rang in his ears. "Ainsley—"

He shook his head on a quelling look at Ruthie and squatted, eye to eye with the three-year-old. "Only if being the puppy's daddy counts."

"Uh-uh." She tossed her chin side to side in an exaggerated negative, glossy pigtails bouncing. "Do you want to be a daddy?"

The reality that getting in over his head with Ruthie meant affecting more lives than his or her own sank in all over again. He tapped his fingers against his thigh and pretended to consider her transparent inquiry. "Looking for a new daddy, are you?"

"Yes." She bobbed her head, a desperate eagerness glinting in her eyes. "Camille wants one too. A nice one."

He could feel the tension radiating off Ruthie without

looking up at her. "You know, Ains, when you're in the market for a dad, you have to take your time, make sure you get exactly the right one—"

"We've already had the wrong one."

The breath whooshed out of him. Damn, he'd negotiated violent arrests less complicated. He wet his lips. "When I was really little, my mother went away, and it was just me and my dad. I spent a lot of time looking for a new mom, and I never found the right one."

"Grandma's book has mommies in it too. You could pick one from there."

He wasn't going to laugh, not when he understood only too well how deadly serious this conversation was. "I'm a little old for a new mommy now. But you know what figured out when I got older, about looking for a mom?"

She shook her head, eyes solemn.

"I realized that all that time I spent wning for a great new mom, I could have spent with the great dad I already had. Maybe..." He chucked her chin and she giggled. "Maybe if you just enjoy being with your mama and your grandma, then the new-daddy thing will take care of itself."

She stared at him a moment, then shifted her gaze to Ruthie's. "Can I have hot chocolate now?"

"Most definitely." Ruthie extended hand and Ainsley wrapped their fingers together. Chris held the door for them. As she passed through, Ruthie touched a finger to his chest.

"Thank you," she whispered.

"Anytime."

She paused, her eyes full of sadness and hot promises all at the same time. "When I get you alone Chris Parker, I'm going to kiss you senseless."

Hell, he was beginning to think letting her turn him stupid with her kisses might not be a bad thing. "Looking forward to it, Ruth Ann Calvert."

"Lucy, you've got some 'splainin' to do. What have you got to say for yourself?"

Chris opened his locker and masked the desire to chuckle with a long-suffering expression. "Troy Lee, anyone ever tell you that you watch too much television?"

"Late nights up with the baby." Troy Lee propped an elbow on his adjacent locker and smacked Chris in the chest. Voices echoed from the hallway outside the officer's locker room. "Spill it, man."

"What the hell are you talking about?" He shrugged out of his uniform shirt and draped it on the locker hook.

"The brunette, you know, the one you were making eyes at in front of the coffee house."

Shit. He swallowed a sigh and tugged his vest from the locker. "Nothing to spill. We're friends."

"Yeah, like Anl and I are friends." A broad grin displayed Troy Lee's white teeth. He punched Chris's shoulder. "This is great."

He struggled into the vest and closed the hook-and-loop straps, making sure the fit was snug and tight with no gaps. "Why is that, Troy Lee?"

"Because if you getting that close to a woman, it means you're facing your issues."

Anger sizzled over his skin. Issues. Hell. Where had that come from? He jerked his shirt from the hook and stabbed his arms into the sleeves. "I don't have issues."

Troy Lee snorted. "Sure you don't."

He buttoned it and shoved his shirttail in, irritation making him clumsy. "Just what issues do you think I have?"

"Hey, man, you missed the back. Let me help you with that." Troy Lee grabbed the rear of his waistband, gun belt and all.

"What the..." His voice emerged a surprised yelp and he elbowed in Troy Lee's direction. "Get the hell off me."

Instead, Troy Lee used the leverage to shift them so Chris's back hit the lockers. Grinning even wider, Troy Lee bracketed

Chris's head with his hands and leaned in, their eyes inches apart. "Let's talk about your issues."

"Troy Lee, what the fuck?"

"Does it bother you to have me this close?"

"It pisses me off." Chris looked sideways at the hall. "Next you thing you know, someone will see this and then everyone's gonna be saying I'm your bitch."

"Nah, most of them think I'm yours on the down-low," Troy Lee drawled. "The stupid ones who can't see that you're about as gay as I am. But no tension, no jumpiness?"

"No." Only if the urge to kill him for being stupid counted. "This is freakin' dumb, Troy Lee. What—?"

"Stay here a sec then and I'll go get Deb out of dispatch. Or even better, Falconetti's upstairs talking to Calvert. Let's see how you react to her this close—"

"Fuck, no." He didn't like where this was going, didn't like Troy Lee—make that *anyone*—having this much insight into how his brain worked. He flattened his palms against Troy Lee's chest and shoved. "Fine, you made your point. I have issues with women in my personal space, okay? Now get off me."

Undisturbed by the animosity, Troy Lee levered away. "But this is good, see? If you can get close to her, especially the way you were looking at her, then you're dealing with the mess."

"You know, if I wanted a fucking therapist, I'd go hire one." He slammed his locker harder than necessary. "But thanks a lot for your opinion."

Troy Lee lounged against the lockers next to him once more. "Hell, I thought for a split second you had. Then I realized it wasn't Tori, although she looks just like her, and that you weren't being stupid enough to scam on Cookie's woman—"

"Troy Lee." He rested his forehead on the locker with a weary sigh. "Shut up."

"You know what stasis means?"

"What?" He should have known Troy Lee would just ignore him and keep talking.

"It's kinda like being suspended, like holding a note in

191

music that doesn't change."

"Fascinating, but what does that have to do with me?"

"Chris, man, you've been in stasis the whole time I've known you. Kind of in the same place, not going anywhere, not changing. The fact you're moving out of that with this woman? It's fantastic."

The memory of Ruthie's shining eyes, the sweet way her touch made him feel shivered over him. "Yeah, it's cool."

Troy Lee landed another guy-to-guy punch on his arm. "Come on. Let's go to work."

Surrounded by the soothing normalcy of his radio crackling, Chris swung the unit onto Durham Street and played the spotlight over the deserted IGA parking lot. Back on the job, back in the groove, he felt more like himself.

A self-derisive grin played around his mouth as he turned in behind the chicken joint. A couple of feral cats froze in the act of raiding the dumpster out back, their eyes glowing in the harsh glare of his spot. Ruthie's promise to kiss him senseless echoed in his head, and all he could think about was how soon he could let her get him alone.

He liked the way she made him feel—alive, stable, normal. They carefully avoided talking about the future and he was grateful for that. It was too soon. Time enough for that once her divorce was final, once he finally found a way to tell her about Kimberly. Right now, being together, growing closer, learning more about one another was almost enough.

Almost. His grin widening, he swung the light over the windows of the upholstery shop and the adjacent insurance agency. Enough would be finding some way to salve the unbearable urge he had to touch her. Taking her hand or arm as they walked, stealing the occasional very chaste kiss wasn't nearly enough.

He wanted more. He wanted everything she had to give him, even if the intense way he wanted everything still scared him. He was going to have to deal with it, though. She was too important not to face the fear.

Another Chandler patrol car sat in the Rite Aid parking lot and he pulled in, easing to a stop, facing the opposite direction. He lowered his window. Slumped in the other car's driver's seat, Troy Lee rested his wrist on the steering wheel and flashed him a grin. "Hey."

"Hey." He fiddled with the air-conditioning vents, turning the flow onto Hound, snoozing in the backseat.

Troy Lee lifted a soda can to his mouth. "Slow night, huh?"

Chris cringed. There existed no better way to jinx a cop's night than to refer to it as "slow". "Man, now why did you have to go and say that—"

The radio squawk cut him off. "Chandler to C-5."

With a rough sigh, Chris reached for his mike. "Go ahead, Chandler."

"10-16, 1112 Boll Weevil Road."

On a groan, he rested his brow on the wheel. A domestic dispute at the Stinsons'. Why wasn't he surprised?

"10-4, Chandler, 10-76." He replaced the microphone and scowled at Troy Lee, who appeared completely unrepentant. "You had to say it, didn't you?"

Troy Lee gunned his motor and grabbed his mike to call himself in as also en route. "Let's go."

They went sans blue lights and sirens, late-night traffic almost nonexistent on the back-country roads, the drive to the Stinsons' rural home taking less than ten minutes. The house sat away from the highway, surrounded by pecan trees. The Stinsons were well known within the sheriff's department; in the nearly four years Stanton Reed had been sheriff, there'd been no less than twelve domestic calls involving the couple at one location or another. Maggie Stinson had gone so far as to leave her husband once the year before, but she'd returned within months, swayed by Jed's sworn promises that he'd never harm her again.

Those promises had held good for maybe a month.

Pulling into the long rutted driveway, Chris had no doubt if they arrested Jed Stinson tonight, Maggie would bail him out before morning.

A bare yellow light bulb illuminated the sagging front porch. Vines climbed up the posts and along the fascia board beneath the roof. Chris killed the engine and headlights, sliding to a silent stop before the porch. Troy Lee's brakes squealed as he pulled in behind him, headlights glaring, and Chris swallowed a groan. He knew better. The kid was too freaking smart not to.

He met Troy Lee at the rear of his own unit, eyeing the front of the house. The front door stood open, the empty living room visible through the torn screen door. No sounds other than loud music emanated from the decrepit home.

Somehow, the silence unnerved him more than the yelling and screaming that usually accompanied a visit to the Stinsons. He reached for his holster and unsnapped it before signaling for Troy Lee to follow him.

They moved quietly up the steps, but the porch boards creaked under their feet and Chris grimaced. He eased the screen door open. The living room looked like it always had when he'd been here before—threadbare furniture, a newspaper slung haphazardly on the floor, a few toys spread over the outdated carpet. The television blared with rock videos.

The smell hit him when he crossed the threshold, filling his senses with the nauseatingly familiar metallic scent, so strong he felt he could bite down and taste it.

Jesus.

"Is that...?" Troy Lee's whisper trailed off behind him.

"Yeah." Too many crime scenes, too many altercations with Kimberly for him to mistake that smell. His gaze darted up the dark stairwell, down the dim hallway that ran the length of the house from the living room. Lights blazed in the kitchen and the remains of a broken mixing bowl littered the cracked linoleum floor.

He slid his gun free, the soft *slick* of Troy Lee doing the same too loud in his ears. Turning his head, he caught Troy

Lee's eye and nodded toward the hallway. Troy Lee's blue eyes were big and dark in his pale face. As long as he didn't get nervous and trigger-happy and shoot Chris in the back, they were good.

The sickening smell of blood and body fluids grew stronger as they drew near the kitchen, easing, covering one another as they passed a couple of doors. His gut clenched with each footstep.

At the kitchen doorway, his stomach fell to his feet. Maggie Stinson sat at the cheap dinette, hands folded before her, staring into space. Flour and congealing eggs smeared the floor, mixing with the blood spattered everywhere.

Everywhere. The floor, the cabinets, the countertops, even the ceiling.

Troy Lee gagged.

Damn it, if he threw up, Chris would throttle him.

At this first glimpse of Jed Stinson's corpse, bile crowded Chris's throat.

Goddamn. Talk about overkill. He'd heard other cops use the term, but had never witnessed it himself. But this...no other description applied.

"I'm glad you're here," Maggie said, her voice a dull monotone. She didn't move, didn't look at them, didn't touch the gore-splashed knife on the table before her. "I did it. I killed him."

Chapter Eleven

That could have been him.

Chris stood in the kitchen doorway and watched the crime scene technicians photograph Jed Stinson's body. God, she'd butchered him. Not one or two stab wounds, but enough that the guy's entrails spilled from the slashes in his gut, his liver protruding. His chest lay open, ribs and lungs and God only knew what else visible.

Damn, would he have looked like that if he hadn't managed to twist sideways in the truck cab that night, kicking Kimberly out of the way and yanking the door closed? She'd had that kind of murder in her eyes, that kind of knife in her hand when she'd come after him.

He fingered the raised puckered line of the scar on his biceps, just under his shirtsleeve. A matching wound trailed down the side of his calf, hidden like the ragged slash on his shoulder blade.

Or the burn on his ribcage, where she'd nailed him with her curling iron.

Or maybe the wound nobody could see, the thin fracture line in his forearm where she'd slammed the iron skillet into it as he'd tried to keep her from bashing his skull in.

Behind him, voices drifted from the living room, Maggie's hitching sobs and Tori Calvert's soothing tones, punctuated by Tick and Cookie's voices, questions and clarifications. What the hell was Maggie crying about anyway? She was still alive. Jed was the one with his fucking organs spilled all over the linoleum.

Footsteps creaked on the hall floorboards.

"Hey." Tick tapped his shoulder. "I need you to take Cookie's unit and run Maggie and Tori to the station, process Maggie in."

Chris didn't turn. "Let Troy Lee do it."

"He's busy puking his guts out."

"Then you or Cookie can take her. Damn if I'm gonna."

He felt, rather than saw, Tick's startled surprise.

"Chris." His voice deepened, taking on greater authority. Chris bristled.

"Threaten me with whatever, Tick. Midnights, suspension, whatever. I ain't doing it."

"What the hell is wrong with you?"

"Nothing." He clenched his teeth so hard his face hurt. "But I am not getting in a vehicle with that woman. I'll give you my badge first."

"Come on." Tick tagged his arm. "Let's go outside and talk."

Like talking was going to change anything. Chris shrugged and followed the older man down the hall, through the living room and out the door into the damp night air. He didn't spare Maggie Stinson a single glance.

They stopped beside his unit. Chris leaned on the passenger door and folded his arms over his chest, staring into the dark behind the Stinson place.

Tick rested his hands at his gun belt. "Chris, talk to me. You're wound tighter than a two-dollar watch. What's going on?"

Jaw tight, Chris shook his head.

"Chris—"

"Fuck off, Calvert, and just leave me the hell alone, all right?" The pushing pissed him off, making his chest tight and angry, his skin itchy. In the car, Hound whined and pawed at the cage.

Anger flushed Tick's cheekbones with dull red. "Maybe you

need to go home, Parker."

"Fine by me." He pulled his keys from his pocket.

The screen door screeched open, and Cookie and Tori walked onto the porch. Over Cookie's shoulder, Chris could see Troy Lee standing in the living room, watching over a still-crying Maggie. Cookie laid a hand at the small of Tori's back as they came down the rickety steps. Chris looked away. Shit, just what he needed—more participants in the freakin' circus of his life tonight. His skin literally crawled, a skittering of tiny bug legs along his nerves.

The pair stopped next to Tick, Tori between her brother and fiancé. The patrol car at Chris's back and the three of them before him, between him and the house, created a box, a nice little corner for him. The jittery feeling running beneath his skin worsened.

He shouldn't have put his back against the car. Damn it, he knew a guy always left himself an out, an exit, and he'd failed to do that this time. Just like the night Kim had come after him. The memories pulsed in his head, the screaming, the invectives she'd hurled at him as he carried his shit to the truck. The jingling of the silverware drawer when she'd pulled it open. He'd known what she was up to as soon as he heard the knives rattle.

She'd nailed him once in the shoulder as he made a break for the door and his truck.

Like an idiot, he'd left the windows down and she'd gotten a piece of his arm as he attempted to jam his keys in the ignition.

She'd sliced into his calf as he tried kicking her away.

A shudder worked over him. Later, he never could remember how he got the window rolled up, the truck started.

Tick continued to regard him like he'd sprouted a third arm, pretty much the way his partner at the Tifton PD had done that night in the emergency room, while the doctor stitched him up—nearly a hundred of them—and Chris lied, again, about what had happened. They'd let him lie too, hadn't wanted to look too deeply into the mess of his life.

Tori smiled at him, full of concern, the way she looked whenever he'd witnessed her dealings with Jed and Maggie Stinson before. "I think Maggie's ready to go now."

Maggie was ready to go? Like she wasn't the suspect, like she got to call the shots. He turned a fierce glare on Tori. "Why are you treating her like the victim here?"

Tori looked taken aback for all of two seconds, her smile disappearing, her eyes narrowing the way Tick's did when he was perturbed. "Because she is."

He looked away. "Fuck."

From the corner of his eye, he caught the way Cookie's entire body tightened.

"Chris," Tick said, his voice calm and quiet but holding a distinct warning. As a red light, it didn't do a damn thing for the anger pulsing through Chris's body. "Go home."

Chris ignored him, all his ire zeroing in on Tori and her absolute naïve belief that of course Maggie hadn't had another choice. His gaze tangled with hers and she tilted her chin to a stubborn angle. He straightened from the car, needing to at least feel like he wasn't standing there with his back against a wall.

"You ever think we had it wrong, that maybe there was more to what went on in this house than just Jed beating the shit out of her?"

"I've dealt with Maggie a long time, Chris—"

"Yeah, haven't we all?" He shrugged, tired of feeling like his skin was two sizes too small. "And maybe we were dealing with the situation wrong the whole way around. Women do lie, you know."

"Not Maggie."

"Sure." He snorted. "You know that for real? Did you see what she did to him? No, that's right. You didn't go past the living room. You didn't see how she cut him from asshole to Adam's apple and spilled his damn guts all over that floor. All you see is her as the fucking victim here."

His voice held a level of meanness he'd never known he

possessed. Cookie's face and stance tightened with each word, but Chris was beyond caring. Let Cook take a swing at him. Chris could take him and at least that attack would come head on, not at his back.

"Chris." If possible, Tick's voice had gone even quieter, softer, and he took a step forward. His relaxed posture held no threat, but Chris stiffened anyway, shaking his head. Damn it, he didn't like Tick approaching him the way he would a difficult subject, with that hushed voice and bland expression. Obviously, the guy didn't get the concept of "fuck off".

Tori held up a quelling hand, her gaze not wavering from Chris's. He didn't like that either, the serene, watchful way she looked at him. He itched under that calm regard.

"Chris-boy," Cookie said, his tone as muted and blank as Tick's, the friendly nickname grating like it never had before. "Why don't you let me drive you home?"

"I can drive my damn self."

Cook nodded. "Go home. Get some sleep. You'll feel better."

Feel better. He rolled his shoulders in a tight shrug. Whatever. He just wanted the hell out of here. The problem was, he couldn't go until they moved, couldn't turn and walk around the rear of the car to get to the driver's side.

He didn't turn his back on anyone. Ever. That lesson he'd learned the hardest way possible.

Tick finally glanced away from his face and reached behind Tori to tag Cookie's beefy arm. "Let's go check on the crime scene techs. Tori can help Troy Lee get Maggie's statement."

They trailed back inside, Tick holding the screen door and allowing the others to precede him. Chris sagged, his knees weak with what felt like an adrenaline crash. He rubbed a hand over his eyes. Shit, he was tired, like when he'd pulled a shift over in Tifton and then Kimberly had wanted to fight all night, yelling and berating.

Yeah, he was that kind of tired.

Maybe sleep really was what he needed.

"What the hell was that with Chris-boy, anyway?"

Signing off on the typed copy of Maggie Stinson's statement, Tick shook his head at Cookie's inquiry. "Damn if I know. Never seen him like that before."

"You have to admit I did good." Cookie slid the initial crime scene reports into a folder and tapped it on his desk. "I didn't whip his ass for turning on Tori."

Tori, feet tucked under her in the desk chair across from Cookie's, gave a ladylike snort but didn't look up from her cell phone, thumbs flying over the keypad. "If you went around handing out ass-whippings to every victim who ever turned on me, you'd be a very busy man, Mark."

Tick jerked his head up, catching Cookie's surprised expression before turning to his sister. "What?"

Her thumbs faltered and she frowned. "Damn it, you made me lose."

"Don't curse." Tick and Cookie laid down the correction simultaneously. Their gazes met again, and Tick, seeing his own questions in his partner's face, waved him on.

Cookie thumped his thumb on the folder he'd laid atop his desk. "What did you mean, victim?"

Tori flipped her phone shut. "What do you want, honey, a dictionary definition?"

Cookie opened his mouth and snapped it closed, frustration jerking his heavy brows together. "Tor."

She made an aggravated moue. "His entire reaction tonight was textbook-victim PTSD. Geez, Tick, you live with Caitlin and you didn't recognize those responses?"

He shook his head, not liking to be reminded of the horror his wife had endured. "Nightmares and anxiety attacks, Tori, and I can't remember the last time she had one of those. I've never seen her act like Parker did tonight." She shot him a disbelieving look and he threw out his hands. "I'm serious. I've never seen that behavior in you, either. What makes you think he's a victim?"

"Instinct and experience." She shrugged and looped her

arms around her knees.

Cookie still frowned. He unwrapped a piece of gum and folded it into his mouth. "A victim of what, exactly?"

She gave him a look. "I'm a psychologist, not a mind-reader. Childhood abuse, maybe, or he grew up seeing violent behavior between his parents. Maybe he's a victim of domestic violence himself."

"Chris?" Tick couldn't help the amused grunt that escaped him and he didn't miss the matching sound that rumbled in Cookie's throat. Tori fixed them both with a withering stare.

Cookie tossed the Stinson folder in his working basket. "You're reaching there, sweetheart."

"Why? Because he's a man? Or because he's a cop?"

"I get that men can be victims of domestic violence, Tor." Tick propped against the counter and rubbed a hand over his tired eyes. Lord, it had been a long night, and that weird stuff with Chris still didn't sit right. But Tori's theory seemed way out there, even as odd as Chris's behavior had been. "But not Chris Parker. No way."

She rolled her eyes and he could almost hear her calling him an idiot. "Why not?"

"Because." Cookie picked up the conversation for him. "We've seen this boy take down suspects by himself that we wouldn't have wanted to tackle together. Believe me, he can handle his own. Kinda hard to imagine him getting his ass kicked by a girl."

Tori held her fiancé's gaze for a long moment before flicking a finger in Tick's direction. "And how many times have you said he's lucky Cait doesn't decide to kick his when she's angry?"

Tick groaned. He got so tired of hearing that crap all the time. He glared at his partner. "Yeah. How many times?"

Cookie leaned back. "Oh shit, here we go. Tor, baby, some things are supposed to stay between us."

Tori eyed him, chin tilted to a challenging angle. "Could she?"

Tick blew out a long breath. Caitlin possessed the same

Quantico training he had, kept her body in top physical condition. He might be taller and bigger, but she could outlast him. And she was strong and agile—he knew that from the playful wrestling that often ended up with them naked and sighing in bed. If she really wanted to, she could take him down and keep him down. "Probably."

"I'm sure you'd broadcast that all over the department if she was."

Like hell.

"Would you tell anyone?" Tori prodded.

He hooked his thumbs in his belt, glanced at Cookie and shook his head. "No."

His sister waved her hands like a magician who'd just made a colorful scarf disappear into thin air. "There you go then."

"Shit," Cookie breathed. Tick understood the single syllable completely.

He jerked his chin at his partner. "That explains why he was so pissed off at you for riding me about hiding out from Cait the other day."

"Explains tonight too."

Frustrated, Tick tugged a hand through his already tousled hair. "So now what do we do?"

Tori unfolded her legs and stretched. "Not much you can do. Pushing him is probably the worst thing you could do under the circumstances. He's got to work through the healing process."

"This thing with his temper flaring is new." Concern glinted in Cookie's eyes. "The guy is usually really controlled. Something's got him stirred up."

This time Tori's Lord-you're-an-idiot look included both of them. "It's Ruthie."

Tick blinked. "Our Ruthie?"

"No. Ruthie Garner from *Today in Georgia.* Yes, our Ruthie."

With a long exhale, Tick shook his head. "Ah, damn it. How do you know that?"

"Because I've seen them together, the way they look at one another. It's obvious."

He resisted an urge to drag his fingers through his hair again. "She's...it's not a good time for her."

"Maybe not." Tori gave another nonchalant roll of her shoulders. "Or maybe it's the best timing in the world. She's healing too. Maybe right now, each of them needs what the other brings to the table. It's pretty clear they're not rushing anything." She smothered a wide yawn. "But you do not need to go pushing there, either. The best thing you can do right now, for both of them, is give them time and space."

He took Cookie's advice and slept.

Once Chris kenneled Hound, he stumbled to his bedroom and somehow managed to divest himself of his shoes and gun belt. He hung his uniform shirt, all brass in place, over the footboard, collapsed facedown across the covers and let the exhaustion take him.

He slept until almost noon, when Hound's hungry whine shook him from a dreamless doze. After emptying his bladder, he fed the dog and turned him loose to run the backyard for a few minutes while he swigged a bottle of water that did little to quell his grumbling stomach. The idea of food set nausea churning in his throat.

Hound was none too happy about returning to his pen, but Chris ignored the big, limpid eyes and shuffled back inside. There, he slumped in the recliner and finished off his water. The light flashed on his answering machine and he ignored the two messages there.

Shit, he was supposed to work tonight, a seven-to-seven. He dragged a hand down his face. He couldn't deal with that. Seven hours should be enough notice. Rolling sideways, he snagged the cordless phone and called in sick to dispatch, something he hadn't done in years.

Not since Kim, anyway.

He didn't feel guilty for it, either. Instead, a blessed

numbness washed through him, the urge to sleep tugging at him. He pushed up and lurched back to his bedroom, letting the dark, soothing slumber take him once more.

That became his routine for the next two days as well. After the jingling of his cell phone woke him late in the evening on the first day, he shut it off without looking at it, turned off the ringer on the landline and let the machine pick up. He didn't bother listening to the messages.

His existence narrowed to sleep, rudimentary care of the dog, water or soda to stave off thirst and hunger, and more sleep. When his body fought back, trying to jerk him into alertness, trying to give his mind time to work, he scrounged up the half a bottle of strong pain pills he still had from the days after Kimberly had gone after him with the knife and used those, a few at a time, to force the drowsing dead-to-the-world state.

Late in the afternoon on the third day, an insistent pounding infiltrated his half-drugged consciousness. He lifted his head, listened for a moment, dropped back to the pillow. If he ignored them, maybe whoever it was would go away. The room spun in a slow, sickening swirl, and he closed his eyes. Desperate hunger gnawed at his stomach, a bitter medicinal aftertaste lingering in his mouth.

The knocking didn't stop. With a frustrated growl, Chris dragged the other pillow over his head. Shit. If he didn't answer the door, that should be a pretty good sign he didn't want company.

The noise faded, whether it really ceased or he couldn't hear it through the heavy down covering his ear. He sighed, sinking back into the drug-induced doze.

"Chris." Tick's voice, a heavy hand shaking his shoulder, bringing him to the surface.

He tried to shrug the older man off. "Go away."

"Wake up." Tick tapped his jaw, hard. "Come on, Parker."

Chris rolled to his back in the opposite direction, an arm shielding his eyes from the too-bright sun slanting in between the blinds. The movement caused another sickening wave of motion to spin through his brain. "Leave me alone."

"Shit." Pills rattled against plastic and the bed dipped hard, Tick shoving his arm aside to grip his chin and flip his eyelids up. "How many of these did you take?"

Chris tried to fight off the firm hold, but his arms felt like lead, heavy and useless.

"Chris. This is important. How many did you take?"

It took him a minute to get his vision focused enough so that Tick's face was something other than a blur. The investigator glowered down at him, deep concern in his eyes and the slashes by his mouth. Chris finally managed to shrug him off. "Four."

"You only took four this time?" Tick rattled the bottle again. "Or you took four total?"

"Four this morning." Chris shifted to sit on the side of the bed. He buried his face in his hands. "Four last night. Four yesterday morning."

"Holy hell." Anger trembled in Tick's deep drawl. "It's a wonder you didn't puke and aspirate. Or stop your damn heart."

Chris didn't respond, trying to fight off a wave of nausea and dizziness.

"Come on. You're getting in the shower." Tick hooked a hand around his biceps and hauled him up. Chris's stomach heaved and fury spurted through him, made hotter by his failure to tug free of Tick's easy hold. "And if you're not out in five minutes, I'm coming in after you."

"Go to hell, Tick."

"It's time to get it together, Parker." With his free hand, Tick gripped his chin again, forcing Chris to look at him. "Ruthie's in the living room. You want her to see you like this?"

The question set him back. Ruthie, here?

Chris shook his head and immediately regretted it, the floor pitching up at a weird angle, making the queasiness quiver in his throat. "You shouldn't have let her come."

Tick's exasperated sigh rumbled between them. "I didn't

have a hell of a lot of choice in the matter. She was hell-bent on checking on you herself, never mind I was coming over here anyway after you called in again today."

Closing his eyes, Chris didn't reply. God, he really wished the house would stop moving around him.

"Come on." Tick tugged him toward the bathroom with a gentle hand. "Shower, shave, get some food in you. You'll feel better."

Once in the bath, with the door closed, shower running and steam beginning to silver the mirror, he glanced at his reflection and wished he hadn't. He looked worse than he felt.

In the shower, he leaned against the tiled wall and tried to pull it together. Hell, he'd really done it this time. If there was a way out of this situation without spilling the entire sad, sorry truth about his life, he didn't see it.

This would be worse than dealing with his partner and sergeant in the emergency room.

He ground the heels of his hands into his eyes. Shit, it would have been good if he'd thought about that before he went off the deep end. The water beat down around him, pattering to the floor. He blew out a long breath. He wasn't sure who he looked less forward to facing—Tick or Ruthie.

Ruthie cracked a couple of eggs into a cereal bowl and whisked in a small amount of milk. The rich smell of coffee perking wrapped around her, the coffeemaker gurgling and hissing as a steady stream of dark liquid fell into the carafe.

Her stomach still felt hollow and jittery with nerves and worry. All the way over here—no, ever since Chris hadn't answered the phone the third time she'd tried to call him yesterday—she'd worried about what they'd find. Something had happened, something her brother wouldn't discuss, and Chris's comment about "not being whole" kept repeating in her mind, taking on implications that horrified her.

Tick's grim expression when he'd strode out of Chris's bedroom moments earlier hadn't eased her mind any. But his only comment had been a terse statement that Chris was in the shower, cleaning up.

He rummaged in the utility room off the kitchen and reappeared with a tennis ball in one hand and a rope toy in the other. "I'm going to go turn the dog loose for a while. Doubt he's had any real exercise the last couple of days. Save me some coffee."

With a quick kiss across her cheek, he disappeared through the sliding glass door. A few seconds later she heard an excited *woof.*

Setting her whisk aside, she tilted the small pan over the burner to allow the melted butter to cover the bottom before pouring in the egg mixture. She was plating the fluffy eggs and a couple of pieces of toast when a door opened down the hallway and quiet footsteps sounded on the carpeted floor. Her heart gave an unsettled leap.

She made sure her face betrayed nothing but friendly concern, not wanting him to know how completely he'd terrified her with his sudden withdrawal from her, from life. She set the plate on the small kitchen table and waited, wrapping her fingers tightly around a mug bearing the ABAC logo.

He appeared in the doorway and her throat tightened. He looked miserable and absolutely awful—his damp hair tousled, blue eyes dull and slightly unfocused, his jaw clean-shaven but cheeks and eyes sunken. Jeans and a pale blue T-shirt hung on his body.

When he met her gaze, something flickered deep in his eyes and his mouth firmed, but not before she witnessed the slight tremble of his chin. She forgot friendly concern, a blend of relief and anguish roiling through her. The empty mug hit the counter with a thump and she went to him, pressing to him, her arms about his waist.

He froze for an instant at her embrace, then he folded her close, his hold on her near-bruising in intensity. She tucked her face into his throat, the clean scents of soap and shampoo and male filling her nose, his skin warm and slightly damp against her lips. He shuddered in her arms, a harsh half-groan, half-sigh rumbling from his chest before he buried his face in her hair.

"Oh hell, Ruthie, I screwed up bad this time."

She flattened her palms on his back and urged him closer. "No, you didn't. It's all right."

He pulled back and ran a hand over his already mussed hair. "You don't understand. When this..." His voice trailed away and he glanced over his shoulder, his expression closing.

"He's outside with Hound." She reached for his hands, rubbing her thumbs over his knuckles. "He's not going to push. As far as anyone is concerned, you've had a stomach flu and took some of your accrued sick leave."

His mouth tightened. "Sure."

"He's worried about you, though." She curved her fingers along his jaw. "So am I."

He looked away on a muttered curse. Ruthie took a step back, holding on to one of his hands. "You need to eat something. I made you some eggs and toast. I'll get you some coffee."

She gave him a light push toward the table and filled the ABAC mug before finding another, this one bearing a sailboat, for herself. Joining him at the table, she found him staring at the food but not eating, one thumb tracing the fork tines.

Folding both hands around her mug, she let the warmth seep into her palms. "Chris?"

He shook his head and slanted a halfhearted grin in her direction. "You shouldn't have to deal with my crap, Ruthie."

She lifted her cup for a quick sip. "I thought of it as offering support to the man I'm falling—"

As she bit the statement off, their gazes met and clung, the unsaid reality of what she'd been about to say hovering between them. He dropped his gaze first, rubbing both hands over his face, elbows resting on the edge of the table. A shaky laugh escaped him. "Damn, I wish I was half as strong as you are."

She shook her head, not believing that he didn't see how damn strong he really was. Or how weak she could really be.

"It's all relative. Now eat."

The food and caffeine made him feel more human, although nerves continued to jitter low in his gut. The feeling only worsened when Tick strode inside, tossed Hound's toys in their basket in the utility room and stopped at the kitchen sink to wash his hands.

The older man helped himself to coffee, fixed Chris with an appraising look before he glanced at Ruthie. "I need to talk with him. Can you give us a minute?"

She darted a look at Chris and nodded. "Sure. I'll step outside and call Mama, check on the children."

Tick waited until she was gone to move. He pulled a chair from the table and eased into it, his hands curved around the mug, his expression troubled. Everything Chris had managed to eat turned to a cold, hard lump in his belly. Oh hell, this was it.

Tick's dark gaze flicked up to his and he tapped his fingers on the heavy ceramic cup. "Listen, I don't know what's going on with you and Ruthie. And I don't know what's going on with you, but I know I can't put you back on patrol until whatever is going on is worked out. Plan on riding a desk for a while."

Desk duty. Chris blew out a long breath. At least Tick wasn't talking suspension. If he'd pulled this stunt over at Tifton, he'd have been looking at thirty days off.

Tick thumped a finger on the table in a sharp staccato. "You're going to have to see someone, a counselor, whatever, to work through this, Chris. You can pick who you want to see, but I'm going to need clearance from whoever it is before I put you back in a car."

Ah, damn it all, he should have seen that one coming. Talk to a counselor?

Oh hell. Just what he needed.

Chapter Twelve

Jennifer wasn't sure which was worse—being stuck with Stephen Chason for days at a time or catching up on her mother's messages when she returned. With a groan, she rested her forehead on her arm, the receiver at her ear.

"How many this time?" Beecham asked, gleeful teasing coloring his voice. She lifted her head to glare at him across the small office they shared.

"Six." She hit the delete code once more. "And guess what? Five of them are about you."

"Me?" That got his attention. With almost comical speed, he abandoned his laptop where he was checking his backlog of email and swiveled to stare at her. "What do you mean, about me?"

"She wants me to come home my next weekend off." Jennifer smirked at him. "And I'm supposed to bring you with me."

He returned his attention to his computer. "Wouldn't have this problem if you hadn't told her about us."

"If I hadn't told her, she'd have me set up with Paul Coleman for the Junior League ball and from there, it's a slippery downhill slope to engraved invitations and bridal registries, Beech. My mother is the master matchmaker."

He snorted but didn't look at her.

Jennifer narrowed her eyes at the back of his head. God, the man was thick sometimes.

"So, how do you feel about the Junior League ball, Beecham?"

"Never been to one."

For a split second, she considered nailing the back of his head with the stuffed pig that graced the shelf behind her desk. "I think you're missing the point—"

"Harrell!" The pleased, vaguely familiar voice filled the tiny area with exuberance. Beecham's body jerked before every muscle stiffened. Jennifer glanced toward the door. The perfectly coifed blonde woman with the trim leopard-spotted jacket over black slacks didn't look like anyone's threat, but Jennifer knew firsthand how a mother's presence could inspire mingled joy and dread. For a man like Harrell Beecham, having his mother in his professional space probably had every molecule in his body crawling.

"Mom." He rose, a taut welcoming smile pinned to his face. He caught her in a tight hug. "What are you doing here?"

"What? A mother can't drop by to see her only child?" Julia Gruen reached up to pat his cheek and Jennifer caught the glimmer of light over a diamond on her third finger, left hand. Her stomach dropped like a stone. Oh, this was not going to be good.

"Flying from Palm Beach to Atlanta is not dropping by." He leaned down to brush a kiss over her cheek and Jennifer knew the instant he caught sight of the engagement ring. If he'd stiffened at his mother's voice, he went downright rigid now, his smile slipping. He recovered quickly. "But I'm glad to see you."

He darted a look in Jennifer's direction and she didn't need a codebook to decipher that expression. She stood, smothering a fake yawn. "I'm going to grab a latte and let you two catch up."

"Oh, Jennifer, you don't have to go." Julia reached for her hands like they were old friends, rather than mere acquaintances who'd met once. She leaned forward to brush a kiss over Jennifer's cheek. "You look lovely, dear."

"Thank you. And I am just going to slip out and—"

"Isn't she lovely, Harrell?" Julia's grip tightened and Jennifer stood still, feeling rather helpless. She could take the older woman, sure, but somehow, using her Bureau training to escape from her secret lover's mother didn't seem like the best route right now.

"Yes, Mom, she is." His gaze slid to Jennifer's and she caught a glimpse of desperation there. If she really wanted to torture him for being thickheaded earlier, this would be the time to do it. Too bad she was crazy in love with the guy.

Gently, she extricated herself from Julia's intense hold. "Wonderful to see you again, Mrs. Gruen—"

"Call me Julia, please."

"Julia." Jennifer smiled so wide her cheeks hurt. Damn it, his mother liked her. She could like the older woman, simply because she'd produced Beecham. "Y'all have a nice visit. Beecham, I'll catch up to you later."

She closed the door behind her with a soft *snick* and leaned against it for a second. Really stupid of her to feel this level of hurt because she had to hide what she felt around his mother.

Really, really stupid. But telling herself that didn't make the hurt any less real.

His mother studied the closed door, lips pursed. "You should snap her up, Harrell. She's smart, beautiful—"

"Mom." Wasn't this just like her, going off on a tangent about how he should hook up with Jennifer, when she was sporting yet another diamond ring? He tapped a fingertip against the gaudy rock. "Is there something you want to tell me?"

The brightness of her smile rivaled the stone's sparkle. "Isn't it wonderful? Barry proposed. We're flying to Vegas this weekend for the wedding."

Oh, good God. He closed his eyes. Not again. "Mom...don't you think this is a little sudden? How long have you known this guy? And it's only been a couple of months since the divorce was final—"

"Harrell, my darling, love is sudden and timeless and—"

"You've been married eight times already." Not to mention the various broken engagements and dead-end relationships.

"Oh, this time it's for sure, darling, and I want you to give me away." Her long, mascaraed lashes fluttered and a trilling laugh fell from her lips. "You'll love Barry, I know you will."

Like hell he would. And like hell he'd play any part in this particular fiasco. Thank God in heaven for this security detail. "I have to work part of the weekend, Mom."

Her face fell and he almost felt guilty. "Can't you get away, sweetie? I so want you to be there."

No sense in blowing this into a huge fuss here in the office. "I'll see, okay? But no promises."

"But you can come to dinner with us tonight." It wasn't a question.

The tentative plans he and Jennifer had tossed around earlier tumbled through his head: dinner at her place, a movie, probably his spending the night over there since they'd been sleeping apart during their days with Chason. Not asking her to go with him to this dinner would get sticky. He knew it, as surely as he knew she'd been angling to get him to go to that damn ball with her.

He sighed. "Sure, Mom. I can do dinner tonight."

And he jolly couldn't wait.

Jennifer curled her bare toes around the edge of the coffee table. She scooped a handful of popcorn from the bowl at her side and popped it in her mouth, chasing it with a bite of Ben & Jerry's Chunky Monkey. On the screen, a massive genetically engineered snake chased a hapless band of jungle adventurers. She really hoped the obnoxious guide who bore a striking resemblance to Harrell Beecham bought it next.

"Oh, don't go in the water, you bimbo." She sighed at the bikini-clad scientist's lack of brain cells. "Snakes can swim."

The beautiful women in these movies were always stunningly stupid. And men with commitment issues never really changed, did they?

She jammed her spoon in the half-empty carton and leaned forward to set it on the table. Telling herself to be patient was all fine and dandy and good as long as she wasn't staring the evidence of his fear in the face.

The doorbell pealed and she paused in mid-grab over the popcorn bowl. With her chest tight, she scrambled from the couch. She'd hoped he wouldn't show up tonight. She wasn't completely sure she could pull off "calm and nontemperamental".

She really needed that pig to throw at his head.

Without bothering to use the peephole, she swung the door open. He stood outside her apartment, still wearing his navy Fibbie suit and carrying a takeout bag from Bone's. A weary smile broke on his face at the sight of her and he stepped forward into the foyer, wrapping her close, the bag tapping against her lower back.

"God, am I glad to see you," he muttered against her hair. She tried to relax in his embrace. He didn't seem to notice, pulling back to brush his mouth over hers and shove the door closed behind him. He cupped her nape and tugged her in for another brief, hard kiss before holding the bag aloft. "I brought you dinner."

She shrugged. "Already ate. But thanks."

Stripping off his tie, he followed as she carried the bag into the kitchen and tossed it in the refrigerator. "I am so glad this night is over."

She closed the refrigerator door softly. So...he went to dinner with his mother, pretended she didn't exist, then showed up at her door to unwind. Yeah. That made calm and nontemperamental easy to do.

"C'mere." He leaned against the pass-through bar and tugged her into his arms. She went, still unable to let go into his touch. He pressed his cheek to hers on a humming sigh, thumbs rubbing at the small of her back. Her skin crept under the easy caress. She caught a glimpse of them in the wavy reflection at the microwave.

He appeared relaxed, the miserable tension draining from his face and posture now that he was in her presence. She wrapped her arms about his waist. The fact he could do that with her eased the lingering hurt somewhat. He nuzzled the side of her neck. "Missed you tonight."

You didn't have to. The words trembled at the tip of her tongue, but she swallowed them. Somehow, they didn't smack of calm and nontemperamental. Besides, pushing that point would lead to an argument, she was sure of it, and he didn't need any further emotional upheaval so soon on the heels of his mother's arrival.

She turned her head and pressed a quick kiss to his cheek. "You too."

He lifted his head, eyes narrowing slightly. "What's wrong?"

"Nothing."

"Yeah. Tell that to someone else." He rubbed at the base of her spine again. "You don't feel right, Jen."

She slipped free of his hold with a light laugh. "Maybe it's you. You're pretty tense."

His brows lowered, he rested his hands on the counter's edge and studied her. She feathered a hand through her hair and turned away. "I left ice cream melting in the living room."

Grateful for the excuse, she escaped. The reprieve proved to be temporary as he followed on her heels. "Pissed off at me, aren't you. For not taking you with me tonight."

She snagged the ice cream carton and bypassed the couch for the armchair. She folded herself into it yoga-style and spooned up a melting mouthful of banana, chocolate and walnut therapy. "Not pissed. Hurt. There's a difference." She shrugged. "I'll get over it."

His shoulders heaved with a rough sigh. "Jen..."

She held up both hands, condensation-dripping carton in one, sticky spoon in the other. "I don't want to talk about it, Harrell. You're not going to change your mind and it's not worth fighting over tonight. Sit down, have some popcorn and watch giant snakes eat stupid people."

He didn't move, hands resting at his waist, his entire body tight with renewed tension. She knew that look. He wasn't going to let this go, which made absolutely no sense. Keeping her a big, dirty secret from everyone was his issue, not hers. He should be glad she was letting him off the hook.

Mouth set in a straight, thin line, he leaned down, grabbed the remote and turned off the television. Jennifer gaped at the blank screen for a moment, a hint of blue still glowing there, then turned a scowl on him. "I was watching that."

"I think this is—"

The phone cut him off. Jennifer swallowed a sharp, humorless giggle. My God, the irony. Only one person would call her after ten o'clock at night. She'd never thought she'd be happy about one of her mother's calls. She lunged for the cordless phone on the coffee table, nearly dumping ice cream and herself on the carpet in the process.

An inarticulate growl grumbled from Beecham's throat. "Jen, let the voice mail—"

"It's my mom." She lifted the phone to her ear and unfolded her legs. "Hello?"

"Jennifer, I didn't wake you, did I?" The soothing familiarity of her mother's serene voice flowed over the line.

"No, I was watching a movie."

"Oh." A long pause vibrated between them. "Are you all right?"

"Yes, of course." A sudden and completely ridiculous urge to cry gripped her throat. She'd never been one for confiding in her maternal parental unit.

"You sound...strained."

"Ice cream. Froze my tongue." She pulled her knees up and wrapped one arm around them, ignoring the stiff way Beecham turned away, his back ramrod straight. "Did you need something, Mom?"

"I need to give Trish a final count on our tickets for the ball. Are you coming home? And should I buy one or two?"

"Yes, I'm coming," she said quietly, her gaze trained on the wall of Beecham's back. Solid, sturdy...unyielding. She blinked away a film of tears. "But you just need one for me."

"So Harrell isn't coming?" She hated the sympathy that entered her mother's tone. Hated even more how the warm emotion weakened her.

"No, he's not coming with me." If anything, Beecham's body stiffened further. Jennifer made a quick dash at her eyes and sucked in a sharp breath. "Mom, I need to go. I'll call you tomorrow."

"Of course, sweetheart. I love you."

"You too. Good night." She laid the phone aside and watched a puddle of condensation gather about the bottom of the ice cream box.

"I guess I'm supposed to feel guilty and agree to go to that damn ball with you?"

"No. I don't want you with me under those circumstances." She slipped from the chair, gathered the popcorn bowl and the remnants of Ben & Jerry's, and took them through to the kitchen.

He followed to hover in the doorway, tension screaming from him. "What do you want from me?"

She slanted a disgusted look at him over her shoulder while she dumped the stale popcorn and rinsed the bowl. "I don't want anything *from* you. I just want you." She turned to face him, clutching the plastic bowl with silly dancing popcorn kernels on it until her hands ached. "Would I like to have you with me when I go home? Of course. It would be nice to sit at my mother's boring dinner parties with you so I didn't have to listen to Allison's husband tell any more of those godawful dentist stories, to dance with you at Trisha's precious ball, to—"

"Is that what I am, Jen? A way for you to compete with your sisters?"

Any fight she had left was gone, completely drained away. She felt like a sickly puddle of goo, like the melted mess of Ben & Jerry's she'd just tossed. "At least my family knows about you."

"Goddamn it, I knew sooner or later we'd get to that." He rolled his eyes heavenward. "This is never going to work."

"Because you don't want it to. You and your self-fulfilling prophecies." She shook her head on a quiet, sad laugh. God, she was exhausted. "You probably told yourself all the way over here we were going to end up fighting about your not telling your mom about me."

His expression gave him away. She held the bowl tighter against her midriff, which felt curiously hollow and achy despite the amount of junk food she'd eaten earlier.

"What will you do when I'm tired of fighting for us, Harrell?"

He gave a rigid shrug but said nothing.

Poignant sorrow filtered through her. "Then you'll be able to tell yourself you were right all along, won't you?"

He glanced away. "Jen—"

"I love you."

The color drained from his face. "Please don't say that."

"You're right. It doesn't really matter, does it?"

His brows lowered in a fierce frown. "It matters too much."

A spurt of inappropriate humor washed through her. "You're an odd duck, Beecham. It matters too much? So, what, you don't want me to say it, because you'd rather not have me love you at all, so you don't risk losing it? I don't get you."

He closed his eyes. "Jennifer—"

"I'm tired." She set the bowl aside and reached to turn off the lights. "You should go."

"If that's what you want." He picked up his tie from the counter where he'd tossed it earlier. He wrapped the red-patterned silk around his hand in a nervous, repetitive motion. "I'll see you in the morning."

Then he was gone, the front door closing quietly behind him. Jennifer covered her eyes with one hand, refusing to give in to the threatening tears. Maybe in the morning she'd know what to do next.

✧

Chris paused in the open doorway to Tori Calvert's office at the women's crisis center. He wasn't sure exactly why he was here, beyond the fact he owed her an apology. And he needed the name of a freaking therapist. A really good one, who he could trust enough to help him get this crap out of his mind.

Her dark head bent over what looked like a budget spreadsheet, Tori tapped a pencil on her desk in a soft, repetitive *thunk*. Hooking his thumbs in the back pockets of his faded jeans, Chris cleared his throat. "Tori?"

She looked up, a quick, genuine smile lighting her face, and set the pencil and paperwork aside. "Hey, Chris. Come on in."

He took a single nervous step forward. Hell, he felt like a kid summoned to the principal's office. Or a rookie called on the carpet for some stupid infraction. He cleared his throat again. "I owe you an apology for the other night. I was completely out of line."

She tilted her head to one side and gave an easy shrug. "It's okay."

"It won't happen again."

"You want to sit down?" She indicated the plush chairs sitting before her desk. He took another step forward, darted a glance back at the empty hallway. She smiled, a winsome expression that reminded him of Ruthie. "You can close the door if that makes you more comfortable."

He did so, the lock catching with a quiet click. The small room seemed to grow smaller and he took a seat, his body tense and uncomfortable. She didn't speak but regarded him with that calm smile.

With a hard swallow, he met her gaze head on. "I was wondering if you could recommend a local counselor. I'm on desk duty until I can get a psych clearance."

"Sure." With a nod, she reached for a brochure from a small stack on the credenza behind her desk. "This is a list of local psychologists and therapists. If you can give me an idea of the type of person you'd be comfortable with, I could make some suggestions. A couple of them specialize in law-enforcement issues—"

"It's not exactly a work-related problem." He shifted in the chair and coughed into his cupped hand. "I know it probably seemed that way the other night, but..."

His voice trailed away. This was Tick's sister. *Ruthie's* sister. How the hell was he supposed to explain this to her, let alone a complete stranger?

She tucked a stray lock of brown hair behind her ear. "You realize anything you tell me is privileged. It never leaves this room."

He darted a look at her, finding her gaze steady on him. "I don't...know where to start."

"Maybe with why you were so upset at the Stinsons' the other night?"

He grimaced. "I was an ass. I overreacted."

"You've seen stabbing victims before." It wasn't a question, but merely a quiet statement of fact.

"It could have been me." He blew out a harsh breath and looked away, the intensity of the admission too much to bear while facing another person.

"How so?"

The next inhale and exhale shuddered through him. "When I was at the Tifton PD, there was a woman, my fiancée. Her name was Kimberly. Kim. We were living together."

"You were pretty young."

"Twenty-four, twenty-five. I met her while I was in the police academy. She was one of the instructor's daughters. Her granddaddy was on the county commission over there."

"You didn't marry her, then?"

He gave a humorless chuckle. "No. It was good the first year. It took me a while to realize what she was doing. First, it was I spent too much time with the guys, not enough with her, and somehow my buddies disappeared from the picture. She wanted me to herself, she said, and I was young and stupid enough to be flattered I meant that much to her. Then I shouldn't spend so much time training. I needed to be with her."

"She isolated you."

He darted a quick look at Tori. "Yeah."

"And she got angry when you didn't comply?"

"That's one way of putting it." When Tori didn't prod, he rubbed both hands down his thighs, a shudder working over him. "It started with yelling and screaming. She'd throw things, but hell, my partner's wife did that too. I didn't think a lot about it, you know? My dad raised me by himself, so it's not like I knew how a couple was supposed to be."

She fiddled with her engagement ring. "I can understand that."

"She threw a book at me one night when I was walking out of the room after I told her I'd heard enough, I was going to bed. Caught me in the middle of the back. Left a hell of a bruise."

"The first bruise."

"Yeah." A harsh sigh shook him. "The first bruise."

"And it didn't stop there."

"No." He shook his head, the memories scraping over him with crushing intensity. "I could handle the hitting and slapping. I think she knew I wasn't going to hurt her and she knew I couldn't very well call the cops. She'd have ruined me. But then the crazy stuff started. I'd come in from a shift, and it would be screaming and fighting all night long. She'd hide my damn keys or mess up my uniform so I'd have to start all over getting it ready."

"Controlling behaviors."

"I guess. Insane behavior, if you ask me. But the physical stuff escalated too. She ended up breaking my arm with a skillet. I was lucky, though, because I really think her aim was to break my skull."

"I'm so sorry, Chris. Truly I am. No one should have to deal with any of that."

He dropped his head with a rueful smile. "Hey, I survived."

"So how did you get out?"

"I was already looking for another job. Figured I'd leave law enforcement if I had to. If I didn't leave her, I was going to end up dead. Packed my stuff. I'd planned to get out while she was gone to classes—she was going to nursing school—but she came home early while I was packing my truck."

Tori made a small encouraging sound. He closed his eyes, the memories beating at the backs of his eyelids, flashes of Kimberly's enraged face.

"She was royally pissed off when she realized what was going on." He lifted his gaze and met Tori's dead-on, his pride demanding that for some reason. He shrugged, an edgy movement. "She came after me with a knife. Got my arm." He ran his index finger down the scar, hidden by his T-shirt. "Slashed into my back at my shoulder blade. And she got my calf as I was trying to get her out of my truck."

A flare of disgust—one he knew not meant for him—flashed in her eyes. "You lied about what happened at the emergency room, didn't you?"

He lifted his eyebrows. "With my sergeant and partner standing there? Hell, yeah. But I didn't go back and a couple of months later, I came here."

"To put your life together again."

"Yeah." Another shrug, his back hurting from how freaking tense he was. "Heard from an old buddy a few months ago that she'd married a guy I used to work the same shift with."

"So at the Stinsons'..."

"I saw what Maggie'd done to Jed—whether he'd hurt her or not, whether he deserved it or not—and thought that could have been me, if Kim...if I hadn't managed to get out that night." He looked away, his jaw tight. "And I turned on you."

"That's understandable."

His head jerked around. "I lost control."

"It happens, Chris."

"Not to me. Not that way." His inability to hold it together had put him on desk-jockey status indefinitely. Even if no one really knew why, the questioning looks, the whispers still lingered.

With one finger, she traced an intricate design on her desk blotter. "It's kind of like a soda bottle that gets shaken up. It can only take so much internalized pressure before it spills over when someone takes the cap off."

"Yeah."

She turned back to the brochure she'd pulled earlier. "So you need a therapist, one who deals extensively with domestic-violence issues—"

"I don't suppose that would be you?" The quiet question surprised even him. Instead of withdrawing the inquiry, however, he waited for her reply.

"It could be, if that's what you wanted, if you're comfortable with that."

He flicked a glance at the small framed snapshot of Cookie by her computer. "What I tell you is private, right?"

"Of course."

He nodded, some of the strain leaving his body on a sharp exhale. "I think I'd rather talk to you than a stranger."

"All right. I tell you what..." She swiveled to snag a thin leather planner from the credenza. "Let's block you out some time. Today's Tuesday. I have some time Thursday morning, around nine?"

"Sounds great." He jerked a thumb toward the door and rose. "I'll get out of here and let you get back to work."

She smiled and her pencil scratched across the calendar. "See you Thursday."

At the door, hand on the knob, he paused and looked back at her. "Tori? I really am sorry for how I treated you the other night."

"I know." Her smiled widened, softened a little. "And it really is okay."

He pulled the door open, a little of the dark weight sloughing away. "See you Thursday morning."

Lunch with his mother and her fiancé was an ordeal. In other circumstances, his mother might have been correct about his liking Barry Kelsey. But not when the man was in line to be ex-stepfather number eight. Inevitably, his mother's relationships ended, and as Harrell had heard once too often, he was the one constant male in her life, the one she could count on.

When Barry was long gone, Harrell would be helping his mother gather the shattered pieces all over again.

He picked at his chicken pasta, not even the spicy allure of his favorite Italian place lifting his mood or piquing his appetite. His mother's happy and excited chatter filled the empty pauses in the conversation, and she sprinkled her words with easy affectionate touches she split between him and Barry.

She laid a gentle palm on his knee. "I wish you'd brought Jennifer with you. She is a lovely girl, Harrell."

The reminder only served to darken his mood. "She was working this afternoon, Mom. And we're partners, not joined at the hip."

She blinked big blue eyes at him. "I simply don't want you to be alone. Is that too much to ask, for a mother to see her son settled and happy?"

At the word "settled", he choked on a sip of water. He wasn't aware it was even in her vocabulary. As for "happy"...

Was there such a thing?

She shook her head and gathered her purse. "I'm going to visit the little girls' room. You boys have a nice chat while I'm gone."

He reserved all comment. Once she was out of sight, he feigned renewed interest in his food.

"You're very important to her," Barry said suddenly in his rich baritone. "She loves you very much."

Harrell laid aside his fork. "I feel the same way about her."

"You're not happy about this marriage, are you, son?"

He bristled at the easygoing endearment. "No, I'm not. I

225

don't want to see her make another mistake, but I'm well aware she's going to do exactly as she wishes. And right now, she wishes to marry you. I can't change that."

"I have every intention of making this her last wedding."

Why, exactly, was the older man declaring his intentions to Harrell? He shifted in his chair, unwilling to prevaricate any further. "Well, that's been her every intention the last eight times. And considering she's only been divorced a couple of months, I don't see how this marriage is going to last any longer than the others."

Barry's odd expression puzzled him. "You think we've only known one another a few months."

Harrell reached for his water glass. "What else am I supposed to think?"

"I've known Julia since before you were born." The quiet statement stunned him. Harrell darted a quick glance at the other man. Barry nodded. "Your mother and I were high school sweethearts. We drifted apart when I went away to college, but I never forgot her, even after I married. When I moved back to Florida last year after my wife died, I looked her up. She was married, of course, so I resigned myself to being merely her friend."

Harrell studied him, trying to gauge his veracity.

"We'll have that renewed friendship as a basis for this marriage. I'm certain we'll succeed. I'm very sorry, Harrell, that you don't share that certainty. As I'm sure you're aware, your doubts are hurtful to your mother, however well-founded they might be."

Harrell cleared his throat, the chastisement making him uncomfortable.

"So." Barry's tone turned brisk. "Are you going to come to Vegas and give your mother away?"

Chapter Thirteen

Worrying her bottom lip with her teeth, Ruthie studied the orders spread over her mother's large kitchen table. She definitely had more here than she was going to be able to fit in the van. Obviously, Tori's lunch-delivery idea had been priceless in jump-starting her fledgling catering business. To add to her excitement, she had her first booking for a dinner party.

Everything seemed to be going so well—the children were adjusting, almost thriving now that John Robert and Camille had started school, her small career was taking off, the divorce was proceeding as planned. For the moment, she had a handle on her life.

Now if she could just get a handle on Chris...

She sighed. That's why she couldn't concentrate this morning. Concern and worry continued to nag at her since that afternoon at his house. In the intervening days, he'd called once or twice, short conversations in which little of substance was said. Tick assured her he seemed better now that he was back at work, even if it was desk duty.

But she wanted to see that for herself. She wanted to see him.

Brows drawn together, she darted a look at her calendar. If he didn't turn up in the next day or so, she would go to him. Maybe prepare a dinner, just for the two of them.

Outside, tires crunched on pea gravel and her heart jumped in her chest.

"Stop being silly," she said aloud, more to settle the

fluttering excitement in her stomach than anything else. "He's working the station. Probably Tick coming to see Mama."

Forcing herself to focus, she began sorting the lunch orders by entrée.

Strong footsteps thudded on the steps beyond the screened porch, followed moments later by a sharp knock at the back door. The barely banked excitement flared anew.

Like she didn't know that knock by now.

Sure enough, Chris waited at the door to the screened porch. He still looked wrung out—pale and heavy-eyed, his strong frame clad in jeans and a T-shirt. As their gazes met, one corner of his mouth curved up in a smile that didn't quite relieve his somber expression. "Hey."

"Hey." Her mouth dry, she stepped back, clinging to the doorknob. "Come in."

As he passed, she caught a whiff of crisp soap and clean male. She turned, right into a hard chest and solid arms. Startled, she looked up, his blue gaze burning into hers. Giving into impulse, she wrapped her arms around him and leaned up, pressing her mouth to his. With a muffled sound halfway between a groan and a moan, he tugged her close and kissed her, hard.

After a moment, she pulled back, touching his chin. "I've missed you."

"You too." He rubbed her spine in a soft caress and glanced away, his gaze settling on the table. "What are you up to?"

"Organizing lunch orders for tomorrow. Planning a menu for a dinner party." She stroked down his arms, loving the warm strength under her palms. Biting her lip, she slanted a look up at him from beneath her lashes, not sure she should even broach the subject uppermost in her mind. "How are you?"

He didn't pretend to misunderstand her. "I'm okay. Riding a desk is the pits, but I'm okay."

She nodded, but didn't speak.

He cleared his throat, glanced away, then swung his gaze back to hers. "I've talked to Tori a couple of times this week."

Her breath hitched. "Really?"

"Yeah." He rubbed a stray strand of her hair between his thumb and forefinger. "One of Tick's caveats was that I see someone, to work through...my past. Tori seemed like a good choice. I mean, I know her and it would feel weird telling some of this stuff to a stranger, you know?"

"I understand." She caressed his arm once more. "Is it helping? Or is it too soon to tell?"

The chuckle that rumbled from his throat was wry, a little self-derisive. "Hell if I know, but at least I managed to get the words out with her. And she doesn't look at me like I'm crazy."

"You were worried about that."

"Yeah." He released her, although the gesture reeked of reluctance. She liked that, the fact he wanted to be close to her. She wanted to be close to him too, especially after the past few days. "Hell, sometimes I wonder if I'm not."

"That sounds familiar." She crossed to the table and resumed sorting the order forms. "I can't tell you the number of times I wondered if Stephen was normal and I was the crazy one. He was good at manipulating my head like that."

"Listen," he said, rubbing a thumb over the edge of the table, "I only stopped by for a moment because I've been missing you. I have to be on the front desk at three and need to go home and change."

"You know how to make a girl feel all giddy inside, you know that?"

He laughed, but sobered quickly, that thumb still moving on the table edge in a nervous back-and-forth motion. "I was thinking maybe we'd have dinner one night this week. Maybe just the two of us? I, uh, need to tell you some things before we, well, before we get in any deeper."

Any deeper? The way she felt about him? "I'm already in way deeper than I ever thought I'd be this soon after Stephen. And the scary thing is I like it."

He moved his hand, that thumb making slow circles on the back of her hand. "Me too. You're...something special, Ruthie."

"And I could love you, Chris Parker, if you'd let me."

"I know. Me too." He caught her chin in an easy grip and leaned in to brush his lips over hers, a quick, firm kiss. "Which is why we're having this conversation, soon."

"I'm pretty sure Mama would watch the kids for me one night. She's enjoying having them around finally and they adore her." She tilted her head to the side. "But let's not go out. I'd rather cook for you."

He nodded, a pleased smile lighting his face. "Okay. Call me and let me know what night."

With another swift, hard kiss, he was gone and she stared at the doorway, rubbing a finger over her tingling lips.

"I just didn't think it was right, to not share my concerns with you." Worry twisted Sara Davis's pretty features and she reached out to touch Ruthie's arm.

"I appreciate it." Ruthie brushed Sara's fingers and glanced across the classroom at John Robert, gathering his things. "We're meeting with the counselor again next week and I'll mention it to him. He says we're looking at a long, tough row, but we can do it."

"I know this whole situation has to be hard on you as well as on the children." Sara folded her arms and leaned on the wall, next to the placard labeling the room as her second-grade domain. "I think he's had a rough week. He's been really withdrawn most days, but when he snapped at the other boys for teasing Camille, there was real anger in it that just didn't feel like anger at them."

"I'll talk to him. Thank you." Ruthie passed her fingers through Ainsley's hair. It had been a clingier day than most, with Ruthie being unable to make a single movement without Ainsley attached to her legs. She smiled at her son as he approached, backpack slung over one shoulder. "Ready to go? Camille should be finished with science club."

John Robert kicked at the molding as they entered the

hallway. "Mama, this is a stupid school. Why can't we go to school at home, like we used to?"

"Because, my precious boy, you need to be around other children, besides your sisters." She tilted his face up with gentle fingers. The sense that whatever bothered him had little to do with school slid through her. "I know it's hard getting used to something new, a different life, but let's give it a good try, all right?"

His shoulders slumped. "All right. I guess."

They collected Camille from the first grade after-school science group, and she bubbled over with enthusiasm, explaining that day's experiment to a wide-eyed Ainsley. John Robert remained quiet as they walked out into the sunlight. A chilly wind ruffled his hair and he squinted across the green area fronting the school.

"My shoe's untied." Ainsley plopped in the middle of the bottom step with customary princess aplomb and extended her left foot.

"All right. Scoot this way so we're not blocking everyone." Setting her bag to one side, she knelt and steadied the small foot on her thigh.

"Mama, there's Chris." John Robert spoke over her head. "I need to talk to him."

"Wait a second." Ruthie glanced over her shoulder. Yes, it was Chris, across the green space at the sidewalk, his Jeep pulled in behind a sheriff's unit. He and the deputy stood behind the vehicles, heads bent in conversation. "Honey, he's—"

"I'll be right back. I have to talk to him."

"John Robert." Her always-obedient child paid her no heed and she didn't know whether to fuss or cheer. She had said she didn't want perfect anymore, hadn't she? She cast an exasperated look in his wake. He hurried across the grass, something about the set of his shoulders bringing to mind the way her father had looked when he'd been pursuing a task with single-minded determination.

"Mama," Camille whispered, her voice full of horrified glee.

"John Robert didn't mind."

"I see that." She made quick work of tying Ainsley's shoe and rose. "Come on, girls."

Interested in this turn of events, Ainsley deigned not to cling, but slipped her hand into Camille's as they hurried after John Robert. They reached the two men and her son in time for her to catch John Robert's apology for interrupting their conversation. A spurt of humor shot through her. At least he remembered his manners when he rebelled.

He turned a slight scowl in Chris's direction. "You went away."

Oh, sweet Lord. Her breath caught, all humor dying, much as Chris's welcoming smile froze.

"You went away," John Robert repeated. "For days. Without saying anything first."

Chris met her gaze for a second, then bent to John Robert's level. "I know. I'm sorry for that."

"You made Camille and Ainsley and"—John Robert darted a look up at Ruthie, his mouth set in mutinous lines—"and Mama unhappy. They missed you."

"I missed all of you too." Raw pain made Chris's words ragged. "I was...I wasn't well those days, John Robert. I didn't mean to hurt any of you. It won't happen again, I promise."

"Daddy used to make promises he didn't keep." Camille released Ainsley's hand and took a step forward, focused on Chris's face.

"I know. But I'm not the same man your father is. When I make a promise, I keep it."

"Like Mama." John Robert lifted his eyes to Ruthie's. "She always keeps her promises."

"I'm sure she does. I haven't met a Calvert who doesn't." Chris extended his hand in John Robert's direction. "I promise, I won't go away without a goodbye first again."

John Robert took his hand in a firm shake.

"Are you *planning* to go away?" Camille asked.

A hint of a genuine smile returned to Chris's mouth. He

rose, his gaze on Ruthie's. "No. I'm not planning on going away."

Ainsley sidled closer to the deputy, who watched the exchange with folded arms and a disbelieving expression. She grasped a handful of his slacks and tugged. "I'm Ainsley."

"Hello, Ainsley." He grinned, displaying white teeth and dimples. "I'm Troy Lee."

Ainsley studied him a moment. "Are you a daddy?"

His brows lifted and Ruthie swallowed a groan. Not now. Chris's muffled snicker didn't help, although anything was better than the hurt and guilt she'd glimpsed in his eyes earlier.

"I am a daddy. Want to see?" At Ainsley's eager nod, Troy Lee pulled his cell phone from his belt and flipped it open. He extended it so Ainsley could inspect the baby picture on the screen.

She sighed in disgust and looked at Ruthie. "Mama, he's already taken, just like the man at the grocery store and the one at the gas station."

"So I hear." Her cheeks hot, she gestured toward the playground. "Why don't y'all go play for just a few minutes while I talk to Chris. You, Master John Robert, can think about what kind of privilege you might lose for ignoring me earlier."

She tousled his hair and he grimaced before the three trooped to the play area. She turned to a still-grinning Troy Lee. "I'm so sorry. She's shopping for a new daddy."

"Don't worry about it." Eyes glimmering with laugher, he waved away her apology and nudged Chris. "In the market for a new daddy, huh?"

"Shut up and go write somebody a ticket."

Unperturbed, Troy Lee consulted his watch. "I have to go make another couple of rounds anyway. Call me about next weekend, Chris."

Once the sheriff's unit had pulled away, Chris turned to Ruthie. "The grocery store *and* the gas station?"

"And the diner and the library and...shall I keep going?"

His attention straying to where the children romped at the

swings, he tucked his hands in his pockets. "I guess we're going to have to give her a steady male presence. One that doesn't just disappear on a whim."

"Chris, it wasn't like that. Please don't—"

"It was selfish, Ruthie. I didn't think about anyone but myself. I can't do that anymore. My life's not just about me any longer."

Did he hear what he was saying? She reached for his hand, rubbed her thumb across his palm. "So about that private dinner...I'm doing a dinner party Saturday night but how about Sunday?"

"Sounds great." He folded his hand around hers, warmth spreading out from the contact of their palms. "We've got a lot to talk about."

If spending two days in Chason's company was bad, spending two days in Chason's company with Beecham gone was even worse.

Jennifer popped a couple of frozen waffles in the toaster and tried to keep her skin from crawling. Banning had stayed over to cover Beecham's absence and the agent sat at the small dinette table with Chason, the *Atlanta Journal-Constitution* spread over the Formica surface. The sense of discomfort and unease Chason inspired deepened every time she was forced into contact with him and the final hours in this rotation stretched before her.

Newsprint rustled behind her, followed by the clink of a coffee cup hitting a saucer. Normal everyday sounds that shouldn't send frissons of nervous tension running over her, but did. Odd how relieved she'd been when Beecham had told her he was going to Vegas with his mother for her wedding. At the time, she'd wanted him gone, far from her, so she'd have time to regain the strength she would need to handle losing him. Now, trapped with Chason, she wanted Beecham here, trusted him to have her back in a way she couldn't explain.

Banning's complacency rattled her.

Her waffles popped up and she lifted them to a plate, hissing a little as they singed her fingertips. Forgoing the syrup, she added a dollop of strawberry jam. She couldn't make herself join the two men at the small table; instead, she leaned against the counter and ate quickly, glancing at the kitchen clock every few minutes. She was ready for Edgewood to be here so she could return to Atlanta, escape Chason's creepy presence.

"Hey, Settles, you're off the next couple of days," Banning said, pulling her from the circular reverie. "Got any plans?"

She found nothing but friendly inquiry in his face. Normally, she liked him—he was funny and easygoing. She sighed. It wasn't his fault Chason made her paranoid.

Ignoring the look Chason flicked in her direction, she shrugged. "I'm going to see my family."

She'd made the decision in the early hours of the morning. Getting out of town would keep her out of Beecham's presence when he returned from Las Vegas. Sure, she was hiding, but right now she didn't care. She wasn't ready to see him yet, beyond interacting with him at work. Somehow, she'd avoided any real conversation with him about their relationship, or lack thereof—probably because he'd been preoccupied with his mother's upcoming nuptials. His decision to go and give his mother away had surprised her, but she shouldn't have been. He loved his mother, even if her multimarried and multidivorced status did drive him insane.

No wonder the guy had issues.

Insurmountable issues, as far as their own relationship went. He was never going to be able to trust in them. He was never going to be able to relax about loving her. It didn't matter how hard she tried, how hard she fought for them...it wouldn't be enough.

The silly tears she'd been fighting for days pricked at her eyes and she blinked rapidly. No way in hell would she cry in front of Banning.

Definitely not in front of Chason.

The rumble of a diesel straight truck sounded outside and she relaxed. The UPS truck bearing Edgewood. Thank God. The sooner she was out of here, the sooner she could be on her way home. Even her mother was preferable to the endless circling of her mind when she had too much time to think.

When Edgewood came through the back door, she escaped to grab her things. The desire to get as far away as possible pulsed in her. At least with Banning working through the next two-day rotation, she wouldn't have to debrief with Edgewood.

Like it mattered what she had to say. Her fellow agents had already decided Chason presented no danger, escape or otherwise. She and Beecham hadn't been able to convince Weston of their concerns, either. What was it with men, anyway, that they latched on to an idea and nothing could make them let go?

Shouldering her bag, she stepped into the hallway. Banning's voice carried from the kitchen. "Damn, that's a bitch, Steve."

Steve? They were calling him Steve now? Good God in heaven.

As she entered the kitchen, Banning handed her the folded newspaper, the legal advertisements face up. "Check it out, Settles."

She skimmed the column he indicated, her nerves shifting to outright fear. Halfway down was a divorce petition, one Ruth Ann Calvert Chason informing Stephen Walter Chason that their marriage would be dissolved in what was now less than thirty days.

"Hell of a note, isn't it?" Edgewood shook his head. "Finding that in the paper?"

Jennifer darted a glance at Chason. He seemed unmoved, his face expressionless as he shrugged and lifted his coffee cup. "It was part of my agreement with the government, that I let her have her way in this."

His level of calm seemed genuine, but a memory flashed in

Jennifer's head, his hands closing around that puppy's small skull while he regarded Ruthie with equal composure.

But as long as he was here, in this house that even the agents assigned to guard him didn't know the location of, Ruthie was safe. It was the later Jennifer worried about, the time when he'd have the anonymity of the Witness Protection Program on his side, when he could go after Ruthie.

Without warning.

And without mercy.

Dinner didn't exactly go as Ruthie had envisioned. The food, the cooking, was no problem. Chris's large kitchen proved easy to work in.

But the meal itself? A dismal failure. Ruthie watched him do more moving his food around the plate with a fork than actual eating.

She moistened her lips. "How was your week?"

"Okay." His shuttered blue gaze flickered to hers, then back to his plate. "It was a week, I guess."

"So it wasn't too bad, being on the desk?"

"It's...interesting. People call about the oddest things."

Disconcerted by the tension hovering at the table, Ruthie popped a shrimp in her mouth and chewed, not really tasting it. He'd been happy to see her, as pleased as she'd been to see him, she'd bet on it. What was going on?

"What about you?" He moved a piece of pasta with his fork. "Business good?"

She nodded. "It's growing."

They lapsed into a taut silence. She didn't get it, either—they were never this ill at ease with one another. Things didn't improve with dessert and relief deluged her once the time came to clear the table. At least she'd have cleaning up to busy her hands.

"You said we needed to talk. Of course, I also promised to kiss you senseless once I had you completely alone, and this is the first chance I've had to do that. So what comes first?" She set the plates she carried on the counter and turned to take the glass casserole from him. He stared at her, his eyes blazing with a sudden fire. Her stomach lifted and turned over, a deep fluttering kicking off lower with a series of tiny, stinging aches.

His Adam's apple bobbed with a swallow. "Having you kiss me senseless sounds pretty damn good right now."

The serving dish hit the countertop with a dull thud. She reached for him first. Arms around his neck, she leaned up and kissed him. With a smothered groan, he wrapped her close and plundered her mouth. She met the ferocity of his possession with an intensity of her own, holding his face and sucking his tongue between her lips.

"God, Ruthie." He backed her into the counter, fumbling at the tiny buttons on her blouse. She went for the hem of his cotton polo and tugged it free of his jeans before rubbing her hands up the sleek warmth of his waist and rib cage. He growled in pleasure and kissed her again, giving up on her buttons and shoving the fabric out of his way instead.

Lost in the heated wonder of his mouth, she arched into him, bare midriff brushing against his stomach. The contact sent sharp desire piercing through her, weakening her legs and filling her with fierce triumph. Stephen had not stolen the ability to need and desire from her. She wanted this, wanted Chris.

He stroked his thumbs across the lower edge of her sternum and sensation danced out from the caress. She loved the hot, rough touch of his skin on hers. Nipping lightly at his bottom lip, she scraped her nails along his waistband, just below the small of his back. His knees dipped, his pelvis bumping hers, almost as though his legs had buckled.

"Jiminy Cricket." The rumble of his choked laughter shivered against her mouth. He brushed his palms back and forth over her waist.

She trailed her fingertips across the light stubble on his jaw. "Take me to bed."

"Hell." His breath rushed out on a shocked exhale and his lashes fell. "Are you sure?"

"Absolutely." She ran her thumb across his lower lip. Leaning closer, she tilted into him and let her tongue take the same path her thumb had. The pale blue of his eyes darkened, grew hot and stormy. "I want you, Chris."

"I don't want to rush this, don't want to mess us up. This isn't why I invited you here—"

She stopped the words with a fingertip atop his lips. "Nothing you could do would mess us up. Do you not get how important you're becoming to me?"

"Ruthie." The warmth of his mouth moved against her skin. "There's—"

"Time for that later." She dropped her hand and leaned in to feather her lips over his. "I need you."

For a long moment, he stared at her before he stepped back, took her hand and led her down the hall. In the dimness of his bedroom, she stood before him, her desire for him making her bold. Holding his gaze, she lifted her hands to unbutton her blouse. Finally, she shrugged free of the thin garment and he wrapped a warm palm around her nape, pulling her in for another of those passion-drugging kisses.

She fisted the hem of his shirt and dragged it upward, over his head. Deeply golden filtered sunlight fell on his torso, highlighting his tightly muscled chest and abdomen. Her mouth dry, she let her hands drift over his shoulders, across firm pectorals, down his arms, to his hands. A long, thin line of puckered flesh ran from shoulder to elbow. He flinched when she brushed it, and she moved her hand quickly to his chest. With scrupulous care, she avoided the scar there, a pale, flat mark at his ribs.

A shaky laugh erupted from his mouth and he buried his face against her hair. His hold at her hips tightened, his fingers seeming to tremble. "Shit, this is a bad idea. I don't know what I'm doing anymore, don't know how to—"

"Chris, stop. It's all right." She whispered the words near his ear. She folded her arms about him and held him closer. With her palms flat on his back, she discovered yet another mark on his shoulder blade, a jagged twin to the one on his arm. She rubbed her cheek against his neck. "Just hold me a moment."

He embraced her, too tightly but somehow just right at the same time. The thin lace of her bra did little to deflect the heat of his skin on her own. She curled into him and scattered tiny kisses along his throat, over his shoulder, all the while playing her hands over his back. Desire with all the burn of fine, smooth whiskey poured through her.

He exhaled hard, stirring her hair. "She ruined me."

Hatred for the unknown woman blazed to life, strong and virulent. Ruthie tamped it away and leaned back to meet his troubled eyes, brimming with mingled despair and desire. "I don't believe that."

"I don't want to be this way with you, awkward and damn near afraid."

"Stop thinking so much. Just...touch me." Taking his wrists, she lifted his hands to her body, molding his palms around the curves of her breasts. Still holding his forearms in a light grasp, she trailed her fingers over the backs of his hands as he shaped and caressed her. Her head fell back and her hair tumbled free from her already messy knot. "Oh yes, like that."

The pads of his thumbs flicked over the lace covering her hardening nipples. Bending his head, he took one into his mouth, teeth grating and tugging through the thin fabric. Need arrowed from the point of intense contact to the throbbing between her thighs.

"I want to go slow, make this so good for you," he murmured. "But it's been a long time, sweetheart, and I don't know if I can."

"Maybe I don't want slow. Maybe I just want you—"

The words died under his mouth and he lifted her against him, before spinning to lay her across the bed and follow her down, his hips between her thighs. "My God, Ruthie, you make me crazy."

"Good." She wiggled against him, her skirt riding high. Denim scratched the tender inside of her thighs. She ran teasing hands down his spine, dipping beneath his jeans to cup his buttocks and pull him into her. Lord, when was the last time she'd felt like this, free and confident, secure in the knowledge a man wanted her? "What are you going to do about it?"

A sound that was half-chuckle, half-growl escaped him and he lowered his head to her breasts once more. "Is that a challenge?"

She slid her hands around to his fly, making short work of the button and zipper. He hissed a curse when she encircled him, stroking and teasing. "It could be."

Hard and heavy, he pushed into her hand, his teeth tearing into his bottom lip. After a second, he caught her hand, stopping the smooth motion. "If you keep doing that, we're really not going to go slow."

He leaned over her, touching his lips to hers in a kiss that was different, softer than the wild exchange they'd shared in the kitchen. When he finally lifted his head, he gazed at her with a softer fire in his eyes, the lines of his face gentled.

"Can't remember the last time I felt like this," he whispered, tracing a fingertip along the curve of her cheek. "Come to think of it, I don't think I've ever felt like this, about anyone."

Again, she reached for him, linking her hands behind his head and pulling him down to her. Lying in the mingled shadows and strips of fading sunlight, they touched and explored, learning the tastes and textures of one another's bodies, the caresses punctuated by sighs and moans and sometimes Chris's deep groan.

Finally, Ruthie shifted restlessly beneath him and slipped a hand down to encircle him once more. "Chris, please, now."

"Sure?" he muttered next to her ear, a teasing hand testing her readiness.

"Yes." She arched into him. "Please, hurry. I want you."

A brief interruption while he rolled on a condom, a readjusting of positions and he moved inside her with a slow, easy thrust, another muffled groan escaping his lips. She inhaled sharply at the intense pleasure of being stretched around him. Fully sheathed within her, he stilled, tendons standing out on his neck and arms with an effort at control. Experimentally, she tilted her hips beneath his, rocking into him, and he gasped.

"Lord, Ruthie, don't, I won't be able to—"

"It doesn't matter." Giddiness bubbled through her, joining the heated desire radiating from the intimate connection of their bodies. "I don't care how long you last. I just want you, want this."

She moved beneath him, a tiny coaxing roll of her pelvis, and he muttered an oath on a smothered moan before he plunged hard against her. She wrapped her arms and legs about him as they moved together in a hurried coupling. Small shivers of an orgasm washed through her and she sighed his name moments before he thrust deeper with a hushed grunt of satiation.

He collapsed into her, one arm holding his weight, his face buried against her shoulder. Eyes closed, Ruthie held him, the sweetness of connection spiraling through her. She stroked a hand over his shoulder and down his back, frowning a little at the ridge of scar tissue on his left shoulder blade. A tear trickled from beneath her lashes, followed by another before she blinked them away. This was no place for tears. The joy and completion he'd brought to her life were too big for tears.

He kissed her shoulder, eased away long enough to dispose of the condom, returned to pull her close once more.

"Ruthie," he whispered, and she warmed to the raw emotion in her name on his lips. She held him tighter, never wanting to let go of the moment or of the man in her arms.

Keeping her close, he rolled to his side and she pillowed her head on his shoulder, rubbing a hand along the line of his ribs. His humming sigh vibrated through her. They lay in silence for long moments, the sun slipping away completely.

Finally, wrapped close, they slept.

The feathery back and forth movement of fingers on his spine brought Chris awake. He smiled into the pillow, his body saturated with a bone-deep contentment. Ruthie kissed his shoulder blade, lips brushing against the jagged scar there, and some of his pleasure drained away. He tensed and her caresses stilled for a moment.

She pressed her cheek to his back before she continued rubbing at his side. He relaxed under that gentle touch. She made being with her so damn easy. He loved that about her, the quiet acceptance, that she didn't try to push beneath his defenses, but waited for him to lower them.

Loved.

He rolled the concept around his mind, testing it, tasting the words. He found himself wanting to give her the words, well aware she already had the emotion from him.

The memory of Kimberly, how much he'd thought he'd loved her at first, how quickly he'd gotten pulled into and wrapped up in her stopped him. Ruthie was nothing like Kim, but at the same time, the swift fierceness of his feelings for her was enough to slow him down a little.

Teasing fingers ran over his side, stopping to tickle at his hipbone, bringing a smile to his mouth again. It died on a rough sigh. She deserved to know why he might be reticent at times, why he needed to take this slow and easy.

He rolled to his back and wrapped an arm around her. She folded her hands on his chest, her chin propped on them, impish dark eyes trained on his. He wrapped a stray tress around his finger, rubbing the silky strands between thumb and forefinger.

"That looks like a serious expression," she said.

"I need to tell you about Kim."

She nodded, silent, waiting, patient.

His stomach knotted and he looked away. Maybe he shouldn't have brought it up, brought Kimberly into what lay between him and Ruthie. Except, if he didn't, *Kim* would always be between him and Ruthie.

"You don't have to do this now."

"Yeah, I do."

Her fingertip moved over his skin, tracing a small figure eight. He shivered under the light touch.

"Kim was...when I was over at the Tifton PD, Kim was my fiancée." He swallowed against a sudden dryness in his mouth. "We lived together for almost a year."

Ruthie remained silent but there was no sense of prodding urgency in her waiting, only a quiet acceptance of whatever he wanted to say.

"She, um, she..." The urge to move, to escape the memories grabbed him with a strong hand and he shifted up against the pillows, looping his arms around his knees. Ruthie reached for the sheet and wound it around her curves, sitting with her feet under her, as pretty and casual as if they sat on her mama's back porch talking. He dropped his head and blew out a long breath, trying to dispel the tension wrapping old tentacles around him.

Ruthie caressed his ankle, the top of his foot, an easy touch designed to soothe. He lifted his gaze to hers. "She was violent. At first, emotionally, screaming and crap when things didn't go the way she wanted them to. Later, physically."

"She did this." Ruthie trailed a finger up the scar on his calf. "And the one on your arm, your back."

"That was the last time. She came after me with a knife. I swear to God, I think she really wanted me dead that night. After that, I didn't go back."

She curved her palm around his calf. "Chris, she had no right... If I could take it away, I would."

"I told you I wasn't whole, Ruthie. She...she messed up my head big time. You shouldn't have to deal with that. You deserve better—"

"Stop." Leaning forward, she halted the flow of words with her mouth. After a swift, sweet kiss, she pulled back, still touching his leg. Her eyes glowed with a fierce light. "I don't think you realize how strong and special you are. I'm very blessed to have you in my life like this, and I know it, so you can just stop running yourself down, Chris Parker, do you hear me?"

An irresistible grin tugged at his mouth. She was definitely a Calvert. How many times had he heard her mother or Tori use that very tone? He laid his hand over hers, trapping her fingers against his skin. "Yes, ma'am."

A naughty expression lit her face. "Oh, I think I like the sound of that, coming from you."

He laughed, surprised by her playfulness. "Come here."

She did, letting him draw her nearer. With their faces close, lips only a breath apart, he found himself staring into her intense gaze, wanting to get lost in her. She pressed a finger to his mouth. "I won't hurt you, Chris. I promise. Let me love you."

Eyes still locked on hers, he nodded. She eased forward, taking his mouth, and he cupped a hand around her nape, pulling her down and under him. With an approving moan, she wrapped herself around him, her touch soothing and arousing once more.

With darkness descending around them, he made love to her, losing himself, finding himself, in her.

Chapter Fourteen

"Do you take this woman to be your lawfully wedded wife..."

As Las Vegas wedding chapels went, Harrell had to concede this one probably wasn't too bad. The understated décor was done in shades of ivory and pale cream, and the officiant wore a somber suit instead of the prerequisite and clichéd Elvis costume.

Swallowing his lingering doubts, he'd walked his mother down an ivory runner scattered with pale pink rose petals— fake, he was pretty sure but nice just the same—and handed her over to Barry. Now, he stood to one side, hands linked behind his back, watching as his mother exchanged vows with husband number nine. The weird thing was, he could almost believe she and Barry could make a go of it. His mother did believe it. Her confidence blew his mind.

And made him ashamed, all at the same time. His mother had the same faith in love Jennifer did. Guilt curled through him with the memory of Jennifer telling him she loved him, of his throwing away her declaration. She was right—hearing her say it, even when he loved her, scared him shitless. He was a fucking coward, willing to let Jennifer hurt because he was too afraid to risk himself.

The knowledge didn't sit well.

"...for better or worse, as long as you both shall live?"

His mother beamed at Barry's "I will". Yes, she was happy, although Harrell had too much experience with her wedded bliss and the resulting heartbreak to fully place his confidence in this union. But for this moment, at least, she was happy. She'd found some happiness, as well, in all of her marriages. For that, she was willing to gamble that her joy with Barry would last.

"Julia, do you take this man…"

He was guaranteeing his unhappiness.

Shrugging off a slight frown, Harrell straightened. Being with Jennifer, however briefly, had brought more peace and contentment into his life than anything ever had before. And he was tossing that aside to ward off future pain.

How fucking twisted was that?

"I now pronounce you husband and wife. You may kiss your bride."

Harrell's mother lifted her face, and Barry leaned in and brushed a firm, chaste kiss over her lips. The other attendees— a couple waiting for their own nuptials and a curvy blonde who'd filled out the necessary paperwork—stepped forward with congratulations and best wishes. Then his mother looked around expectantly, and Harrell pinned on a bright smile and gathered her in a close hug. She held on to him a moment, her perfume whispering a childhood memory over him, before she let him go. He shook Barry's hand, offering congratulations.

She tucked her hand through Harrell's arm as they prepared to leave. "We should go for a really nice dinner and celebrate."

An impatience to be back in Atlanta, to fix what he'd screwed to hell with Jennifer, simmered under his skin, warring with his sense of duty to his mother. He didn't want to dim that glow on her face.

Keeping his smile in place, he nodded. "Sure thing, but I have to leave right after, Mom. I need to get back to Atlanta. There's something I have to take care of."

Somehow, being at home helped. Never in her wildest imaginings would Jennifer have believed that being surrounded by her mother and sisters would make her feel better, but oddly, it did, so much so that she waited until insanely early Monday to leave for Atlanta. Finally feeling like she was getting her equilibrium back, she ignored her cell phone both times it rang and displayed Beecham's number on the caller ID.

Eyes still burning from the tears she'd shed on her mother's shoulder, she fought through Atlanta's early morning traffic to arrive at her apartment a little before seven. Time enough to change for the office, grab some orange juice and a bagel, begin getting over Harrell Beecham.

Shit. She braked too hard as she caught a glimpse of his familiar sedan in the lot before her building. Clad in a dark blue suit, he sat on the front steps. Damn it, what was he doing here?

Lifting her chin, she zipped into a parking spot at the end of the row. Straightening her shoulders, she tugged her overnight bag free and marched up the sidewalk. He rose at her approach, but she didn't spare him a glance on her way up the stairs. He followed, heavy footsteps ringing on the treads. At her door, he reached for her bag as she juggled for the right key. She let him take it. She was finished fighting with him.

Bag in hand, he leaned a shoulder against the wall as she unlocked the door. "I tried calling you."

"Yeah." She pushed the door inwards. "I know."

"Jen—"

"I have to change. Give me fifteen minutes." She tossed her keys on the table in the small foyer. "Raid the fridge if you like."

Her bag hit the floor and he reached for her, pulling her around to face him. He looked down at her, his eyes stormy. "Jennifer, please."

"No." Anger and renewed strength pulsed deep in her. "Not again."

He didn't loosen his grip. However, a very real fear lurked in his eyes. "Hear me out. I know I screwed up. I know that by not trusting in you, in us, the way we feel, that I destroyed your faith in us, in me. Give me a chance to make it right, baby, please."

"No." She blinked hard, the urge to cry hitting her all over again, making her already irritated eyes burn. "I don't want to live my life like this, Beecham. I won't live my life like this, wondering when you're going to pull everything out from under me—"

"I won't." He cradled her face, desperation spiraling through his voice. "God, Jen, I stood there yesterday, watching my mother put herself out there and realized what a damn coward I was, that I was sacrificing you to keep myself safe, and it made me sick, to think I'd do that to you, to us."

She pulled away, afraid of succumbing to his touch, his words. "And what's different now? What's going to keep you from doing the same thing?"

"You." His voice lowered, intensity vibrating in the deep tones. "You will, because, goddamn it, I love you, Jen, and I don't want to waste another second being afraid. I just want to love you every second I can."

"Don't. Don't do this. I can't keep—" To her horror, she choked up, her voice breaking on the words, the weak tears falling once more.

Swearing, he stepped forward and wrapped her close. She struggled against him, but he merely tightened his arms. Finally, she gave in, clinging to him as the hurt spent itself in rough sobs.

He kissed the curve of her neck, buried his face against her, mouth close to her ear. "Tell me you love me too, Jen," he whispered. "Give me that, just that. I'll prove myself to you, I promise. You won't have to doubt me again."

She closed her eyes, so tempted to believe in him, so afraid of falling once more.

Their cell phones rang simultaneously. He stiffened and she stilled, pulling free.

"Weston," Beecham said.

"Janice." Jennifer named Weston's secretary. Unease traveled over her, lifting a wave of fine gooseflesh in its wake.

She flipped the phone open and lifted it to her ear. "Agent Settles."

Janice's terse message did little to assuage the lingering trepidation. Ending the call, Jennifer faced Beecham, sure he'd gotten the same communication she had—Banning and Edgewood had both failed to make scheduled check-ins; neither were answering their cells.

This was not good.

"We've got to go," she said as Beecham snapped his own phone closed, his mouth a grim line. She brushed at her still-damp lashes. Her jeans and pink polo would have to do; she wasn't taking time to change, not with every nerve singing with tension, not when she was ninety-nine percent sure her fears about Chason had come to fruition.

Beecham nodded, brows lowering in a frown. "Jen, about—"

"No. No more." She moved toward the door, jingling her keys. "Let's go."

His whole being taut with a vibrating pressure, he accompanied her to the car. He didn't try to broach the subject of what lay, or didn't lay, between them, or actually speak at all as she navigated Atlanta's morning gridlock. She was grateful too.

He didn't speak, but as she tailed the BuCar with Weston and another senior agent to the safe house, she felt his gaze on her occasionally, as heavy and palpable as a touch. With each mile, her own apprehension grew, a weird blend of professional and personal anxiety that pulsed through her body.

When they reached the safe house, the nervousness solidified into a grim certainty. The front door stood ajar. No way Banning and Edgewood, however complacent they might have grown with Chason, would be that sloppy.

The smells hit her as they approached the door and she didn't even have to go farther to know what they'd find. The sharp metallic odor of blood blended with bodily fluids and decay. Jennifer's empty stomach curdled.

Weston pushed the door inward. "Shit."

Chason was nowhere in the house. They found Banning in the living room. Jennifer stared, a rough shudder moving over her. Blood congealed into a sticky pool around Banning's head, his throat slit.

Beecham brushed her arm. "Let's check the bedrooms."

Upstairs, Edgewood's body still lay in bed, a gaping slash in his neck as well. Beecham eyed the body, touched one arm tentatively.

"Rigor's already passed. Looks like lividity's set in. They've been dead a while, at least twenty-four hours." Beecham's terse statement confirmed Jennifer's own thoughts.

"Call Calvert," she said quietly, aware of Weston's voice below them as he called in the deaths and requested the evidence response team. "You know where Chason's going. He doesn't have anything left to lose now, Beecham."

With a sharp nod, Beecham pulled his phone from his belt. Half-listening to his brief, strained conversation, she studied the brutal wound on Edgewood's body and tried to figure out how far a lead on them Chason had.

Oh, please let it not be too late for them to keep Ruthie safe.

The house sat empty and quiet, early sunlight slanting in through the kitchen window and splashing bright puddles on the floor and counters. Ruthie set out the ingredients she'd need for the day's lunch entrée—tomatoes, bell peppers, onions, boneless chicken breasts.

John Robert and Camille had boarded the school bus just minutes earlier and Mama had taken Ainsley with her for a church meeting. That had become part of their easy routine, Ainsley spending time with her beloved grandmother while Ruthie passed the morning cooking and preparing lunches, then her daughter accompanying her on the deliveries before they picked up John Robert and Camille from school.

Tonight, they were all having dinner at Chris's, and John

Robert couldn't stop talking about it. Ruthie smiled and made short work of slicing bell peppers into julienne strips. The children were fast falling into adoration with his quiet strength, drinking it in. She shivered a little, at the memory of having that same strength all over her, his hands and mouth on her. She adored him too.

Life was good, better than it had been in as long as she could remember.

The side door opened and closed with a soft snick.

She reached for another pepper and applied her knife to it. "Mama? Did you forget something?"

Footfalls whispered in the hallway, but not her mother's light steps. Not Tick's easy stride or Chris's sure tread, either. Apprehension prickled over her. There'd been no sounds of an engine outside, no crunching of tires on pea gravel. Someone could have parked on the grass, beneath the trees but...

She stilled, tightening her grip on the knife, and edged toward the back door, keeping the table between her and the hallway door as she did so. Something about those steady, measured steps was too familiar.

She glanced toward the phone, gauging the distance between it and the door. If she went for the phone, she'd be cornered. If she went outside, the nearest house was two miles away.

He stepped into the doorway. A chilly certainty settled over her. Her palms damp, she clutched the knife, blade pointed in his direction. She'd defied him, ruined everything for him. He wouldn't let that go unpunished.

He wouldn't let *her* go.

"Hello, Ruth," Stephen said, his tone quiet and even. "Put the knife down and come here, darling."

Just like he always had. Just like he expected her to obey instantly. Did he really not get that she'd escaped him, that there was never any going back?

The reality of his appearance slowly settled in. He was sweaty, disheveled, his clothes and hands stained with dirt, caked mud, grass...and what looked like blood. Seconds for that to penetrate her mind, seconds for the implications to sink in.

"Ruth," he repeated softly. "Come here."

"No."

Familiar controlled fury flickered in his brown eyes. "I told you to—"

"You don't do that anymore, Stephen." Her fingers slipped on the knife and she tightened her grip until her knuckles hurt. "Now go. Leave."

He took a step forward. "I'm not going anywhere. Get over—"

"I said get out." She lifted the knife, holding it in front of her, the handle pressed hard against her stomach for support. The blade quivered wildly. The beginnings of fear and adrenaline filtered through her, trying to cloud her brain, and she shoved them down. If she got scared, if she let the panic take over, she was dead. She knew it as certainly as she knew at this point, it was him or her.

His face tightened. "I'm only going to tell you one more time, Ruth."

The phone's sharp shrill shattered the standoff. Startled, Ruthie glanced at it.

Stephen lunged, hands curled into claws.

She threw up a hand to ward him off. His hand closed on her wrist with bruising intensity, dragging her toward him.

The phone rang again.

The blade sank home with a sickeningly wet squishing sound. The impact shimmered up her arm, and shock and surprise bloomed in his eyes. A muffled *oomph* escaped his parted lips.

He looked down, his knees buckling as he took one staggering step back. With a shuddery breath, Ruthie held tight to the shank. It slid free, thick red blood coating the wide surface. Two, then three fat drops fell to the floor, splattering. The phone half-rang, stopping in midnote.

Another step backward and he sank to his knees, still

clutching his chest, still staring at the massive flow of blood over his fingers. His stunned gaze lifted to hers.

My God, what had she done?

He slumped forward, one hand going forward to break his fall, his body sliding to a heap on her mama's spotless white tile floor.

Oh, sweet Jesus, had she killed him? One stab wound couldn't do that, could it? Surely not. She lifted a trembling hand to her forehead, the other still gripping the bloody knife. Down the hallway, the side door slammed open. Running footsteps on polished hardwood.

"Ruthie?" Fear and concern coated Tick's voice. She pressed against the counter. Oh Lord oh Lord oh Lord...

"Are you all right?" The words shook. He stood in the doorway, face white, his gaze jumping from her to the knife to Stephen's motionless form and back to her.

"I...yes, I'm..." Over her brother's shoulder, she caught a glimpse of Chris. Her heart stuttered. No. He couldn't see this, not her standing here over Stephen, blood beginning to spread over the floor, blood on the knife she held. What would he think?

Whatever he thought, she couldn't tell from his pale expressionless face, his blank eyes.

"Chris," Tick said, his tone evening out, taking on a hint of deep authority. "I need the scene kit from the car. And call dispatch. Tell them we need the GBI over here."

Chris's gaze darted from Tick to her and back again. "Sure. I'll be right back."

She sagged against the counter, eyes closed. Just like that, he was gone and it was over. It had to be, after what he'd seen. He wouldn't want her now.

"Ruthie, are you hurt?" Tick's voice, from below, and she lifted heavy lids to find him crouched beside Stephen's motionless form.

"No." She shook her head in a slow side-to-side roll, tremors running through her whole being. "Is he...?"

With a sharp nod, Tick rose. "He's dead."

"Oh, God." She clutched at the counter, the knife clattering to the tile top. Her children's father. She'd killed her babies' father. How would she...what would they...? She held on harder, afraid her legs were going to give out and dump her on the floor. What had she done?

"Ruthie." Tick's warm hands closed on her shoulders, a steady grip that kept her standing. "It's all right, okay? I'm here, Chris is here, it's over. Everything is over and it's all right."

"Oh, sweet Jesus," she whispered. Her heart beat too fast, thumping against her sternum, wanting to get out of its captivity. And why did she feel like she was floating, like her head was somewhere detached from her body, a helium-light sphere headed for the ceiling? "Oh my Lord, Tick."

"I know." He kneaded her shoulders. "I'm going to get Tori over here for you and we'll take care of you, I swear. I can't investigate this, but I need you to tell me everything that happened, baby girl, okay?"

Baby girl. She hadn't heard that endearment in years, not since the last time her father had used it, on his way out of the house, on his way to the airstrip. She'd been fifteen, a little gawky and awkward, but still her daddy's baby girl. She'd been in this very room, standing at the table, just beyond where Stephen's body lay, and Daddy had tousled her hair and hugged her close...and she'd never seen him again. The plane had gone down and he'd died, she'd been lost without him and Stephen had called to that empty place in her once she met him...

Camille and Ainsley. She'd taken their father, put them in the same position.

"Ruthie." Desperation sharpened Tick's voice, tightened the angles of his face. "Please. Stay with me. I need you to tell me everything."

"I killed him. I was cooking, chopping peppers for lunches, and I heard the door open. I thought it was Mama but then when those footsteps came down the hall...I...it was him or me, I knew that but...oh my God, Tick." She glanced up at him, around the kitchen in a wild arc. Nausea barreled into her throat. "I killed him. I *killed* him. I'm going to be sick."

She spun, gripping the counter as she leaned over the sink, helpless as her stomach emptied itself of its own volition, acid and bile burning her throat. Sudden hot tears spurted from her eyes, mixing with the mucous that poured from her nose. Tick sheltered her, holding her hair from her face, his forehead pressed to her shoulder, so she felt the tremors that moved through his body as well.

Why was he shaking? He wasn't the one who'd just gutted someone in their mama's kitchen.

"Tick." Chris's calm voice barely penetrated the miserable haze of her retching and heaves. "I'm taping off the house. GBI and the coroner are en route, so is Cookie. I told him to bring Tori with him."

Tick nodded, not lifting his head from Ruthie's shoulder. "Good. Thanks."

When the heaving finally stopped, the sobs started, choking her, tearing from her raw throat until they sounded more like wails. Through it all her brother held her, his arm about her waist keeping her from sliding to the blood-slick floor.

"It's all right, Ruthie," he murmured over and over. "It's done now, it's all right."

How could he say that? How could anything ever be all right after this?

He smoothed her damp hair from her wet cheeks, found a rag and washed her face. He didn't touch her bloody hands. She shuddered. She didn't want him doing this. She wanted Chris, needed Chris, and he wanted nothing to do with her. He couldn't, not now.

She sucked in a shuddery breath and straightened, stiffening her body and dislodging her brother's supportive hold. She'd cope. She could. No matter what, she'd deal with it. Calverts didn't cave. She hadn't let Stephen break her completely and she wouldn't let this either, even if it cost her Chris.

Even if it cost her everything.

The following minutes and hours settled into a blur of GBI agents and questions. Tori appeared at her side, strong, capable, loving, and stayed there, picking up where Tick had left off. She'd not been allowed to change clothes or clean up, really, until crime scene technicians took pictures of the scene, photographed her hands and arms. At some point, Autry Reed appeared, and under her protective presence, Ruthie repeated the story over and over, until it didn't seem real anymore, but rather something out of a horrific movie she'd seen once upon a time.

"We're almost finished here, I think." Tori sat beside her on the back porch glider and pressed a cup of cool water into her hands, which she'd finally been able to wash, although she felt a little like Lady Macbeth—that not enough water or perfume existed to cleanse them. "Just a little while longer and we'll get you some clean clothes. I'm pretty sure you'd like a shower too."

Ruthie nodded, fingers wrapped around the plastic cup. Through the window, she could see Chris, standing in the hall doorway, arms folded over his chest as he watched the GBI investigators and crime scene unit work. Tick spoke to him and Chris lowered his head, listening a moment before he nodded. They disappeared down the dim hallway.

Her lungs emptied in a shaky exhale. Tori laid a warm hand on her knee.

"My children, Tor," Ruthie whispered, closing her eyes. "I killed their father. How do I live with that?"

"By remembering that he put you in the position where you had no choice." Tori's fingers tightened. "You did what you had to. This is not your fault, Ruthie."

"What am I going to say to them?" The tears pushed at her eyes again, scratching and burning.

Tori wrapped an arm about her shoulders, pressing her forehead to Ruthie's temple. "We'll deal with it together. I'll help you. We'll get you through this, I promise."

Holding back a sob, Ruthie nodded but knew the acquiescence was a lie. She didn't see how she'd ever survive this intact.

"The ME thinks the knife severed his aorta. Death was probably nearly instantaneous." A quiet female tone drifted out to them, one of the GBI agents from Moultrie. "The initial impression of the scene supports her story."

Her story. Like it was something she'd sit down and write, with a beginning and middle and end. Something she'd tell, with Ainsley curled up on her lap, waiting for happily-ever-after. Her sharp inhale was half-sob, half-laugh.

Tori stroked her arm. "I'm going to see if it's okay if we leave. You don't need to be here anymore."

Ruthie stared out at the shimmering surface of the pond. She wanted to close her burning eyes, but she knew what images awaited her if she did: the fury in Stephen's eyes, the sight of that knife slipping roughly into his flesh, the blood.

Chris's blank gaze.

She gave herself a sharp shake. No. She wasn't thinking about that. There was no point, too much else to worry about. She rubbed a thumb over the bruises on her wrist, perfect impressions of Stephen's fingers.

In minutes, Tori returned, holding a small bundle of clothing and Ruthie's purse. "Come on. Let's get you out of here."

As they slipped out the back door, Chris's quiet voice flowed from the open kitchen door, his murmured words indistinct. Ruthie didn't look back. There was no point in doing so.

They were over.

With Beecham at her side, Jennifer jogged up the steps of Lenora Calvert's home. During the short flight from Atlanta to Albany, they'd received word of Stephen Chason's death at Ruthie's hands. Knowing Ruthie was safe had settled Jennifer's nerves somewhat, but she still wanted to see for herself. A weird sense of deja vu pulsed under her skin as they entered the house, memories of searching this house in the dark night filtering through her mind.

In the hallway off the kitchen, Calvert leaned against the wall, a tall deputy at his side, both of them watching the agents and crime scene technicians swarming over the kitchen.

His gaze skittered over Jennifer before latching on Beecham's grim face. With a curt nod, Calvert pushed away from the wall and shook Beecham's hand. "Hey."

Jennifer surveyed the room beyond him, sparing only one hard glance at Chason's corpse as it was lifted into a gaping body bag. "How's Ruthie?"

The deputy seemed to stiffen slightly. Calvert's dark eyes flickered over her. "Physically, she's fine. Emotionally? She's in shock. My baby sister took her back to her place."

Beside Jennifer, Beecham slumped visibly, some of the tension draining from his body. During the flight he'd remained tense and silent. She hadn't had to ask to know he'd been thinking of Tessa Marlow and how that attempt at protection had gone horribly wrong as well.

"What happened, exactly?" Beecham jerked his chin toward the body bag.

Calvert's eyes narrowed and turned cool. "Y'all screwed up and let him get away. The son of a bitch came after my sister."

Beecham blew out a long breath. "We've got two dead agents, Tick, two good men. I don't need your shit too. You know as well as I do that sometimes crap happens, even with all necessary precautions. Now what happened?"

Jennifer listened, horrified, as Calvert briefly outlined what had transpired in the house. The images he described tumbled through her mind and she wrapped her arms over her midriff, filled with empathy for Ruthie.

When Calvert finished, she caught his gaze again. "I'd like to see her," she said quietly.

"I'll take you." The deputy spoke for the first time. A look passed between him and Calvert, some indefinable nonverbal message that Jennifer didn't quite understand. Calvert nodded.

"I'm staying here." Beecham didn't meet her eyes.

She stepped away from him, glad to escape his presence. "I'll see you later then."

Long years of training provided Chris the restraint not to abandon Agent Settles at the car and sprint up the stairs to Tori's apartment. Images beat in his head—Chason's body, the bloody knife, the horrified fear on Ruthie's pale face. He'd wanted nothing more than to snatch her close, shield her, never let her go. That terror had stopped him, given him the impetus to step back and yield to Tick's easy authority. He'd have died before doing anything to make that pain and horror worse.

Not knowing what awaited him beyond the door at the top of the stairs scared the hell out of him. He just needed...he needed to know she was okay, that she was whole and that Chason hadn't succeeded in killing off the strength and joy that lay deep inside her. He needed her to be all right.

He made himself follow the aloof agent, made himself let her take the lead. A hollowness settled in his stomach as he approached the door. Settles knocked and the cold emptiness worsened as quiet echoed from the apartment. What if she wasn't okay? Memories of her withdrawing, shrinking into silence, beat in his head.

After a long, pulse-pounding pause, the door swung inward. Tori regarded them with a mixture of reserve and protectiveness. Chris cleared his throat. "Tori, this is Agent Settles. She wanted to see Ruthie—"

"I'm not involved with the investigation here." Settles' soft voice cut across his. "I knew her from Charleston. I needed to see if she was all right."

Tori stepped back to allow them entrance. "She's lying down but I don't think she's asleep. It's...she's having a hard time."

His heart crushed in on itself. Chris darted a look toward the open bedroom door. "Do you think she'd want to see me?"

Tori's eyes glittered. "I think she'd love to see you." She

turned to Settles. "Thank you for coming to check on her, but she's fragile. I'd advise you to wait before talking to her."

Settles nodded, folding her arms to grasp her elbows. "Of course. I understand."

"But she needs you." Tori reached for Chris's hand, her fingers squeezing around his, and his eyes burned. "Go to her."

Blinking hard, he pressed Tori's hand and let go. Trepidation pounded in his chest with each of his footfalls on the wooden floor. Damn it, he was afraid of what lay beyond the bedroom door, of what he would find.

What he found was Ruthie hunched on Tori's bed, knees drawn up, her back to the door. He sucked in a breath, dragging up strength from deep inside. One thing was for sure—he wouldn't leave her alone to face this. With the carpet now muffling his steps, he came around the foot of the bed. She wasn't sleeping, her bruised, dark gaze trained on the opposite wall.

He hunkered down by the bed. A hand under her cheek, she lay curled on her side, a sense of being utterly lost in her eyes. He fought down the craving to touch her. "Hey."

Her eyes filled and her mouth quivered wildly before her teeth sank into the lower lip, steadying it. "Hey."

With his fingers resting on the floor for stability, he let his gaze rove her pale face. He swallowed, hard. "Ruthie, I need to touch you, sweetheart, to know for myself you're okay. I need to hold you. But I won't, not unless you tell me that it's all right."

With her chin trembling, she blinked several times. Still, the tears spilled over, wetting her cheeks. "You can't know how much I want that."

Relief crashed into him, and he closed his eyes for a second, riding out the wave. When he opened them, he reached out to brush a fingertip over her damp cheeks. "Baby, I'm sorry. You don't know how damn sorry I am that you had to go through this."

Her face crumpled. "I didn't want him dead, Chris. I never wanted him *dead*. I just wanted…"

On a cracked sob, her voice failed. Unable to stand anymore, he came to his feet, to sit on the side of the bed and gather her against his chest. Arms wrapped tight around her, he pressed his face to her hair. Her entire body shook against him, sobs choking her.

She clung to him, fingers digging into his back. "I didn't want..."

"I know, baby."

A shuddering breath trembled through her body and she turned her cheek against his chest. "Chris, what am I going to do?"

"Meet it. Get through it." He pulled her closer, remembered fear still gripping him. He'd been so damned afraid entering that house. What if it had gone the other way? "I'll be here. I'll help you, if that's what you want. Whatever you need...I'll be it."

She lifted her head, swiping at wet cheeks, pushing back damp, disheveled hair. "How can you be this way? You saw him, what I did...it had to be like when—"

"No." He framed her face, his own hands shaking. "Nothing like that. I know you and there's no doubt you only did what you had to." He swallowed, fighting the lump gripping his throat with an iron fist. He spread his fingers, caressing, cherishing every inch of her face he could reach, and expelled a long exhale. "I love you, Ruthie, and you have to believe nothing will ever change that. Nothing. You told me once that you'd love me if I'd let you, and this may be the absolute wrong time to say this...but when you're ready, I'll be here, standing by to let you."

"I already love you." Muted joy shot through him with the words, but she folded her face into his neck, the tears falling. "God, Chris, I'm scared."

He held her tighter, doing everything he could to absorb that fear, take it away. The hell of it was that he couldn't make it go away, not really. Only time could do that. But he could be here for her, stand by her, love her. That he could do. He pressed his mouth against her temple. "I know, baby, I know. Whatever happens, I'm here. We'll face it all together, I promise."

It was all over but the paperwork. Meetings and debriefings had stretched into the evening hours. Through it all, Harrell had watched Jennifer after she'd returned to the Chandler County Sheriff's Office. He didn't have to look far for the cause of her tense silence. Any mirror would have given him a great look at himself.

He was a stupid ass. He'd hurt her, had ruined everything with his foolish fear and reticence. Now he faced the very real prospect that he'd hidden behind that fear too long, that it was too late to win her back. Because his declaration of love that morning sure as hell hadn't made her happy. Worry settled low in his belly, a tight, cold knot.

"I'm headed home." Tick ran both hands down his face. He looked completely wiped out, his face drawn and pale, eyes rimmed with red. "Are you staying tonight or going back to Atlanta?"

"We're staying the night." He cast a quick look at the back of Jennifer's head. "Weston wants us to meet one more time with the GBI agent in charge before we head back."

Jennifer didn't look up from where she sat at an empty desk, transcribing notes. He cleared his throat. "Jen, are you ready?"

"Of course." She didn't spare him a glance. Once her things were stowed in her bag, they walked out of the cramped sheriff's department to the rental car in silence. The heavy quiet hovered over them throughout the short drive to the motel. Once there, she gathered her bag and jacket and slid from the car. His stomach plummeted. It really was as bad as he thought, then.

However, on the sidewalk, she waited before their respective doors, watching him with guarded eyes. "I suppose you want to talk about this morning."

Relief washed over him, followed by an instantaneous flow of foreboding. "I think we should, don't you?"

With a shrug, she swiped the card through the lock and

went inside, leaving the door open for him to follow. He closed it behind him and stood, waiting. With extreme precision, she placed her laptop carrier atop the table and folded her jacket over a nearby chair. Her shoulders moved in a deep breath and she sat on the end of one bed, her hands folded in her lap. She lifted infinitely sad eyes to his. "I don't know what to do, Beech."

He dared to sit beside her, but didn't touch. "What do you mean, baby?"

"You say you love me, but they're just words, really. They can't trump the fear. It's too deeply seated in you. I love you, but if I walk away to protect myself, then what am I doing, except what you've seen your mother do all along, which is give up when it gets difficult. All that will accomplish is making it even harder for you to trust anyone, and I don't want to do that to you, Harrell. I *love* you. I don't want it to be this way."

Silence pulsed between them. Harrell sucked in a harsh breath.

"You're right. They're just words and at this moment, they're not enough because I've been a stupid, stubborn son of a bitch where you're concerned." He closed his eyes, just for a second, steeling himself. Opening them, he reached for her hand, aligning their palms, but not twining his fingers tightly through hers the way he wanted to. "Maybe what we need right now is time, for the actions to make the words enough. Do you think we can do that?"

On a small sniffle, she nodded, and when she did turn to him, tears washed her eyes although her mouth curved in a tremulous smile. "I have all the time in the world for you."

Flooded with gratitude for grace he didn't deserve, he leaned in to kiss her. Her lips, warm and still trembling, moved beneath his, and she lifted a hand to his nape. Healing swept through him, warming him.

"I do love you, Jen," he murmured against her lips. "I'll show you. Let me and I'll prove it to you."

"Yes," she whispered, kissing the corner of his mouth. "Yes."

He rubbed his fingers down her spine in a soothing caress.

"About that ball…"

She pulled back, frowning. "You don't have to—"

"I want to." With his arm about her waist, he drew her close again. "But we'll need an extra pair of tickets."

She snuggled into him, her palms against his chest. "An extra pair? For who?"

"My mom and Barry." Her simple touch, her nearness, made his heart rate accelerate. He traced the back of knuckles along her jaw. Hope uncurled within him. "When I tell her about you, she's going to be thrilled and she's going to want to spend as much time as possible getting to know you."

Happiness flashed over her face, the vestiges of hurt and fear slipping away. He finally relaxed completely. They were going to be okay. He could do this, could make this commitment and be the man she needed, and she would help him along the way. She leaned in to kiss him. "I can't wait."

Ruthie stirred from an uneasy doze filled with nightmarish images of a blood-spattered white floor. She blinked, the fuzzy outlines of Tick's living room coming into a slow soft-focus. She cringed at the immediate reality shoving in on her—Stephen dead at her hands, her mother and the children here at Tick and Caitlin's because the house remained a closed crime scene. She laid a palm over her stinging eyes and released a shuddery breath.

"Ruthie?" Fingers threaded through her hair. She dropped her hand to meet Chris's steady gaze, shuttered with concern. He brushed his mouth over her cheek. "Okay?"

She caught his wrist, the skin warm and real under her cold fingers, and turned her head to bury her lips against his palm. "I'm so glad you're here."

"I'm not going anywhere." He hunkered by the sofa, much as he'd done by Tori's bed earlier. He curved his fingers along her jaw.

A memory flashed in her head, this same gentleness of his, his stable presence and reassurance when she'd had to tell the children what she'd done. She held his gaze, the fear and anxiety still jumping within her, but tempered by his soothing touch. "Promise?"

His expression softened further and he leaned in to whisper a feathery kiss on her mouth. "Promise. And I always keep mine."

Epilogue

"Let's go to bed."

Her husband murmured the words near her ear, and Ruthie Parker's body went warm and melting, little thrills of pleasure trailing down her spine. She shivered as his hands spread over her abdomen, fingers plucking at her apron tie. She'd heard him come in the sliding glass door in the den minutes earlier, but he'd gone to the bedrooms first, checking in on the children, as he always did at the end of a 3-to-11 shift.

"Chris, I have to...oh." She closed her eyes on a sigh as his mouth found that perfect spot at the juncture of her neck and shoulder. Swallowing, she tried to quell the tingly desire firing to life in her belly. She covered his hands with her own. "I have to finish decorating this cake. It's for that party Tick and Cait are throwing Harrell and Jennifer, to celebrate their engagement."

"Finish it later. Hound's in the kennel, the kids are asleep, I'm 10-6 for the night." Leather creaked behind her as he widened his stance and pulled her back into him slightly. The pepper-spray case pressed into the small of her back, and higher, she could feel his badge imprinted through her thin blouse. He nipped at her neck, a silent chuckle shimmering over her skin. "Come on, Ruthie, you know you want to."

Her soft laugh fell between them. She did want to, she always wanted to. Something about the intense, steady way he loved her turned her inside out all the time. Nearly a year of dating, almost six months of marriage hadn't changed that.

"Fifteen minutes." She turned her head and pressed a kiss to his hair. "Time for me to finish this layer and you to shower. I'll meet you there."

"Deal." He squeezed her close one last time, rubbed his palm down her hip and strode down the hall.

With anticipation humming in her body, she made quick work of smoothing the fondant and stowed the completed layer with its twin in the industrial fridge they'd tucked in one corner of the kitchen, just for her thriving catering endeavor. Once the prep area was clean, she hurried down the hall as well. She entered the bedroom just as Chris, damp and naked, emerged from the bathroom.

He jerked his chin at her. "Get over here, beautiful."

Giddiness bubbled up in her throat. "No, you get over here."

Love and laughter gleamed in his eyes under raised brows, but he obeyed. She expected him to begin undoing the buttons on her blouse, but instead, he wrapped his arms around her and hugged her close, his face buried in her neck. A deep sigh of contentment rolled through his body.

She embraced him, just as tightly, that same sense of completion and happiness warming her. Unable to resist the temptation of his bare skin, she ran her palms down his back. "I thought you were eager."

"I am, but I like holding you." He trailed a single fingertip along her spine. "Besides, we have all night."

"No," she murmured, tucked against his heart, "we have the rest of our lives."

"You're right." He found that spot at her shoulder again. "And I can't wait to spend it with you."

About the Author

How does a high school English teacher end up plotting murders? She uses her experiences as a cop's wife to become a writer of romantic suspense! Linda Winfree lives in a quintessential small Georgia town with her husband and two children. By day, she teaches American Literature, advises the student government and coaches the drama team; by night she pens sultry books full of murder and mayhem.

To learn more about Linda and her books, visit her website at www.lindawinfree.com or join her Yahoo newsletter group at http://groups.yahoo.com/group/linda_winfree. Linda loves hearing from readers. Feel free to drop her an email at linda_winfree@yahoo.com.

As their passion catches fire, so does a killer's vengeance…

Love Me Tomorrow
© *2009 Dee Tenorio*
A Rancho del Cielo romance.

In the sleepy town of Rancho del Cielo, a killer arsonist is targeting firefighter Josh Whittaker's friends, family and most importantly…the love of his life.

As fires encircle Josh's life, his troubles mount. His best friend is dead. The woman he'd give his life to protect is pregnant. Secrets he's held on to for years are spilling free. If he could just find his equilibrium, he could pull himself together. What he doesn't know is that someone is dead-set on tearing everything he knows apart.

Losing a lifelong friend has finally awakened Miranda McTiernan to how much of her life has been spent in limbo. Now that she's pregnant, a dream she never believed could happen, the reality isn't quite what she'd expected. Instead of being happy and secure, she's scared and hiding a secret that could ruin the future she's worked so hard to create.

Assuming she has a future…

Warning: Includes a heroine out to get her man, a hero determined to do the wrong thing for the right reasons, and hormones gone wild. Reading with cookies recommended.

Available now in ebook and print from Samhain Publishing.

LaVergne, TN USA
25 February 2010
174265LV00003B/46/P